SEDUCTION

A DARK BRATVA FAKE MARRIAGE ROMANCE

WICKED VOWS
BOOK 3

JANE HENRY

Seduction: A Dark Bratva Fake Marriage Romance

Cover photography by *Michelle Lancaster* (www.michellelancaster.com)

Cover art by *Popkitty*

ISBN: 978-1-961866-07-2

Cover art for Alternate Cover Print Edition by *Haya in Designs*

ISBN: 978-1-961866-13-3 (Alternate Cover Print Edition)

Playlist

Scan QR Code to listen to the playlist for 'Seduction: A Dark Bratva Fake Marriage Romance" on Spotify©

My mission is simple yet deadly—pose as the newly hired bodyguard for Vera Ivanova and assassinate her father.

But Vera, clever and defiant, doesn't want a bodyguard. Instead, she proposes a dangerous game: I'll be her fake husband in public.

Vera is unlike anyone I've encountered—intelligent, gorgeous, untamed and untouched. Everything I want and nothing I can have.

The utter destruction and demise of my ultimate plan.

Consumed by desire, I choose a new tactic: seduction.

I vow to show her a world of both pleasure and pain, a world she's only imagined in her darkest fantasies and the pages of her books. Yet, Vera proves to be more than a match for me, ensnaring me in her own game of temptation and turning me into a man obsessed.

Now, caught in a war between duty and passion... I'm torn

between the loyalty to my family and my seductive love for
the enemy.

CHAPTER ONE

Nikko

MY FOOTSTEPS POUND on the pavement like the relentless beating of a drum. My lungs feel like they're going to burst, and my legs ache. I barely notice the rush of cherry blossoms as I pass or the pedestrians by the park; I'm so blinded by the sweat in my eyes. I push myself harder, faster, *longer*. It's a mind game, a mind fuck.

Everything is.

I turn the left corner between Maple and Tower Streets and see my destination in front of me. I'm so far away it's merely a blur, but as long as I can clearly see what's in front of me, I can keep going.

My mentor Kolya told me that any training—*all* training— should be faced as if your life was on the line. Nothing's in vain. You're not running for the sake of a healthy heart or stronger lungs; you're running from an enemy who's going to slit your throat when he catches you.

So when I finally arrive at Mikhail and Aria's house, I come to a stop, hands laced behind my head, heaving with the effort to catch my breath. I barely feel the brush of wind, a promise of stagnant summer heat later in the day.

I notice cars outside. Aleks and Harper are here, likely with their small crew of kids. Mom's car is here, but no Polina. Viktor. Lev.

Frowning, I take out my phone and look down. I never miss a call or text, and today's no different. Nothing missed. Then why's everyone here?

I run my arm across my sweaty brow to clear my vision and trot up the stairs.

"There he is." Mikhail jerks his head in greeting as he walks past the doorway, his one-year-old son Sasha in his arms. It's fitting as *pakhan* to the Romanov family and older brother to all that Mikhail had the first child. It was time.

My brother Aleksandr holds his infant son beside his wife Harper, who's holding the second twin. Both babies have their daddy's bright blue eyes and mama's honey-blonde hair. I turn to the sound of a child's laugh and see my mom walking toward the dining room hand-in-hand with Harper's toddler, Ivy.

Our family has grown in leaps and bounds as Mikhail and Aria's baby just turned one, and Aleksandr and his wife just had twins. With Harper's toddler completing the ensemble, my mother is in her absolute glory with four grandchildren. I haven't seen her this happy in years.

It had to happen. If we're going to establish ourselves as the premier Bratva group in the Cove, the area of New York nestled between Coney Island and Manhattan and the stomping grounds we own and operate, we needed to establish roots. Recruiting and expanding only go so far.

"Where've you been?" Mikhail snaps.

I gesture down to the sleeveless workout tee slicked with sweat and clinging to my body, my running shorts, and my running shoes. "Thought I'd try out my suit for the gala. Prepare for the paparazzi and all that."

"He's swimming in sweat from head to toe," Harper responds. "I can smell him from here. Either he's just come in from a run, or no one's told us the zombie apocalypse is upon us."

Aleksandr chuckles. shaking his head. "Nikko *always* goes for a run on Sunday at noon, Mikhail. You know that. Monday through Friday, you can set a clock by his five a.m. workouts, but he takes a break on Sunday and only goes for a run."

"That's why I pay you to keep track of this sh—stuff," Mikhail says, scowling. The presence of children slows his roll. I'd bet he misses the days he could curse at whim.

I walk past both of them and head to the kitchen. "Did I miss something? Why's everyone here?"

The two of them exchange a look as I grab a bottle of water. Mikhail nods. "Yeah. We have an urgent matter to discuss, but we wanted to wait and do it in person. Just us."

In other words, they waited for my mother to come so she could watch the kids. None of the nannies work Sundays.

Interesting.

I toss the empty water bottle, reach into the fridge, and grab a protein shake, twist the cap off, and down half of it in a few gulps. "What is it?"

Mikhail frowns. "We've discovered a connection between the attempt at poisoning Harper and the attack on Lev."

I stand up straighter, instantly alert. The type of retribution demanded by this situation will fall squarely on my shoulders.

When someone needs to die, I'm the one called.

Seven minutes later, I'm freshly showered and dressed, sitting on Mikhail's balcony that overlooks the ocean. Aleks sits on my left, and my younger brother Viktor is to my right, nursing a cup of coffee. Mikhail's on his way because he had to consult with his wife, Aria, our head hacker and cybersecurity pro.

"Aleks, what's going on?" I ask.

Aleksandr, who works alongside Aria, broods, looking over the Manhattan skyline visible from Mikhail's balcony.

He shakes his head. "Wait for Mikhail. We all need to be present."

Viktor, silent and hulking, sits brooding. Our group heavy's mere presence— hulking, tattooed, and typically dressed in leather— can be enough to ward off enemies. And if it isn't, he's willing and able to get shit done.

Lev, however, gets to his feet and begins to pace. Our youngest brother by several years, Lev is a trained fighter and our team strategist. With his athletic build, he's the one we send in to maneuver through tricky situations and defend himself if needed. Confident, with a magnetic personality that makes women swoon, Lev doesn't ever get romantically entangled. He's too occupied with other things.

"Ollie joining us?" Lev asks, his jaw tight.

"Remotely."

Jesus. It's been over a year since Mikhail and Aria had their son Sasha and our brother Ollie's been working in Moscow. He came home for Sasha's baptism, then went straight back to Moscow.

"When's he coming home?"

Aleks shakes his head, a muscle twitching in his jaw. "Don't know."

"We're stronger when we're together," I say, shaking my head.

"While that might be true," Mikhail says from the balcony doorway as he comes out to meet us, "in this case, it might not be."

What does that mean?

Mikhail joins us and shuts the door behind him. I watch him curiously. I know that look on his face. Whatever he needs to tell us is big.

"Aria and Aleks unlocked some prime intel," Mikhail says, walking past the chairs toward the edge of the balcony. He leans against the wrought iron fence and crosses his arm on his chest. His deep-set dark brown eyes beneath heavy brows, golden, tanned skin, and dark brown hair tinged with flecks of gold make him look almost godlike. And while

Mikhail might appear a bit more civilized than the rest of us, there's a reason he's called the Siberian tiger.

"You know we've been on the trail of those who attacked us for some time now. We've narrowed it down to rival Bratva and a few subsidiary groups. In recent weeks, Aria has discovered that the subsidiaries weren't actually behind any of the attacks but funded by the larger groups." His tone grows sober as his eyes harden. Mikhail is known as the Siberian tiger for a reason.

"We have names."

Unlike other rival groups in New York, ours is one of the only not held together by blood. Like other Russian factions before us, our father decided he would ensure allegiance to our family by adopting all of us. But blood isn't what bonds us all together.

Loyalty. Honor. Trust. The ties of familial bonds run deep despite the way we came into the family.

When Mikhail calls us by name, it's like a call to arms. A summoning. A flare that lights the night sky, calling all of us to action. Any one of us would lay down his life for the other, a claim some of our rivals could never make.

"Names," Lev says, his jaw tightening. Recent years have hardened the softer features of his younger face. He suffered during an all-out attack, resulting in a beating that left him hospitalized shortly after Mikhail was made *pakhan* in the wake of our father's death. He was outnumbered and left for dead outside a nightclub.

Mikhail straightens. While Lev was personally attacked,

Mikhail's wife was nearly poisoned to death. "Ivanov. Petr Ivanov."

"Son of a bitch," Lev says under his breath, shaking his head. "After all we did for him."

"Right."

When my father was still here and we were a fledgling group, we ran surveillance for Ivanov at our own risk for what turned out to be a pittance in hindsight.

"He doesn't care. He knows we own The Cove, and he wants in." Mikhail shakes his head; no further explanation is needed. They all want in.

After my father's death, we took down our greatest rival, Fyodor Volkov. But after his death, other groups vied for power and attention in the coveted Cove.

Ivanov.

A chill runs through me at the knowledge that we have a target. This is where *my* area of expertise comes into play. I stand and straighten my shoulders. "Tell me everything."

Mikhail shakes his head.

"The problem with the Ivanovs is that Petr is untouchable. He's invested more time and money in his own protection than most invest in their entire family. Classic textbook narcissist. So he's surrounded by an army of monsters who will stop at nothing to keep him safe."

I snort. "Like I fucking care. Give me a sniper rifle and a sight and I'll take him down no matter the protection he's put around him. You know I will."

Mikhail nods. "I know you will, but it isn't worth the risk. Kolya and I have consulted, and we have what we believe to be a better plan."

Fire thrums in my veins. This is my family that was attacked. I want to do what I do best.

"Mikhail. A better plan? Better than sending me to take him out once and for all?"

"Sit down, Nikko," Mikhail says calmly. "I'd bet my fucking life on you exacting revenge. But then what? It's more complicated than that. What if this was only the beginning of a much larger plan to take us down? What if he's acting on behalf of another man in a position of power? What if the assassination of Petr Ivanov is the first domino we strike down, only to start something too big for us to handle? We do need to take Ivanov out, but we have to have a crystal clear strategy before we do."

He has a point. I cross my arms over my chest while I listen and finally give a reluctant nod. "Go on."

"I have more details that will help us form our plan." Kolya's voice comes from behind me. I turn to see him entering the balcony. Ten years Mikhail's senior, he was one of my father's best friends in the military. He became an older brother to us, a mentor who trained us in hand-to-hand combat and so much more. While Mikhail has become the patriarch of our family, Kolya will forever be our advisor.

We're all ears.

Kolya strolls onto the balcony, stroking his chin. He looks at each of us, a storm brewing in his eyes when his gaze meets mine. This is personal. "Ivanov has two daughters. One is engaged to be married to a high-ranking captain of the *Ledyanoye Bratstvo*."

A shadow passes over Viktor's features but passes so quickly that I wonder if I've imagined it. Always the face of a stoic, it's unlike him to betray any show of emotion. A muscle ticks in his jaw. Does he know more about them than he's letting on?

"But his younger daughter, Vera Ivanova, is single. Brilliant. And stunning."

Mikhail's eyes are fixed on me as he continues where Kolya left off.

"Vera Ivanova's been selected to join a prestigious graduate student program for gifted medical students in Moscow. Thanks to my wife's impeccable research, I have it on good authority that he cares more about his reputation than he does his actual family. He hasn't shared a bed with his wife in twenty years and has a different mistress in every major city in Russia. He has nothing to do with his daughters. He wanted a son."

Classic. I roll my eyes but nod.

"His wife, Zofia Ivanova, has insisted her daughter bring a bodyguard to Moscow. She also despises her husband's homeland and forbade her daughter from learning the language, which puts her at a disadvantage."

"Ahh," Viktor says, his deep rumble of a voice getting all our attention since he rarely speaks during meetings. Or, honestly, at all. "I see where you're going with this."

I think I see, too, but I want to hear Mikhail explicitly state what he's thinking. I'm slow to make decisions, and I don't ever jump to conclusions.

Mikhail nods. "No one's ever met this new bodyguard. Vera has no idea what he looks like, and Vera's father won't be anywhere near her. . . at least at first. And we only need a few weeks."

"I could go," Viktor says. "I could pretend to be her bodyguard—"

Mikhail nods. "You will go, Viktor. You'll take out the current bodyguard." Mikhail's eyes ice over. "We happen to know for a fact that the man was only hired as a favor to his Moscow mistress, as he is her nephew. He's been convicted on charges of child abuse and possession of child pornography and only released because of his connection to Ivanov." Mikhail scowls. "I want you to know who you're dealing with before you end him, Viktor." He leans forward. "Be silent. Be decisive. We'll do away with his body so there's no evidence. But for the love of Christ, make it fucking hurt."

Viktor is someone we rely on, but he does better work when he has a clear motive. He has no qualms about taking the life of an enemy but considers it an act of justice to do away with someone whose actions he considers heinous and reprehensible.

Fuck. He's chosen Viktor instead of me for whatever reason. If he—

Mikhail turns to me. "Nikko. You'll go with him."

It takes me a second to register what he just said. "Me?"

Mikhail nods. "You most closely match the profile of the man hired to protect her. With a few small tweaks, you'd pass for him at a distance. The others would stand out too much." Mikhail holds my gaze. "Listen carefully. Your job is to pretend to be her bodyguard. Get close to her, Nikko. Find out everything you can about her father and his operation. And when the time is right," he pauses, his words weighing heavily as he lays out my objective. "You'll end him."

I nod. I'll accept this responsibility. It's the only choice I have. And even if I had another, this is the one that I'd choose. I'm dedicated to protecting my family, no matter the cost.

"You said she speaks no Russian," I say thoughtfully, tapping my chin. "Should make things interesting since *I* don't speak any English."

Lev snorts, Aleks grins at me, and even Kolya cracks a reluctant smile. "That will absolutely make it easier for you to gather intel," Kolya admits with a shrug. "To a degree."

"When do I leave?"

Aleks takes out an iPad and pulls up an itinerary. "This is Vera Ivanova's schedule. Aria's set a drone in place to map her for a few days so you can get an idea of her habits, how she operates, where she goes, and what she does. I've tapped into her mobile and online browsing as well." He shakes his head. "I'm telling you, Mikhail, the fact that Aria and I run cybersecurity for you guys puts you head and shoulders above everyone. They don't even have biometric sensors or quantum encryption GPS trackers in place." He shakes his head and curses in Russian, obviously disgusted.

I have no idea what the fuck a quantum encryption GPS tracker is, and only the vaguest idea that the biometric sensors monitor our health and location remotely, but I take his word that it's important and maybe even necessary.

"Her father's set it up so that her new bodyguard will accompany her from America to Moscow. They're scheduled to meet in three days at the airport, where she'll fly to Moscow. And you, as Vera's bodyguard, will go with her. It doesn't matter if anyone sees you since no one else has met the real bodyguard. The only person who can't see you is her father's mistress, but those chances are slim to none." He jerks his chin at Viktor. "And thanks to Viktor, no one will notice he's gone."

I've never had such a mammoth task before. An assassination is a clear instruction, something easy to accomplish with the right tools. This is something entirely different—an assassination with a twist.

"Perfect." I love a challenge.

"Here," Aleks says, taking a file out of his laptop bag and handing it to me. "This is everything we've complied on Vera Ivanova for you to familiarize yourself with before you go in."

I open the file and immediately school my features so I don't give away my shock at seeing her. Delicate features are framed by long, chestnut hair that cascades in loose waves around her shoulders. Emerald-green eyes are highlighted with long, thick lashes, displaying intelligence and curiosity, but the slight upturn of her little nose hints at mischief. A smattering of freckles adds to her wholesome appeal. Despite her slender frame, there's a quiet strength in her posture and movements, hinting at hidden reserves of determination.

I stare at the portrait of the most beautiful woman I've ever laid eyes on. A woman I can't have.

Kolya looks over my shoulder as I continue to read the specs. "You've been trained for this, Nikko. Pretend she's poison. Tell yourself that if you touch her, you turn to stone."

Mikhail grows cold. "Tell yourself that if you touch her, you'll die."

I nod. Stay completely detached. Made of stone. Impermeable.

Stay focused on my job because I have an obligation to kill her father.

CHAPTER TWO

ONE, *two, three, four, five.* I count the bags I'm bringing with me on my flight one more time.

Is it too much? I have a tendency to overpack because I want to be prepared, but the last thing I want is to stand out. Does a grad student moving to an international study program *really* need that many bags? Thankfully, I've condensed the books I need into one heavy suitcase, and everything else fits in the lightweight luggage I bought especially for this trip.

Knock, knock, knock.

"Come in!" I straighten my shoulders and bite my lip as I glance at the clock. I need to leave in an hour if I'm going to arrive two hours and twenty minutes before my scheduled flight. I've never flown at a regular airport before, always using my father's private jets, but it's time, and my research says two hours and twenty minutes is a perfect plan.

"Oh, honey. *Vera.*" My mother's voice wavers from the doorway. Her short hair, once a thick, glossy black, is speckled with gray, but the lines around her eyes hint at someone who loves to laugh and does so often. Now, however, her eyes are brimming with tears.

I swallow a lump in my own throat.

"Is this real?" She walks over to me and takes me in her arms, holding me away a little to look in my eyes. "You look so grown up."

Oh, no. No, no, no. If *she* starts to cry, then *I'm* going to cry, and I can't do that. Nope. Not now.

But my mother's a strong woman, and she raised me to be the same. I take a deep, calming breath and start to tell her I'll call her every night and FaceTime every Sunday because that's the best time I can fit in a call with my rigorous schedule. But when I open my mouth, all that comes out is, "Oh, Mom. I'm going to miss you so much."

Then we're both crying and hugging each other. It's a good thing I don't wear make-up because I'm sure it would be smeared all over the place with these fat, ugly tears. I'm leaving my best friend.

"I wish I could go with you," she whispers. "Are you *sure* I can't? I could take up an apartment downtown or rent a house a bit away. I could—"

"Mom," I tell her gently. "You're needed here. You're planning Lydia's wedding, and I won't even have time to see you if you *did* come. My schedule's insane. Makes my undergrad days look like a cakewalk. But I promise I'll be in touch, and it's only six months."

Only six months. It sounds like an eternity to be in a foreign land, away from home. I love my home. While it's been unconventional, to say the least, my mother did everything she could to keep our childhood normal.

I glance at my watch. Half an hour left.

"Alright," she says with a sigh. "I'll put on my big girl panties and deal with it. I cried when I sent you to kinder-garten, you know."

I smile. "I know." She's told me this story a hundred times. My father was away on business, and it was my first day. Apparently, I 'bravely soldiered on' even though I'm mostly quiet and introverted, while my mother hung back and called *her* mother, and they both sobbed about it together on the phone.

"Your grandmother came to see you before you go. She's downstairs. Come, let's have a cup of tea together, and you can tell her all about what you'll be doing there."

I hide a smile because it's kind of cute. My mom wants me to explain to my grandmother because she doesn't quite understand it herself. It's alright, though. I'd be surprised if my father even knew where I was going.

"My only regret now is never teaching you Russian," she says, biting her lip.

I wave my hand at her. "Mom, the majority of the people I'll be spending my time with are American anyway. I'll pick up what I need to. And anyway, they say the best way to learn a language is full immersion, so I've got that covered." I force a laugh. I'm skilled at medicine and particularly good at all things science, but linguistics, not so much. Lydia got all those genes.

I am admittedly a little nervous that I don't speak the language, but I only found out two weeks ago I was accepted into the program because of an additional grant. There was no time to learn the language.

My mother never taught me Russian because she hates my father. That's no secret. So she did her best to make sure that I was fully raised American in every way she could. A descendant of Polish immigrants, my mother had no use for the Russian language, and my father is too self-absorbed and absent to ever really care.

Mom reaches for the bag. "Oh, Mom, not that one. It's got my books in it, and it's so heavy."

She strains under the weight but winks at me. "It's fine. Go on, now. Let's go see your grandmother."

"Mom, seriously. Take the lighter one."

I manage to wrestle the heavy bag out of her hands and cajole her into taking the backpack.

"Alright, alright," she says. "Let's get these downstairs. I have something to tell you before you go." When she doesn't meet my eyes, my curiosity is piqued.

I carry two of my bags to the bottom of the stairs then go back for the remaining two. When my father's here, he prefers to have hired staff help with things like this, but when he's gone, Mom dismisses all staff. I like to be as normal as possible and don't want to draw unwanted attention to myself.

"What did you need to tell me?" I ask as we head to the living room, where I'll be able to see when the Uber arrives and can visit with my grandmother before I go.

"Your father called this morning," she says, walking beside me and not meeting my eyes.

"Yes? Does he want to meet me at the airport? Go out to dinner when I arrive?" I roll my eyes. He likes to pretend he's a doting father, but she and I both know better. He'll do neither of those things.

"No," she says carefully. "He. . . he's insisting you have a bodyguard while you're traveling."

My jaw drops open, and I freeze in place as I stare at her. "*What?*"

Mom's kind blue eyes grow concerned, and her brows draw together, the lines around her mouth softening. "I tried to talk him out of it because I know how you are, Vera. I know how badly you want to have your independence. But he says Moscow isn't safe, and he *insists.*" She looks away and finally admits in a little voice. "And I have to agree, he's right. It *isn't* safe. I'll feel so much better knowing you're under the protection of someone when you're not with me or your father."

I stare at her. "Mom! I can't have a bodyguard. I'm a grad student! I don't want anyone to know where I come from or who I really am."

Her eyes narrow at that, and she stands taller. "You be proud of who you are, Vera Ivanova. You got into this program of your own volition, with no interference from your father. I saw to that. No one needs to know who your father is."

"So I just show up with a *bodyguard* and people won't think anything of it? There are only five of us in the program!" I stifle a groan, tempted to moan out loud like a thwarted teen. This is the worst possible news.

"You'll find a way to keep your distance. No one will even know he's with you. He can stand far away from you and only stay there in case of emergency."

I sigh and pinch the bridge of my nose. "Is there *anything* I can say to change his mind?"

Mom sighs. "No, especially because, in this instance, I agree with him. Now, go honey. See your grandma before your ride gets here."

With a sigh, I enter the living room. Grandma sits ramrod straight, a teacup in hand. Her eyes twinkle at me, and she pats the seat beside her with an impish little smile. "Vera," she says in her wobbly voice, her accent thick. "Maybe he'll be handsome. You can tell me all about it and give an old lady a chance to live vicariously for once. Now come in here and tell me all about it." She wags a well-manicured red nail at me. "And don't argue with your mother before you're on your way over the Big Pond."

I kiss Grandma's cheeks and take a seat next to her. "I'm not arguing with her, I just—"

"I know what arguing sounds like," Grandma says, taking another sip of tea. Her eyes harden. "Don't argue with your mother."

I stifle a groan. These two are my biggest supporters, so when I don't have their backing, I don't stand a chance. I lived a sheltered life for so long and hoped this would be my first chance to escape the confines of my strict upbringing.

I close my mouth and don't talk back because what's even the point now? My ride is on the way and when I get to the airport, I'm going to meet *him*. My new bodyguard. If he's anything like my father's past guards, I know exactly what to expect. To put it mildly, Grandma will be sorely disappointed by the 'handsome bodyguard.'

"So tell me, Vera. Tell me everything you'll be doing."

I can't help but smile. This is my *jam*. "I'll be at the Advanced Academy of Biomedical Research and Innovation in Moscow for the next six months—"

"It's exclusive," Mom interrupts. "They've combined cutting-edge medical research with practical field study." I hide a smirk. Mom studied the program guide back and forward. "Her grad studies are paid in full because she's a *genius, matka*."

I shake my head. "I'm not a genius."

"Vera, don't be self-deprecating," Mom says with a wave of her hand. "You're going into a field that has the potential of making such a huge difference for high-risk medical conditions! They have rigorous admissions, and only exceptional candidates are accepted."

I smile and turn to my grandmother, who already looks a bit confused. "The curriculum is designed by some of the leaders in the field of military medicine, disaster response, and emergency medical services. We finally get to combine theory with extensive hands-on training and real-world simulations."

"Really," Grandma says, intrigued. "Like what?"

My heartbeat quickens. This is my passion, my baby. I love talking about this. "Like how to give advanced trauma support in a combat situation, how to complete emergency surgical procedures without standard preparation, or how to handle a mass outbreak of biological warfare."

Grandma blinks at me. "It sounds like a TV show."

I can't help but grin. "I did have a professor who was a consultant for a production studio in Hollywood." My heart is heavy, though. I'll miss her and my mother. They were my rocks my whole childhood. And even though they both heavily sheltered me, it almost made up for the lack of any real presence from my father.

My mother looks out the window as a white SUV pulls up out front. Her breath catches as my eyes water.

How do you say goodbye to the only person who ever truly loved you?

I had to do it at one point, but I didn't expect this to feel like such a blow. I kiss Mom's cheek and don't try to stop myself from crying since it's pointless. "I'll miss you," I whisper in her ear. "I'll miss you so much."

"Don't forget to call," Grandma says, wiping her own eyes with a handkerchief.

"Of course not!"

"And you will visit at the holidays?"

"I'll be home by the time we have any holidays of importance," I say with a sad smile. I have to be the brave one here. I turn to the door and grab my bags but stop and stare when the back door of the car opens.

"Mom," I say over my shoulder. "You said my bodyguard was meeting me at the airport. Who's this?"

I stare. This is no tall, lanky man. He's. . . *enormous*. Well over six feet tall. Muscled. Tattooed, probably from head to toe. With a menacing scowl, a sharp jawline, and steely eyes that pierce right through me, I feel like I'm staring at a darker, more lethal version of Superman.

Imposing. Rugged. Primal.

Hot.

His dark hair is cropped short, accentuating his chiseled jawline and piercing gaze. Despite his intimidating appearance, there's a sense of controlled power about him, evident in his precise movements and calculated demeanor.

Did my father just make up for an entire lifetime of neglecting me by going overboard with the bodyguard?

"Oh my God," Mom whispers beside me. "If Jason Bourne were real. . . And on steroids."

That's who I couldn't quite place. He looks like the assassin from those books I loved and the movies my mother did.

"He's coming this way," I whisper to my mother. "Oh my God, he's coming over."

I stick my hand out like some weirdo. He stares for a minute and finally engulfs my much smaller hand in his larger, rougher one. I shiver and hope he doesn't notice.

"I'm Vera," I say because I always make a point to be polite. "And you are?"

"Markov." His voice is deep, his tone short and clipped. I barely register the touch of his rough, warm palm against mine before he recoils and bends to take the bags.

Grandma stares at me and gives a knowing nod. My cheeks heat.

"Oh, be careful, that one's heavy," I say when he reaches for the book bag, but he lifts it as if it weighs nothing at all. "I can help." He still doesn't respond but just takes the bags and puts them in the back of the car. Even the driver doesn't get out. Wordlessly, he holds the door open and gestures for me to follow.

"Well," I say in a whisper to my mom and grandma. "I guess this is it. Thankfully he doesn't seem like he's into small talk. I hate small talk. Maybe this won't be so bad after all."

"It won't be," my mother says in my ear, kissing my cheek. "I am *so proud* of you, Vera. Go, sweetie. Go catch your flight and call me the minute you touch down!"

"Honey, you don't need to do any talking with a man like that," my grandma says, her eyes wide but twinkling.

"Mom!" My mother looks abashed. "That's her *bodyguard*."

My grandma only shrugs. "Even better. Let an old woman have her fun."

I laugh despite the tears that brim in my eyes.

My new bodyguard stands aloof. Waiting. Hot, yes, but he might as well be carved from stone.

It feels a bit surreal, like I'm on a movie set or something, as I get into the seat, and he shuts the door behind me. It's warm in here and smells faintly of cinnamon. The driver nods and lifts a hand to me. "Don't bother talkin' to that guy," he says. "He only speaks Russian."

I sigh and lean back in my seat as he joins me. Suspicion confirmed.

I guess I would feel a bit safer around a man like him if he didn't look at me like *I* was the enemy.

CHAPTER THREE

Nikko

I KNEW what I had to do, and I was prepared.

I watched every single goddamn thing Vera Ivanova did over the past few days. I watched her online history and tracked her phone. Listened in on her conversations. Perused her bank account to see where she spent her money. I even know her astrological sign and the way she takes her coffee.

But no amount of sleuthing, spying, or stalking prepared me for meeting her in person.

I knew she was beautiful. She took my breath away the first time I saw her picture. In person...I can hardly look away.

I have to.

Her clothes are suitable for a long flight—black yoga pants that hug every perfect curve and a pale green long-sleeved tee that makes her eyes pop. So unassuming. So completely mesmerizing.

But it's obvious the second I'm in her presence that there's more to Vera than meets the eye. Despite her slender, petite frame, there's a quiet strength in her posture and movements. A decided elegance in the way she holds herself and the way she speaks. She's grace personified.

From what I've read about her, this woman's fucking brilliant, too, having been accepted into one of the most prestigious grad programs in Europe. The combination of mischief and challenge, grace and intelligence, would outdo a man with lesser self-control than I have. But I've learned how to govern my emotions.

I have to remain aloof. Detached. I shield myself in public and always have, and for that, I'm grateful because I've never needed it more.

Vera gives me a curious look. "Have you ever flown before?" I can't quite decipher the look she's giving me, but to keep up the charade, I only shrug.

She and the driver share a look. Good, my plan worked. I managed to communicate to him that I didn't speak English, and in the short time it took me to load her bags in the car, he must've told her.

I watch as she makes a little finger motion like an airplane flying and give her another shrug as if I still have no idea what she's saying, because her attempts at communicating are sort of cute. I flick my fingers in the air, and she says more clearly and louder this time, *"Plane. You?"*

I shrug and nod. Yes, I've flown before, many times.

I point my finger at her and make a flying motion.

She sits up straighter and shakes her head. "Uh, no. I've never been on a plane."

Shit. Seriously? Her first flight from New York to Moscow will be about ten hours long.

Great. Will she be afraid? Does she know anything about airport protocol? I noticed when she got in the car that her eyes were a bit misty and red-rimmed. Is she afraid of flying, or is there another reason she looks like she was crying?

Doesn't matter, though. My goal is to infiltrate her family's security and get to her father. Vera is just a means to an end.

"I brought some books to read," she says quietly, drumming her fingers on her knees. It's almost like she's talking to herself rather than me, which makes sense since she thinks I don't speak her language. She chooses her words thoughtfully, but I can tell she's more anxious than she's letting on.

Body language conveys more than people know. I note the way she doesn't look at me when she talks. The way her gaze is fixed out the window and her foot taps.

The slight fluttering of her fingertips at her collarbone signifies more than nerves, though.

Has she ever been in close proximity to a man like me before? How sheltered has she been?

She continues, her voice a bit wobbly. "I have some puzzle books. My phone, of course, but my eyes get tired looking at screens after studying, and I'm so over looking at my phone. I hope there's WiFi. Maybe I'll nap, but I don't like the idea of napping in public because I'll let my guard down, and I

—" She gives me a sidelong glance. "Huh. I suppose no one will give me a difficult time if I'm sitting anywhere near you. Maybe I *will* nap."

I'm glad she doesn't think I speak English because I would assure her she'd be absolutely fine to sleep next to me. I'd promise her utter safety and protection, but I can't risk getting too close to her.

"My mother was so overprotective," she explains. "I'm kind of glad we don't speak the same language because that means I can say things maybe I normally wouldn't."

The driver looks at her in the mirror.

"Maybe he's lying."

I stare straight ahead and pretend I didn't hear a thing. Asshole should mind his own business. I don't even have the benefit of being able to give him a dirty look, or I could give myself away.

"You think he's lying?" She gives the driver a quizzical look. "Interesting."

"I didn't say he was. Just saying it's a possibility."

I pretend I don't feel the laser-sharp focus of her assessing gaze.

"Well, then," Vera says, leaning closer to me. She lowers her voice so the driver can't hear her. "What if I were to say things that would make him blush? If he didn't speak English, he wouldn't react, would he?"

What the fuck is she doing?

I give her a dismissive look like she's an annoying little sister who needs to go away, then pull out my phone and pretend to scroll.

"So," she says in a whisper as she casually picks at her cuticles. "I don't like to sleep with pajamas on. Just saying."

Jesus.

I stare at my phone and don't look at her. I barely move.

"I don't like the feel of clothes between me and the blankets," she continues in a whisper. "I wonder if you do."

When I don't respond, she heaves a big sigh.

Maybe Vera Ivanova isn't as innocent as she looks. Appearances can be deceiving.

With a sigh, she talks to the driver again. "I think you're wrong. I think it's actually true." She lowers her voice. "Either that or I don't have the effect on him I'd hoped for."

Oh, but she does.

"Alright, bodyguard," she says again in her plain, straightforward voice. "I've told you one of my biggest secrets. Now I'm going to tell you one more because you don't have a clue what I'm saying."

I keep my eyes stoically on my phone as I flip through various notifications. I cast a mildly curious glance at her.

"No one knows I read all the Bourne books. And I have a major, *huge* crush on Jason Bourne." She leans in. "And you look *just* like him. Like *just. Like. Him.*"

Interesting. Jason Bourne was an assassin and she has a major crush on him.

But it's so tempting to respond. So tempting.

Don't react. Don't react.

I slide my phone into my pocket and look straight ahead while Vera pulls out her phone with a sigh. She puts headphones in and mouths something to herself. I could check to see what she's doing on the screen mirroring app I have, but she's sitting right next to me. I don't want to take risks.

My most important job right now is to get her on that plane. Once we're in the air, the chances of me being discovered lessen.

The second most important job is to engage with the Ivanov Bratva and make them believe I am who I say I am.

I check the driver's GPS on the dash and see we're only two minutes out. I need to prepare.

Most people think airports are adventurous, unless they travel a lot for work, in which case they might find them tiresome and tedious. Some of us, however, know them for what they truly are—dangerous hot zones for criminals, enemies, and anyone you don't trust. Fugitives escape under false identities, people are robbed and kidnapped. I trust no one, especially at an airport.

It's late at night when we pull into the drop-off area. I haven't flown with normal civilians in years. Her father's an asshole for allowing it. If my sister Polina went on a trip to Moscow, not only would she have a *team* of bodyguards with her, they'd be in constant contact with us and she'd fly privately. I never understood why some Bratva don't take care of their women.

But that's none of my business. She's nothing to me.

I exit the car and go to Vera's door to open it for her. I may not be her real bodyguard, but I'll play the part. She's young and innocent. Beautiful and vulnerable. She needs a bodyguard, and goddamn if I'll let anyone hurt her.

I won't think of what I have to do.

When I open the door for her, she looks up at me with her wide, intelligent eyes.

"*Spasibo*," she says with a smug little smile. *Thank you.*

Ah. So that's what she was doing on her phone. Studying Russian.

I can't help but smile at her and nod. "*Pozhaluysta.*"

You're welcome.

The driver looks at both of us, tapping his steering wheel, but doesn't make a move to get our bags. Asshole. I tap the trunk of the car for him to open it so I can get our bags and look in surprise when Vera reaches for one. I don't think so. My mother raised me better than that, and I'll be damned if she carries her bags on my watch. I give her a silent shake of my head and a stern look. "*Nyet.*"

When she huffs at me and reaches for the heavy bag to outright *defy* me, I make my decision. I turn to her and pick her up, hands under her armpits, before I deposit her on the sidewalk. When she flails and lets go of the bag, I take them and point to her little purse. *There. You can take that.*

"I'm a modern woman, you know," she says with a little huff, but the slight flush to her cheeks tells me she's a little flustered by being manhandled. Is she, now?

I'm arranging all our bags on a cart to take them inside when she tries to march away from me. Apparently, her little Russian tutorial failed to teach her the Russian way of telling me to fuck off, which makes it a lot easier for me to ignore her.

Instinctively, I grab the cart handle in my left hand and reach for her with my right. My fingers tighten on her slender arm, not too hard to hurt but enough to stop her.

"Let go of me!"

I don't bother to try to communicate but snap at her in Russian. *"Ne uhodi ot menya v aeroportu!"*

Do not walk away from me in an airport.

Jesus, what is she thinking?

Of course she doesn't understand a word I say, so I only keep my grip on her arm and repeat what I said.

"I'm just getting one of those things for the luggage," she says, pointing about twenty feet away to a stack of trolleys. I scoff and shake my head and get one myself.

"Well, this is gonna be fun," she mutters under her breath. "An overprotective bodyguard I can't talk to?"

What kind of bodyguards has she had?

We stalk in tense silence to check-in, where I plunk our bags down beside the kiosk and glare at her.

"Fine!" she snaps. "I won't pick up the bags, okay?"

Guess I communicated that clearly enough. Good. She's damn lucky she isn't mine with an attitude like that.

I shake my head and scan our boarding passes. I notice her stiffen beside me.

"Um. You cannot take that on a plane," she whispers.

I look up in surprise to see she's looking at my back. The gun I'm carrying is secured in the waistband of my jeans at the small of my back.

I shrug. She leans in closer to me, laying her hand on my back.

Christ.

My skin heats at how near she is, a flare of warmth from her touch, and the faint, lingering smell of warmed toffee and spice surrounds me. Her mouth gets near to my ear, and she tries again, repeating herself. "You can't take a gun on a *plane.*" She presses it into my back to emphasize her point.

Oh yeah? *Watch me.* I only smile at her and shake my head. It'll be fine.

At security, I head immediately to the security guard Aleks told me to go to. I've been in touch with the Ivanov security team but they've given me minimal instructions. Why am I not surprised?

The security guard smiles at me when I turn my arm over and show him the tattoo that marks me as Bratva.

"Hello, sir. This way, please." Behind closed doors, I discreetly hand him the cash we agreed on, and he swiftly moves us aside and down a VIP aisle to get past security to get to our gate.

"You did not just do that," she says, shaking her head. "Jesus, I wish you'd speak English. I'd tell you that was, like…" Her voice trails off when she realizes I'm not responding. "*Hot,*" she says to herself. "No, on second thought, I wouldn't tell you that."

An interesting observation.

We're early for our flight but comfortable in a VIP lounge we've secured beforehand.

"Okay, so this is nice," she says as she walks to a snack station with complimentary drinks and snacks. She points to the food and then her belly. "I'm starving. You?"

I have no idea how long it'll be before we eat again, and I have no intention of sleeping on that plane, so I join her. We feast on sandwiches, chips, and fruit, and when she helps herself to a cookie, I decline.

"Watching those macros, huh? Of course you are. You can't be built like *that* and eat carbs all day long." She sighs. "I, on the other hand, couldn't care less about macros."

She isn't wrong. I don't eat that shit.

I keep my face deliberately impassive, but she's quirky and kind of cute, so it's getting harder to do.

"Macro shmacro," she says, happily munching on a second cookie. "I'll happily sleep, seduced into a sugar coma."

I pretend to busy myself on my phone, but I'm checking the mirroring app on hers. I have no idea how anyone can function with twenty apps open at a time, but she's moving from one thing to the next seamlessly – Russian translating app, a website with "must-know Russian phrases," a little jewel matching game, and an app for reading. Interesting. I have to work extra hard to school my expression when I see the titles. I'd call it. . . eclectic and telling. What can you learn by the titles someone reads?

Dominated by the Billionaire Hitman

The Future of Medical Biometrics

Beauty and the Bodyguard

Mastering His Lady

The Newbies Guide to Russian

"Ladies and gentlemen, flight 5834 for Russia is preparing to board in twenty minutes. Please make any necessary last-minute purchases or trips to the restroom. We will begin shortly with priority seating."

Vera stands and points to a restroom. "I need to use the bathroom before we go, okay?"

When I nod and stand with her, her eyes widen in horror, but I only shake my head and point to the floor outside the restroom. I am not going into the restroom with her.

I will, however, be vigilant to ensure no one's waiting to hurt her or is ready to rob her and watch every exit and entrance.

I read through the list of profiles of the other passengers, as well as the flight attendants. Nothing seems out of place. Maybe she doesn't have a target on her back like others do. Maybe Ivanov's lack of interest in her paid off. Or maybe I just haven't seen anything yet.

The burner phone in my back pocket vibrates with a text. It belongs to Markov Pashnik, whose body lies, weighted, at the bottom of the East River by now.

Markov was less than inspired when he created his contact list.

Did you get her

I respond with one word:

yes

Nothing else. Someone's checking off a box to make sure she's here but doesn't give a shit beyond that.

Works for me.

I pull out my own phone while she's in there and quickly shoot a message to Aleks.

All clear. You see anything?

No one suspects a thing. All good here. Markov is gone, and good riddance. He had few friends. Our plan is working. Once you're there, you're golden. Ivanov is traveling and no one else will know you. You'll meet with the Ivanov Bratva but keep it brief. None of them have met Markov yet but the less contact you have with them the better

Perfect

I slide my phone into my pocket just as she exits and we leave to board.

"I should have had a stiff drink," she says, her voice shaking. I stare straight ahead and pretend I don't notice the way her slim shoulders tremble.

Vera takes a step closer to me.

I can tell she's trying to keep herself calm with deep breaths, as she squares her shoulders and looks straight ahead. We have our carry-on bags with us, but she insisted we take the one that feels like it's loaded with bricks on board. I carry that one and walk behind her as we board.

I am definitely not used to the size of these seats. Whoever booked these tickets was only considering her and not a potential add-on. I hardly fit. Again, I mentally curse her asshole father for shortchanging her. She should be flying business class, in the lap of luxury, not crammed next to me in coach on a ten-hour flight.

"Wow," she says in a whisper. "Uh, tight quarters."

She looks over at me and shakes her head.

"Markov, that can't be comfortable for you."

No matter how hard I try, half my body is practically in her seat. I lean back, cross my arms over my chest, and shake my head at her. I have a job, and I'm going to do it.

Once we get to Moscow, I'll have access to her father's whereabouts as well as his inner circle of acquaintances. But for now, I have one job to do, and I aim to do it well.

An hour in, and my muscles ache from holding myself away from her. I adjust to no avail, and a toddler sitting in front of us with his mother begins to wail.

I know the feeling, buddy.

"Oh, poor thing," Vera says. "Probably his ears."

The mother tries all manner of things with him, but the little guy can't be soothed. I stifle a grumble. If I have to keep myself stuffed into this little seat and listen to a screaming kid for nine more hours. . .

Vera looks through the hole between the two seats and tickles the little boy's foot. He stops. I give her a sharp look. It isn't the safest method, instigating contact with strangers, but she doesn't seem to give a shit. Excellent.

I sit up straight and try to ignore the little guy who's now avidly poking little things through the gap between the seats.

"I don't like flying either," she whispers to him. "I'm scared. Are you scared?"

He looks through the hole from me to her, then back to me. "Scared," he whispers. With wide brown eyes and curly blond hair, he looks about my niece Ivy's age, three or four. The little guy's cheeks are red from crying. His mother smiles at Vera as she talks to him.

"The man next to me, he's my friend but he scares me, too. I mean, look at him."

What's that supposed to mean?

The boy stares at me, and his lower lip trembles. *Shit.*

"Oh no!" Vera says, quickly backtracking. "I just meant he *looks* scary. He's quite nice! You don't need to be afraid of him."

Right, easier said than done.

And how does she know I'm nice?

When he opens his mouth to scream again, I quickly cover my face with my hand. After a few seconds, when I know I have his undivided attention, I peek through my fingers to see him staring. We begin a fast-paced game of peekaboo which has him giggling with laughter.

Finally, the mother gives the little guy a snack, and a few minutes later, he's half asleep against her shoulder.

Vera smiles but doesn't say anything.

The longer we fly, the less comfortable this is, though.

Jesus.

This is bullshit. I pull out my phone when she's busy reading and text Aleks.

> We're in the smallest seats known to man and I'm spilling half into her lap. Help.

It's the middle of the night, but thankfully, Aleks is usually a light sleeper, and the kids keep him up. He responds quickly.

> Shit, sorry bro. Let me see what I can do.

> Tell them to make it sound like a mistake. I don't want to make anyone suspicious.

When the flight attendant, a young woman with blonde hair in a tight bun at the back of her head, comes up to us a few minutes later, Vera startles. She's deep into one of the books she brought in her carry-on.

"Vera Ivanova and Markov Pashnik?" she asks with a smile. "Please come with me."

Aleks pulled through.

She turns to Vera. "You were meant to have an upgrade to first-class. I'm so sorry for the mix-up." She says the same to me in Russian.

"Oh, thank God," Vera says. "You speak Russian and English. Can you translate for us?"

The flight attendant nods. "Of course. First, let's get you settled in your new seats. Unless it's an urgent matter?"

Vera shakes her head. "Not at all."

I take my phone and our carry-ons, and she takes her puzzle books, phone, ginger ale, and headphones, balancing them all precariously in her arms. I reach over and take a few of her things to add to my pile.

"Why, thank you."

I nod silently and follow them to where the plane connects to the first-class section. I breathe a sigh of relief when we see our new seats. The spaciousness and comfort immediately put me at ease. Unlike our previous seats, these fully recline into flat beds. We have a little less than nine hours left, and I don't know if I could've stood much longer in a seat built for a toddler.

"Oh, now this is better," Vera breathes, laying back on her seat. "I might even get a nap here. It's like each seat is its own little cocoon."

"She says these are better seats, and she might even be able to rest," the flight attendant repeats to me in Russian.

I'm a little disappointed she's so far away now, but I know it's just as well.

"Excellent," I respond in Russian. "Please tell her it will be wise to rest before we arrive. Also, tell her she can rest easy; I will watch over her while she does."

The flight attendant's eyes go a little soft, the way a woman's does when she sees a man do something particularly endearing. She relays the message to Vera.

"Before you go," Vera says. "Can you please tell him thank you for everything?"

The flight attendant looks from me to her and back to me. "She says thank you."

In Russian, I respond. "Please tell her, of course, it is my job."

She looks at Vera and smiles. "He says it is his pleasure."

That's not exactly what I said, but the flush of Vera's cheeks when she says it makes me wish that I had.

With more space between us, it's easy for me to turn my phone to the side to see what she's doing. She's reading again. I take a peek. There's a feather on the front and a silver lock.

Dominated by The Billionaire Hitman

Author B.N. Honey takes readers on a whirlwind journey into the lavish world of billionaire Maxwell Rodino, a ruthless businessman with a penchant for control. When the young and talented artist enters his world, she's enraptured in a world of intrigue, luxury, and power. . .

Well, then. Isn't that interesting, little Miss Vera.

I see a link for a sample preview and quickly click it.

> *"No, sir," I said, shaking my head as he circled round me, the short riding crop nearly vibrating with the electric connection between us. "I know better than to make myself come without your permission."*

My phone clatters to the floor. Vera looks up at me in surprise while I quickly grab it before she can see what's on my screen.

Vera Ivanova is reading a book about rich, powerful men and submission and domination.

It's just a book. Fiction. Fantasy. It doesn't mean she's actually. . . into any of that.

And even if she was, it's none of my business.

None.

I steal a glance at her when she's reading again. I notice her breathing has accelerated, and her cheeks are faintly flushed. It's risky, mirroring her phone and seeing the exact place where she's reading, but now that I've peeked. . . I have to know.

Before I can change my mind, I'm tapping on the app and her phone screen is popping up in front of me. I've never read anything like this in my life, but within minutes, I'm wrapped up in the filthiest sex scene I could've imagined.

I look back at the cover.

Feather and lock, my ass. Who knew what was hiding behind a cover like that?

I startle when Vera's head falls to the side.

She's sleeping. Only sleeping.

I didn't realize I was holding my breath. Here in first class, we have ample room, freedom to move, and the luxury of space to sleep in. However, if someone flops around. . . which is exactly what Vera does. . . one can find oneself in close proximity.

Her hair's tickling my arm. Her fragrance envelops me, and as I watch, her hand rests gently on her chest.

What is she dreaming about? A scene about being dominated by a powerful alpha male? Losing total control. . .

She's lived a sheltered life, that much I know. She hides behind her books and big words, and if I've learned anything, it's that she lacks world experience. She has no current boyfriend, and based on what I've researched, she hasn't had any serious relationships.

Yeah. I'd bet good money Vera Ivanova's a virgin.

For one second too long, I allow myself time to fantasize. What would it be like to show her the world she only reads about? To dominate her, master her, see her sweet lips part in ecstasy and hear her seductive moan...

I shut the door on those thoughts with a ferocity that disallows anything more than perfect abstinence. I've done nothing but guard my emotions, yet I find myself attuned to her responses.

I remember how soft her hand felt when I shook it. How slight her body was when I moved her away from the luggage.

It would be a man's greatest honor to dominate a woman like her. That level of *trust*. . . A challenge, yes, but one that I'd relish.

But I know I can't allow myself to be swayed or to show weakness in any way, no matter how tantalizing she is.

I lean back in my chair and plan my next move.

CHAPTER FOUR

Vera

I STARTLE AWAKE to the plane shaking so badly at first I think I must be dreaming. When I realize it isn't a dream, I gasp and try to stand but am quickly pulled down by large, strong hands.

"*Nyet.*" Markov is holding me tight against him, his arms like vice gripping me. The overhead speaker crackles.

"Ladies and gentlemen, we've hit a bit of turbulence. There is nothing to fear. Please remain seated and be sure your safety belts are fastened. We should be able to navigate out of this pocket short—"

His words are cut off when the plane takes a sudden deep nosedive. Screams drown out any more thoughts, mine along with everyone else's. Panic swoops over me. I squeeze my eyes shut and feel tears escape between my lids.

A calm, collected voice beside me anchors me to safety. "*Vsyo budet khorosho.*"

His tone, for the first time, is softened and reassuring. I have no idea what he's saying, but somehow, it puts me at ease. I breathe in through my nose and out through my mouth when a large, warm hand comes to rest on my thigh.

I open my eyes to see him staring straight ahead, ever the picture of stoicism. His jaw clenches, but he shows no fear. My mind swirls in a tempest of fear – what if we crash? Would we survive? My scientific mind immediately calculates how far up we are, our location, the chances of survival. I can hardly form a cohesive thought. What if we – what if I--

Just as soon as the turbulence began, it stops. The plane flies calmly now in the inky darkness of the night sky.

I draw in a deep breath and let it out slowly. My breathing regulates.

"*Spasibo.*"

I'm glad I brushed up a bit on my phone.

Markov gives me a silent nod.

I look down at his hand resting on my thigh. We realize at the same time he's touching me in a way my bodyguard has no business touching me. He was only reassuring me, yes, but the continued intimacy of his hand on my thigh has crossed a line we should never cross.

My cheeks flame, and a warm trickle of awareness flutters between my thighs.

Maybe I shouldn't have spent the last hour before I fell asleep reading about dominant, perfect, sexy as fuck billionaires, especially when I'm in such close proximity to the sexiest Russian I've ever laid eyes on.

I lay my hand on top of his and, with great reluctance, push his hand off of me.

I feel his eyes on me but don't return his gaze as the flight attendant comes to us.

"I'm so sorry about that."

I shake my head. "Unless you're personally responsible for the behavior of the sky, I don't think it's your fault. But thank you."

Markov says something to her in rapid Russian that makes her laugh. She responds, and he gives her a glimmer of a smile.

An unexpected stab of jealousy hits me straight in the solar plexus. I want to know what he said to her. I didn't even know the man was capable of humor.

I want to be the one that makes him smile. Or, *almost* smile anyway.

They continue chattering, and I pick up my book. Fine, have a conversation that doesn't include me. I'll just read my book and pine away with unrealistic expectations, no big deal.

"He says to tell you he was only trying to comfort you and apologizes if he was untoward."

I blink and look up at the flight attendant. "Excuse me?"

She repeats herself. I look over to see him staring straight at me, as serious as always.

I clear my throat.

"Please tell him thank you." I want to say so much more, but for once, I'm grateful for the language barrier.

I glance at the time, surprised to see I slept through most of the flight. We land in an hour.

"Can I get you a snack?" The flight attendant offers the two of us a basket. I recognize little packets of trail mix and a few candies, but there are other snacks I've never seen. *Русское Поле,* some sort of rye crisp, and a variety of chocolates with names like *Коркунов.*

"Those are excellent," she says. "Do you like chocolate?"

"Mmm. Of course."

"Here," she says with a smile. "Take a few of each."

I'm not surprised when Markov declines a snack and drink, considering the fact that he probably subsists on egg white omelets and protein shakes. A man does not carve out a body like that on potato chips and chocolate.

I eat my snacks and comment on them, pretending he can understand me, only because the silence between us feels heavy and weighted. "Mmm. I like the delicate flavor of the chocolate," I say, like I'm doing some kind of review. "Though the subtle hint of roasted nuts is quite nice. Not quite an M&M, but it will do."

He just continues to stare straight ahead. What causes someone to be so serious?

I turn back to my book and lose myself in a fake world with fake promises that won't ever happen in real life.

I wish my father hadn't insisted I take a bodyguard with me.

Despite Markov's silence and stony disposition, he snaps into action as soon as we land. I don't even bother fighting him when it comes to carrying my bags. At this point, I figure I might as well enjoy the bit of pampering, or whatever it is you want to call it. I don't know how he quite manages it, but he holds our bags, escorts me off the plane, and seamlessly guides me toward the exit.

Though it was a ten-hour flight to Moscow, due to the time difference, we arrived in Moscow midday. It feels strange, honestly, as if we've skipped a whole day. The sun hangs high in the clear blue sky in contrast to the inky night we left behind. As we exit the plane, the brisk air of Moscow greets us, a welcome change from the stale cabin air we've endured. The hustle and bustle of Sheremetyevo Airport greets us with travelers and locals alike navigating terminals with practiced ease. The diverse mix of accents and languages around us create a lively hum. My body feels weighted from jet lag, but there's an underlying current of excitement. I've never left my country. This is a new chapter of my life filled with promise.

We gather our luggage and head to the pick-up area. "I was told there would be a car waiting for us—um, me," I amend. I'm not sure how I'm going to explain his presence to the people I'll be working with. I sigh when he stares at me and pull out my phone to bring up the translation app when I see a driver standing beside a large SUV with a sign that says *Vera Ivanova* in bold black lettering.

I point. "There, that's for us."

Markov gives the man a flinty look and nods, carrying our bags. A tall woman who looks vaguely familiar waves excitedly to me. I realize when we get closer to her that I recognize Professor Irina Kuznetsova with her sharp, intelligent eyes, slender frame, and short silver hair. She's the woman I did a teleconference with a few weeks ago, the one in charge of the program. Wow. I had no idea she'd come all the way here just to see me.

"Vera! Welcome!" she says in perfect English. She gives Markov a curious look.

"Professor Kuznetsova?" I say, reaching a tentative hand out to her. "You came all the way to get me at the airport? I'm honored, really."

"Please, call me Irina," she says sheepishly. "You and another one of your classmates, Jake Thomas, took the same flight. I had no time to introduce you two or I would have made sure you made each other's acquaintance well before the flight."

Markov stands stoically to the side.

"You brought a guest?" she asks, her brow furrowed.

God. Here we go.

"Looks more like a bodyguard to me," a booming voice says in English behind me. I turn to see a man who could be the poster child for 'All-American' standing behind me—light brown hair, perfect teeth, pale blue eyes, and an athletic build.

He looks like a child next to Markov.

"Jake Thomas," he says, extending his hand to me. "We were on the same flight but not all of us got mysteriously upgraded to first class." He circles his neck as if pained from sleeping in coach and gives me a wink.

I turn away, my cheeks flushing. Markov narrows his eyes.

"Bodyguard?" Irina asks. Oh, God. I can't stand the idea of anyone thinking I brought a bodyguard with me. Nobody knows who I am or where I come from.

What if she sends me home? After everything I've done and everything I've gone through to get into this program...

My cheeks flush hot as I shake my head and remember that Markov can't speak English. "No, no," I say with a forced laugh, trying not to panic. I wasn't supposed to bring anyone with me. I should be here alone. Goddamn my father for not thinking about the finer details. It's so typical of him to pronounce something that will have a direct impact on my life without caring about the ramifications for *me*.

I say the first thing that comes to mind. "This is—this is my husband." Markov thankfully doesn't react because he has no idea I just told such a bold-faced lie.

Irina stares but quickly composes herself.

"Oh! Of course!" Irina says. "If you'll excuse me for a moment."

She takes out her mobile and makes a quick call. I can't understand what she's saying but it seems as if she's pleading with someone. Markov listens carefully, his face darkening.

Shit.

She comes back a minute later, smiling broadly. "All set," she says. "You can come with me. I've arranged a car ride back to the school and will only have to make a minor adjustment to the room situation."

Oh dear God.

The room situation.

"Have you two met on the way here?" Irina says, a wide smile in place. "Mr. Thomas didn't come from too far away, Ms. Ivanov," she says. "You hail from the Midwest, don't you?"

"I do," he says, sticking his hands in his pockets as if he's being modest. "Though the last few years I studied at Harvard."

Oh, God, name-dropping an Ivy League. Lovely.

The bustling atmosphere of the airport surrounding us makes me feel even more exhausted than ever. I stifle a yawn.

"You must be exhausted after that flight. Come, we'll get you situated in your rooms and give you time to rest before we have a formal dinner tonight to introduce everyone."

Get you situated in your rooms.

What have I done?

"Thank you."

I have to tell Markov. If he hears from anyone else what happened. . . what if he tells them I lied? That he is actually my bodyguard?

How am I going to tell him?

Markov fits the luggage in an overhead rack on the roof of the car, which is admittedly handy. Jake gets into the car first, and I go to follow, but Markov takes me by the arm and shakes his head. "*Nyet.*"

He jerks his head behind him and makes me step aside so that he can sit beside Jake.

"Heh," Jake says. "I guess if it were my wife, I wouldn't want her sandwiched between us either." He gives me a smile. I'm glad *somebody* can be a good sport about things.

A part of me is admittedly thankful, though. I don't know Markov well, but I know him better than Jake, and if I'm going to be sitting side-by-side with a man, stuffed so close together we're like sardines in a can, I'd rather be next to Markov than a stranger I don't trust.

It doesn't really dawn on me that, for all intents and purposes, *Markov* is a stranger I don't trust.

We're squeezed together on the ride to the school while Jake and Irina chatter on in Russian and I fight to keep my eyes open. Why did I say he was my husband? I had the entire flight to come up with a plan but feel like I'm flailing. What will they do with a married couple in the program? *Ugh.*

Markov sits upright, constantly scanning our surroundings as if looking for a potential threat while he keeps his facade in place. I guess that's his job. Is he always this vigilant?

My eyelids are heavy, but I try to keep them open. I don't want to miss anything. As we approach the campus in Moscow, the vibrant energy of the city excites me. The streets are alive with a mix of people—students hurrying along with laptop bags and backpacks, street vendors selling foods, and business professionals in suits and skirts hurrying from one place to the next. I notice Moscow's famous metro buses and trams snaking their way through the crowd.

For the first time, I'm glad I have Markov with me. It's overwhelming to think of being totally alone.

I stifle a yawn. I like my sleep and hardly got any last night. The car is warm, and Markov's like an electric heater beside me. I fight to stay awake but still find Markov gently shaking my shoulder as we arrive.

"We have housing adjacent to the dorms for our grad students in specialty fields. It's nothing fancy and really, glorified dorms, but they're at least semi-private."

I look at Markov, but he doesn't respond. I discreetly take out my phone and type a message in the translator app I downloaded. I have to tell him what I told her. He has to be able to play the part.

"I'm sorry, but there was a miscommunication. For now, just for now, you have to pretend to be my husband. Okay?"

I stare at the foreign words in front of me, unable to read them. Is that really what I want to say? Do I have a choice? I translate the words back and forth until I'm satisfied and I have no more time. We're almost there.

I tap Markov's shoulder and show him the translation before I lose my courage.

I watch him read it. What will he do? What if he insists on telling the truth? Within seconds, his eyes narrow, and then he gestures for my phone. I nod, handing it over. He switches over to the Russian keyboard option. I watch, my mouth dry. My cheeks heat with embarrassment.

I stare when he shows me the phone and his reply. It feels somehow intimate communicating with him like this.

Why didn't you tell the truth?

I can almost hear the admonition in his rough, deep voice, his tone harsh.

I type in a response and hit the translator button again. It's a clumsy way of communicating but it's all we've got.

I don't want them to know you're my bodyguard!

I expect him to want to type out another message, shoves my phone back to me, then he gives one sharp cut of his hand to dismiss me and looks out the window.

I turn away and roll my eyes as we pull up to the college.

I never lived at college because of my strict upbringing, so a college atmosphere is quite new to me. The college itself is flanked on either side by imposing buildings, the architecture at once intricate and modern. My heart thumps. *I'm really here. I made it.*

"Oh, it's beautiful."

"Where did you grow up?" Jake asks me.

"New York."

"Ah, you're a city girl. I imagine Moscow and New York are still very different places."

"Yes, but not all of New York is city. I spent some time in

Upstate New York and more recently in a suburb just outside the city itself. Still, it is definitely not Moscow."

I shrug and feel a heavy hand on my thigh. The doors to the car open, and everyone begins to exit, but I take a minute to look up at Markov. "What?" I whisper.

He gestures for my phone again, scowling, and taps something out on the Russian keypad before handing it back to me. I hit translate.

Do not trust.

Ah, of course my bodyguard's telling me not to trust another man. I roll my eyes at him and tuck my phone in my pocket. I exit the door opposite him.

He predictably grabs our bags, a few at a time, and lines them up on the sidewalk. Irina says something in Russian. She gushes and praises, but he only shrugs and asks a question in return.

"He is such a gentleman," she says in English. "It will be so refreshing to have such a nice married couple here with us! Come, I'll show you your room. You must be so tired."

As we walk, Jake walks beside me. "I've read your work," he says in a low voice. He gives me a crooked smile, and I'm starting to wonder if pretending Markov is my husband was a good idea. What if I meet someone here? After all my sheltering, I've never had a chance like this before.

"Have you?"

"Yes," Jake says. I notice when he smiles, there's a little dimple on his cheek. "Your peer-reviewed analysis on improvised tourniquet techniques in field trauma care was exceptionally well done. I was impressed with the risks you took by applying unorthodox methods and the results you achieved. Truly impressive work."

My chest swells with pride. "Thank you. I led the study but couldn't have done it without the aid of the others I studied with."

Jake smiles, his eyes warming at me. "Humble, too. You'd better have a flaw somewhere, Ms. Ivanov," he says with a wink before he joins Irina.

Markov, as usual, walks beside me with a flinty expression on his face.

Seriously, why did I pretend we were married? I inwardly groan.

I need to make sure no one here knows who I really am, or who he is. This is my chance.

I think Markov and I are beginning to have some marital troubles.

CHAPTER FIVE

Nikko

I TAKE in every detail as we enter the campus.

I've begun to realize that my initial strategy—remaining the aloof bodyguard and finding my way into her family's trust—won't work now because of Vera's lie. I'll have to pivot.

Maybe... just maybe it isn't a curse from the gods to have us share a room. Maybe I don't have to be stoic and detached. As I watch her with the American pretty boy, her eyes all wide and her cheeks flushed, I have a realization: Vera Ivanova is starving for attention.

Hidden from the world, sheltered, she's thrown herself into her studies and made something of herself. I hardly know her, and even I'm damn proud.

But she craves more than recognition.

I've taken note.

"The accommodations are better than you'd find in a typical college dorm," Irina explains, "but we're utilitarian with the space we use and the way we've set things up here." She moves in a little closer to Vera. "I did make a call, and you will have the one room with a private bath. Perhaps Markov can join us for more of the social events we'll have."

Vera blanches but quickly covers it up and nods. "Thank you."

Yes. If there's anything I've learned as an assassin, it's to stay calm under pressure. Prepare for a change of plans. Be ruthless in the execution of Plan B.

"Here," Irina says, handing Vera a set of keys and gesturing to a set of buildings nestled into the campus but slightly offset. "Please get some rest and get settled in. You'll find a map of the campus and an itinerary in your room. We'll meet at the dining area for dinner in three hours."

She flashes me a smile, and she's gone. The American has already found his room.

Vera stares at the door as if it's a snake coiled in wait, ready to snap. Why the sudden panic? She made her choice.

I remember my plan and place the bags down. She opens the door with shaking hands and groans when she pushes it open.

It's a typical Russian bedroom you'd find on a college campus. The modest-sized double bed is the focal point of the otherwise utilitarian room and is made up with four pillows and a lightweight, traditionally patterned duvet. A built-in closet gives us minimal room for storage, but it will do, and there's a small desk with a hard-backed chair. Everything is modern, pragmatic, and compact.

"There isn't even so much as a couch for me to sleep on," she groans. "How is this possibly going to work? I can't tell her I lied now; I'll lose total credibility, and we just *got* here."

I know the feeling.

After bringing in the luggage, I lock the door behind her. I check all locks on the doors and windows. There's no deadbolt, only one shitty lock that wobbles. A teen with a screwdriver could open the damn thing.

I'll take care of that.

I nod at the bed and gesture for her to give me her phone.

I tap the app.

You'll take the bed. I will sleep on the floor.

Her eyes widen as she reads the message. I watch as her lower lip juts out, and she frowns, typing out another message.

No way.

It's time to put my plan into action.

I type another message on the phone. I saw how she responded to the American. I listened to what he said to her.

You are the one who's worked hard to get here. I'm only here to protect you. It's important you sleep well. You will take the bed.

I hand her the phone and walk away. That conversation is over.

I hear her sigh as I head to check out the rest of the room. Fortunately, the locks are the only part of the room that is unsafe. I gesture to the dresser's four drawers and pull out the bottom one, where I'll store my few clothes and weapons. I open my backpack and quickly arrange everything I've brought, then tap the rest of the drawers and point to her.

Yours.

"Thank you," she says, her voice a bit softer this time. Maybe she's touched by my display. Maybe she's honored I'm taking her job here seriously. In any event, she's ignorant to the fact that I'm here to bring justice to my family through the death of her father, and we're going to keep it that way.

I check my phones while she uses the bathroom. Then I look out the window, not far from the streets of Moscow, where I was orphaned. I remember who I was. I remember who I am now. The Romanov family took me in when I had no one. When I had nothing.

Vera Ivanova is the daughter of my enemy.

A plan begins to grow in my mind, taking on a life of its own. I suspect I know exactly how to work this angle...

"I'm tired, Markov," Vera says. I look over my shoulder to see her sitting on the edge of the bed, phone in hand. She's taken off her shoes and changed, now wearing a pair of sweats and a tiny tee.

I didn't know sweats and a tee could be so damn sexy. I intentionally let my gaze roam a little longer than's respectable. Just enough to let her know I see her and fucking like what I see before I can reel myself in.

"Are you tired?" she asks, making a gesture for sleeping and patting the edge of the bed. "You're a big guy, and I don't move in my sleep. You can't sleep on the floor. Rest here, and I'll sleep on the edge of the bed."

I shake my head as if I'm fighting it. Resisting. I will be in that bed tonight, and I will be up close and personal.

After we have a better lock in place.

"Alright, then," she says on a yawn. "You do whatever it is bodyguards do, and I'm going to take a nap."

I turn away from her as she lays down and opens up the book app on her phone, but not long after, I hear her phone plop to the bed with a little thump. She's fast asleep.

I take the opportunity to check in back home.

How are things going? I've tracked you to the campus

We've arrived. All good so far. I'm working on building trust with her so I can get closer to where I need to be. Have you found the location of where the rest meet in Moscow?

The plan is for me to find where the rest of the men of the Ivanov Bratva meet in Moscow. According to the brief texts I've received, they're disorganized at best. We have a small window of time, but it's enough for me to find out what I need to about Petr Ivanov.

If anyone suspects who I am, they'll conveniently disappear, like the real Markov. Many things could go wrong, but I'm prepared to pivot.

I end my conversation with Aleks and pull out the screen mirroring app.

The first thing I notice is that she hasn't progressed much further in her book. For a woman as intelligent as she is, it's a little interesting.

That's when I notice the highlights.

Vera has highlighted certain sections of the book. Maybe she's been rereading them?

Maybe *I* need to read them.

My eyes grow wide as I take in the highlighted portions of the book, and I feel my lips curl into a smile.

His hand curls at the back of my neck.

His warm hand rests on my upper thigh, a possessive touch. . .

"Beg to come, little girl. Don't you ever come without Daddy's permission."

"Disobey Daddy again, and I'll take you over my knee, young lady."

Vera Ivanova's a kinky little girl, and I aim to use that to my full advantage. I'm hard as hell just learning about what she likes, imagining what I could do to her. The fun we could have.

How much of what she reads is fiction, and how much would she actually like?

To follow through with this type of thing, I need to build trust with her.

Kolya taught us years ago that one of the ways to garner trust from an enemy was to use the slightest bit of truth to color a lie. Use your real first name. Speak something from the heart. Reveal a bit of your weakness and human nature is such that people will believe you are trustworthy. It will appear you've exposed your full hand when, in reality, you've only shown a few cards. Just a shadow of truth.

Slowly, I'll reveal just enough for her to let her guard down.

I'm going to break this woman's heart, but it's the only way forward.

I will do whatever it takes to bring my family justice.

No matter the cost.

CHAPTER SIX

Vera

SOMEONE'S SHAKING MY SHOULDER. I'm dead asleep, warm and cozy in bed. It feels so good to sleep. Why is someone waking me in the middle of the night?

I open my blurry eyes and see a tall man standing over me. I'm completely overshadowed by the breadth of his body. I jerk back and gasp.

What the hell?

Caught between sleep and waking, I startle and flail. Tangled in the sheets, I almost fall out of bed. Just in time, he bends and catches me. I'm immediately aware of his clean, woodsy scent and the warmth and confidence of his touch.

Wait.

I recognize that sharp jawline and piercing eyes.

And the familiar perpetual scowl. "It's just me. Relax."

I blink, trying to clear my brain.

Did he just speak English?

Is he still. . . holding me?

His warm arms around me feel nice. He's strong and sturdy, and I've always fantasized about what it would be like to be held by a strong man. . . like him.

It feels better than it did, even in my wildest fantasies.

I stare into the depths of those green eyes.

He *definitely* spoke English. There is way more to this man than he lets on.

"Let me go," I whisper, even though a part of me wants to ask him to hold me tighter. Even though a part of me wants to reach out and run my fingers along the scruff on his strong, masculine jaw. We're alone, just the two of us. What happens in Russia stays in Russia, right?

I half expect him to drop me on the bed like a sack of potatoes, but instead he gently releases me.

"You have to get ready to go."

I sit up on the bed and stare at him. "Did you magically learn another language while I napped? Or have you been lying to me, Markov?"

He sits on the edge of the bed, which bows under his weight.

"I made a decision while you were sleeping." He speaks with a thick Russian accent, but his English is perfect. "We must communicate more clearly if I'm to keep you safe. I never told you I didn't speak English."

I stare at him. Yeah, right. "Oh, don't play that game with me. You know that you led me to believe you didn't speak English. And here you are. . ." I gesture with my hands in confusion.

He shrugs. "I knew that you and I would be sharing quarters, though I didn't know it would be"—he gestures to the bed—"quite this close. I thought it would be in your best interest and mine if we had distance between us. If we couldn't communicate, we could remain professional. But I realize now that puts your safety at risk."

My cheeks heat with a sudden realization of what he's implying. "Do you think just because I've lived a sheltered life that I'm going to fall for the first hot guy I see as soon as I leave my parents' home?"

His brows snap together. "*Nyet.*" It seems even when he's trying to speak English, his Russian still makes an appearance. "I did not think that about you."

Oh dear God. The memory of what I said earlier comes back in a rush...how he could take what I've said. I spoke too freely. Divulged too much.

I told him I don't wear clothes to bed.

I told him he looked like Jason Bourne.

I should have kept my damn mouth shut.

Also? Who the hell am I kidding? He's not just the first hot guy I've met, but he is sexy as hell and exudes every vibe of the dominant nature that makes me crazy. He's the hero of a romance novel in real life, the classic Byronic hero.

If I'm Jane Eyre. . . he's my Mr. Rochester.

I can't think like that. I won't allow myself.

But I have to admit I love hearing him speak.

I cannot allow myself to have a crush on this guy. He works for my father, and anybody who works for my father must be a dick.

Though he's giving me an earnest look, the sharp cut of his jaw and the deep timbre of his voice remind me that he is no boy. "It is my job to protect you. You're a beautiful, intelligent woman. But you're my boss's daughter. If I so much as touched you, he would kill me." His eyes, a striking shade of steel blue, hold mine with an intensity that underscores his solemn vow.

He continues speaking, outlining the boundaries he must never cross, the lines drawn so rigidly by duty and honor. Yet, I'm still caught up in his earlier words—*beautiful, intelligent woman.* He said it with such natural conviction, as if stating something as undebatable as the sky being blue. No underlying charm, no playful smirk to soften the edges of his professionalism. Just plain fact.

Blood thunders in my ears, a relentless drum that makes it difficult to focus on anything but the man in front of me. His presence is commanding, his commitment palpable, and it sends a flurry of butterflies through my stomach. I swallow hard, trying to steady my voice, to appear as unaffected as he is disciplined. But it's a formidable challenge, when every fiber of my being reacts to the proximity of him —this man who might see me as more than a duty...

He glances at his phone, the light casting a glow on his steely features. "I'm sorry we started off this way. It's time that I told you the truth. I speak English as well as anybody here. Maybe then I can... communicate more effectively with the American." The way he says *communicate more effectively* sends chills down my spine. The underlying threat in his tone is unmistakable.

I swallow hard. "Markov, you need to leave him alone. He's in the program with me."

The flash of his eyes is almost predatory and makes my heart quicken with a mix of fear and anticipation.

"He's hot for you, and he's a dick. I'll take care of it. Now get up and ready so we're not late."

I shake my head in disbelief, my thoughts a whirlwind of confusion and alarm, when I glance at the time. "Oh my God! We have to be there in ten minutes!"

"Do you need more time than that?" His question comes casually, as if our earlier exchange hasn't altered the dynamics of our relationship. It's so strange that all of a sudden he's speaking English. I can hardly wrap my brain around the sudden shift. Part of me is relieved-- now, I actually have an ally here, one I can communicate with.

But can I trust him? Doubt gnaws at me, unsettling my thoughts. There I go again, thinking like we're in a romance novel.

We *have* no relationship beyond the professional. There is no foundation of trust or affection. He works for my father and is my bodyguard. Period. End of story.

But is anything really that simple?

"Okay, listen. I can get ready in ten minutes, but for future reference, I typically need a little more than that."

I gesture in my hair. "My hair alone can take ten minutes.
"

"Why?" He looks genuinely confounded.

"It goes all frizzy when I sleep. I can't walk out in public like this."

He shakes his head. Even though he speaks English, it still feels like he has a language barrier.

"You could braid it? I've heard my sister say that helps." He averts his eyes for a moment as if he shouldn't have said that. Huh.

"Well, I don't know how to braid it. Not on myself anyway. And that would make me look so young. I'm already basically the youngest one in the program. . ."

Markov scowls. "We have no time to argue details. Look, I can braid it for you. And you don't look young. You come off too collected and mature to look like a child. That American, though, *he* looks like a child. Do you have a hair tie?"

Wait. Did I actually wake up, or am I still dreaming?

I stare at him before replying. "I have a hair tie."

We have no time to waste, and he's right. . . it would help me get ready. Braiding will quickly tame it, and then I can dash on some makeup and change into some nice clothes. Next thing I know, I'm rummaging through my bag, trying to find a hair tie.

"You're already dressed! Did you do that while I was sleeping? Did you even get any rest?"

"Yes, I changed when you were sleeping. No, I didn't sleep but it's no matter. Give me the hair tie."

Am I really going to let him braid my hair?

Do I have much choice other than doing a messy and weird bun? While I wouldn't call myself vain, I'd like to avoid the mad scientist look if I can help it.

He gestures for me to sit at the desk chair while he stands behind me. It feels strangely intimate when he runs my brush through my hair. I quickly take it from him and shake my head. "I can do this part." My cheeks are hot again, the heat creeping down my neck. I hope he doesn't notice.

I brush my hair, pulling out the tangles, and I know exactly what it looks like now. The tangle-free fluffy mess is reminiscent of cotton candy.

"Where did you learn how to braid hair?"

"My brother has a stepchild. My niece. She's three years old and has long blonde hair. I'm one of her favorites. So I learned. It's not hard. "

Ugh, that's adorable. Dammit.

He quickly gathers the hair at the nape of my neck, sending little tingles down my spine. It's the sexiest thing a man has ever done to me, which is really pretty pathetic if you think about it.

I like the feel of his warm hand on the back of my neck. Separating the hair into strands, and with a tenderness that belies the way he's been until now, he plaits my hair. When he's done, he surprises me by giving it a little tug.

"Hey! What was that?"

"For talking back to me earlier." He leans down, not quite touching me, but so close that the warmth of his breath tickles my neck. "Don't do that again. Behave yourself, Vera. Remember, I'm your husband. You should show your husband some respect."

Before I can gather up my thoughts or somehow slow the rapid beating of my heart, he's gone, and I'm left wondering. . . Is Markov flirting with me? Or was he serious? I can't look at him because I'm afraid that if he sees my eyes, he'll somehow know that that little threat made me all kinds of hot and bothered. My God.

I go to get clothes out of my bag only to find that he's already unpacked and layered everything in the drawers. "You unpacked for me?"

He shrugs. "I was bored, and I knew that you wouldn't have much time to get dressed. And we need to go."

It was kind of nice of him to do that, but still. . . what did I have in those bags he saw?

"Um, thanks." I guess if he's my bodyguard and pretend husband, I might have to give up a little of my privacy. But I'm mentally cringing at the memory of the plain white underwear and plain white bras that I packed. Why would I wear anything sexy? It was just supposed to be me. I don't even own anything sexy.

I quickly grab a clean skirt and a top. Something business casual. He's wearing a light blue button-down dress shirt and navy pants that fit him like a glove. He looks effortlessly put together and casual.

Markov scowls. "Five minutes until we have to go. Skip the makeup."

Okay, now he's stepping too far.

"No. My face is all blotchy from all that travel. I at least need a little lip gloss." I turn my back to him and grab my little bag. "And excuse me, but fake husband that you may be, you are not the boss of me." I need to hold my own with this one.

He presses his lips together and narrows his eyes at me. "I'm your husband. You should obey your husband."

Oh no, he doesn't. I glare at him. I'm suddenly reminded of the way he told me to behave myself.

I open my mouth to protest in some effective, persuasive way, but instead, I turn, run to the bathroom, and slam the door behind me.

Good one, Vera. Very graceful.

I toss makeup on quickly as if my life depended on it and join him back in the room. He gives me a quick look of appraisal and turns away.

"I'm sorry that I didn't tell you the truth. I should have. I was pulled from another mission to be put on this one, and I made some quick decisions. It won't happen again."

It's hard to hold a grudge with an apology that's so honest and direct. I'm so relieved we can actually talk to one another that I'm quick to forgive.

"Thank you. So, do you want that American dude to know that you speak English?

"Believe me," he says with a smile. "He's going to know that very quickly."

"Remember, this is my professional job here, Markov. . ."

"I'll remember." His eyes darken. "And so will he."

We have no more time to chat. Why do I all of a sudden feel so shy in front of him now that we can communicate more freely? That layer of protection between us isn't there anymore.

When he opens the door, I walk past him. He leans in and whispers in my ear, "I know what my job is, Vera. Do you know yours? That little attitude you gave me a few minutes ago? I'll remember that." He smiles and nods. "After you, *wife*."

Oh, my God, I really need to start reading romcom instead of all that erotic romance. Seriously. Maybe thrillers.

"I studied the map while you were sleeping," he says. "It's this way." He reaches for my hand.

"Markov—"

"You're supposed to be my wife," he says in a whisper. "You were the one that chose this, Vera."

 Shit. He's right. I take his hand and practically have to trot to keep up with his long strides.

"We need to solidify the story," he says in a low voice only meant for me to hear.

"What story?"

"How we met. When we got married. All of that."

Something about just hearing him so those words... those events that I've longed for and mostly given up hope of ever happening... just hearing him speak them aloud makes my heart thump in my chest.

Why did I do this?

"Okay. Um. Alright, we can tell them we were high school sweethearts. We went our separate ways after graduation and reunited at a friend's wedding."

"High school sweethearts? That can't work. I'm way older than you. "

I didn't even think of that. "Are you? How old are you?"

"I'm thirty-one. You're, what, twenty-two, twenty-three? Next idea."

"Right. Um. . . I was on vacation, hiking in the mountains of Switzerland, and you were my tour guide?"

He shakes his head. "Do I really look like someone who could be a Swiss tour guide? And what if they ask me about it? The only thing I can tell you about Switzerland is that the chocolate's good."

I snort. "Okay, so, what's your genius idea?"

He purses his lips and scowls. "Online dating service. The algorithm matched us as compatible, even though we come from two very different backgrounds. You were too busy with grad school to date, but we hit it off immediately. After only three months of dating, we eloped, much to our parents' chagrin. That was a year ago."

My romance lover's heart thumps. This is a dangerous place

to be, but I can already see the dining hall and Irina waiting for us. We don't have any more time.

"Deal."

"Vera! Markov! I hope you got some rest," Irina says, greeting us at the door. "We're still waiting for a few guests, but please go on in and introduce yourselves."

Markov opens the door and rests his hand on the small of my back. He leans in and whispers in my ear, "Remember what I said about the American and about behaving your-self. I expect an obedient wife, Vera."

I discreetly stick my tongue out at him and relish the look of challenge in his eyes. If he thinks he's going to tell me what to do, he can think again.

If I behave myself, he might stop threatening me. But a girl needs to live a little. He can't actually touch me, so I'll have my fun.

Jake stands beside a tall, lithe man with short silver hair. When I realize who it is, I forget all about Markov and tamp down the need to fangirl. I want to pinch myself. The man beside Jake is none other than Dr. Antoly Morozov, the scholar I've idealized since grade school. When he sees me, he smiles widely in greeting.

"Welcome. You must be Vera Ivanova. And this is. . ."

"My husband, Markov." Markov and I shake hands with him.

"I'm Professor Morozov," the professor says, extending his hand. "Allow me to introduce the rest. Liam O'Sullivan." He points to another tall man with fiery red hair who looks friendly enough, but I notice a guardedness in his posture. Maybe he's just a reserved Irishman.

"Sophia Lang." A petite woman with jet-black hair and striking blue eyes. Despite her delicate appearance, she seems to carry herself with confidence. "So nice to meet you," she says in a clipped accent.

"And Maxim Smith."

A blond man with wire-rimmed glasses extends a hand to me.

"Hello! Are you also American?"

He shakes his head. "My mother is Russian, and my father is American, hence my name. But I've spent most of my life here in Moscow. "

Markov nods. "As did I. Whereabouts?"

They continue their discussion in Russian, and I'm glad Markov might have at least made an acquaintance. His presence here seems natural, which makes me want to breathe a sigh of relief.

Jake sidles up next to me while Irina pours wine and Markov is busy talking to Maxim. "I thought your husband didn't speak English?"

"Of course he does. He's just a man of few words."

Still, Jake regards him warily. "I'm glad you're not alone. It can be lonely out here without somebody's company. Especially when we get to the fieldwork." Markov looks over at us.

I don't respond because I'm not exactly sure what to say to him, but apparently, Markov does. He leans over and rests an arm on the table beside me. The scent of the woods and spice somehow reassures me. "She most definitely won't be going alone on fieldwork."

"Is that allowed?" Jake asks, undeterred. He takes a sip of wine and keeps his face impassive.

Markov doesn't respond, but he looks like he wants to deck him. Professor Morozov smiles and holds his glass of wine up in a toast. "Absolutely. My own wife occasionally accompanies us as well. With today's political climate, I think we'd be wise to bring a bodyguard-type with us, don't you?"

While everyone else laughs, I nearly choke on my wine. Markov, however, only winks at me. It appears he has a charming side he's been hiding all along.

Can they all know who he really is?

But how much do *I* know?

CHAPTER SEVEN

Nikko

I LISTEN as Vera makes small talk with the rest of the group. Her latest peer-reviewed published research is the topic of conversation, thanks to Dr. Morozov. She's amazing to watch. Not only is she well-spoken, she's intelligent, obviously driven, and charismatic. I doubt she even realizes she's the center of attention; she's so focused on and passionate about what she's talking about. Though it's a small group, she quickly becomes the epicenter of it while everybody else fades away.

I love how avidly she speaks about her work. I understand most of what she says, but only peripherally. When she dives into the details of it, I'm a little lost. So is the American pretty boy, though he tries to pretend he isn't.

The only time Vera's confidence wavers is when someone brings attention back to her and not the actual subject of the research. It seems as if she will talk about her field all day long but can't stand too much attention on herself. She bites her lip and flushes a bit pink.

I want to excuse her from this situation. Tell everyone she has a headache or whatever and needs to sleep. Thank them for their hospitality but tell them it's time my wife got some rest.

But I don't, not yet. I cannot overstep. One thing I've learned in my line of work is how to fade into the woodwork, which is not an easy task when you're 6'4" and built like me. This is her time to shine, and she can't hide from it.

So I busy myself observing her classmates and professors. This is my job. I need to see who might pose a future risk.

"How do you find your accommodations, Markov?" Irina asks in Russian. While the rest of the group is talking to Vera, she's made her way to me. It seems as if she's standing a little too close. Either she suspects I am not who I say I am, or something else is going on.

I've been told I see danger everywhere I go, but I'm instantly on guard.

"They're fine, thank you. I do have an issue with the locks, though, and must insist on replacing them. They are not safe. I can install them myself but wanted to mention it before I make any changes to our housing."

Irina looks apologetic. "Of course. I love that you're concerned about Vera and want to protect her. There's no need for you to take that on yourself. I'll see that it's done first thing tomorrow."

"Thank you. I'll also ask that I be allowed to accompany her in her studies."

"Of course," Irene says with a smile. "While it's not standard for our students to have their spouses accompany them, we're going to make an exception and allow you to partake in as many of our activities as you'd like." She gives me an obvious wink.

I nod. Either Irina's gotten the memo about who the Ivanovs really are and doesn't want to rock the boat, or she has other plans. In any event, I want to stay as close to Vera as I can.

We take our seats, Vera right beside me as they bring out platters of beef stroganoff with thick noodles, salads, and rolls. My mouth waters. I've missed the traditional food of my homeland.

The American sits beside Vera, of course. We'll have to have a word. Discreetly. I can't fuck up his pretty little face without recourse, but he knows that Vera is my wife and thinks it's alright to hit on her. For an intelligent man, he needs some more education.

I watch all of them keenly, but the rest of our meal goes without a hitch.

"Were you in the military?" the slight woman with black hair asks me. "You cut your food and eat with such precision."

You can tell a lot by someone's tone and body posture. She's not judging or giving me a hard time but is genuinely curious. I'm amongst a group of exceptionally brilliant people, so I'm not surprised.

"For a while, yes," I tell her. "When I was younger."

The gray-haired professor laughs. "When he was younger," he says with a gentle shake of his head. "If I could bottle up the youth elixir in one of these labs, I would. Oh, to be *thirty* again."

How does he know how old I am? It might just be an educated guess, but I still trust none of them.

Any one of them could have been placed here by one of our enemies—hers or mine. It's unlikely that anyone has suspected who I am and why I'm here, but it's a possibility I can't ignore.

Predictably, the American monopolizes the conversation, dropping names from Harvard. The ass hat. Irina and Morozov listen intently, but Vera is speaking less and less frequently. I can tell by the way she keeps stifling a yawn that she's exhausted, and the wine hasn't helped.

I watch Maxim only make a small plate of vegetables and rice, then take his leave after a few minutes of socialization.

I will watch that one. Who am I kidding? I'll watch every one of them. No one's anymore trustworthy than the next.

"Let's go," I say in Vera's ear. "You need rest, and I've had enough socializing."

Vera nods, agreeing with me for once.

Irina thankfully adjourns our meeting. "Thank you all for indulging us. It was lovely meeting you. But now, since every-one's exhausted after a long day of travel, we will call it a night and meet first thing in the morning. Our first lab is at seven."

Vera leans over and whispers, "Are you a morning person?"

I nod, leaning in further to make sure nobody hears us. "I like to go for a run at five. Join me?"

"Sure," she says. "I'd love to." I happen to know that she does love to go for a run. I also know she likes to run the same route over and over again, listen to the same playlist, and never alter her routine. That will need to change because it isn't safe.

"Alright then, we will go for the run at four forty-five," I announce, testing her resolve. I want to see how much she likes to be pushed. How she responds when I do exactly what she's been reading about in those books of hers.

Vera wrinkles her nose. "Um. That's a little early, isn't it?"

"We'll need to shower and eat breakfast after the run if we're to be ready by seven."

Though she blows out a breath, she agrees. "True."

Everyone part ways, and we walk once again hand-in-hand back to our dorm apartment.

"What did you think?" she asks.

"The food was excellent. I've missed food like that. You?"

"Some of it was good, but I can already tell I'm going to miss some of my American food." She smiles. "I wasn't asking about the food, though, Markov. What did you think of the *people?*"

I suspected that's what she meant.

"I don't trust anybody, so I'm the last person to ask."

We walk in silence for a moment.

"Who do you find particularly untrustworthy? Besides the American?"

"The silent blond guy. Hid himself from everyone. I would suspect he either feels as if he's above everyone, or he doesn't belong at all. But I don't trust people who don't interact when socialization is expected. I'm not a social guy myself, but I know how to behave. "

"I see. Interesting. You talk a lot about behavior and how people behave," she says. With the way she flutters her fingertips across her neckline, I wonder how thirsty Vera is. . .

I shrug. "It's true. It's who I am. I don't play bullshit games, Vera." I give her a wink. "As for the rest, time will tell. The Irishman is a bit arrogant but intelligent, and he knows his place. Jake wants recognition from everyone—a stereotypical Ivy League pretty boy raised by wealthy parents. Hopefully, being in a program like this will take him down a peg or two. The girl seems nice enough, though you'll need to watch her competitive streak. I like Morozov and Irina. They seem to be good mentors, and I hope they treat you well."

Her brows shoot up her forehead. "Good observations."

"It's my job."

When we arrive back at the room, the little hairs on the back of my neck rise. I reach for her and hold her back before she can enter.

"What?"

I can practically fucking smell it in the air.

"Don't move."

"What's wrong?" she whispers.

"It's a feeling I have." And I'd rather be wrong than step right into a dangerous situation. Both of us are Bratva. We both are moving targets, for different reasons.

I open the door to the room and make her stand right behind me while I scan everything.

The air in the room feels different, subtly charged from a presence that lingers like smoke after a fire. Everything seems untouched, yet it smacks of an intrusion. "Somebody's been in here. "

They were careful, but I know they were here.

"Markov, I think you're overreacting. I was in a bit of a rush when we were leaving, remember? I kind of left things all over the place. "

I shake my head. "Trust me. Somebody was in here. Look through your belongings and tell me if you're missing anything."

"Everything's fine, Markov," she begins, giving me a look that tells me she's not amused by this current line of thinking. "We weren't gone very long."

"*Look.*"

"If you insist." She goes through her clothing and finds nothing amiss, then heads to the bathroom. "I told you everything is—" She stops mid-sentence, staring into the bathroom. "Wait. Nothing's missing, but. . . this is not where I put things. Everything's been. . . moved. My toothbrush was on the left of the sink, and now it's on the right. I always brush with my non-dominant hand on purpose. I put my shampoo on the top shelf and the conditioner on the bottom because that's always how I do things, and now they've been switched."

She spins around and stares at me. "You're right. Someone's been in here. Do we need to move? Find another room? We need to tell somebody—"

I shake my head and take a step so that I can be closer to her. I can tell she's on the verge of panicking.

"Markov, I've never been away from home before. What if I'm a target? What if you are? What if somebody doesn't want me to be in this program?"

I reach my hand to her arm to steady her, to calm her down. "You're fine. I'm fine. Fucking no one is going to hurt you when I'm around. You do not go anywhere without me, Vera. I mean that. Of course you're a target. You're an Ivanov."

When she shakes her head, I decide to lay down the law about my expectations. It will have the dual effect of making sure she stays safe and testing the waters.

I tip my finger under her chin and lift her gaze to mine. "Am I clear?"

She swallows and nods, her eyes widening. "Are you sure it's safe for us to stay here tonight?"

I smile at her. "I dare anyone to come back in this room when I'm here. I've already spoken to Irina. The locks will be fixed tomorrow. You're safe. Someone came in here to rattle you. They achieved that. And when I find out who it is, I'll personally deal with them." She shivers but nods.

I crook a finger at her. "Come here," I instruct softly, my voice laced with feigned calm, for her sake.

Vera hesitates, her body trembling, her eyes wide and haunted. She's shaking like a leaf. Rage simmers within me, ignited by the invasion of our privacy and her reaction, but I push it aside.

This is a good opportunity for me to take the next step with her.

Stepping forward, I pull her into my arms, mindful of her delicate, much smaller frame against my larger one. She fits almost perfectly, like a missing piece I hadn't known I needed. I cup the back of her head, my hand large enough to cradle it and envelop her in a chaste hug. I want to be a barrier against the chaos of the world. "I promise you, Vera, you're safe. No one's going to hurt you. Can you trust me?"

Her eyes, wide and searching, meet mine. The flush of pink in her round cheeks speaks volumes of how she truly feels. "I don't know if I have a choice?"

"You always have a choice. But listen, you are exhausted. Go get ready for bed and I'll take care of things here. I'm going to barricade the door and make some phone calls. Everything is going to be alright."

Her eyes linger on mine for a moment longer, as if searching for reassurance, then slowly, she nods. "If you say so. This is your job, after all."

It is. It so fucking is.

When she goes to the bathroom to dress, I move our luggage and place the dresser in front of the door. The windows don't really concern me because they're too small for anyone to get in.

Who was it? Who is in this room? I check both of my phones. I hate this dual identity, but it's what I have to do for now.

> Aleks: How are things?

> Someone broke into our room when we were at dinner. No idea who it was.

> Are you fucking kidding me?

> We need surveillance

> Aria and I are on it.

> Is everything OK at home?

> Great. Sasha started walking. The twins are lifting their heads up now. Polina's planning her graduation and causing mayhem as usual. Mom is already planning the next gala. We have a lead on donations for it

The pang that hits my chest takes me by surprise.

I miss everyone at home. Who knew I'd be homesick?

Every year, my family hosts a large gathering, and we invite the most distinguished people we know. We raise millions of dollars for charity, solidifying our place as upstanding members of society.

> I'll scout some artwork in Russia while I'm here.

Mom will love that. How's your charge?

Beautiful. Brilliant. Fucking perfect.

She's fine. Mouthy, but I'm not gonna put up with it.

Of course not. You know I've been there. You need anything, you know where to find me.

I tuck my phone away and text the Ivanov captain.

There was evidence that our room was broken into while we were gone.

There's no response. I wait. And wait. Sons of bitches.

I put both phones away just as Vera enters the room.

"So why don't you just. . . forget about what I said I wear to bed earlier."

Ah, that's right. She said quite a few things when she didn't know I could understand her, didn't she?

Now she's wearing sweats and a tee.

"So you lied about what you wear to bed?" I stroke my chin. "You aren't allowed to lie to me."

Her back is to me while she puts her clothes away so I can't tell if her cheeks have colored.

"We're sharing that bed tonight, Vera. I don't care about sleeping on the floor, but I want to be sure I'm right next to you in case anything happens."

"Good. That's fine. We can ...do this, Markov."

We can do this.

We can sleep next to each other and not fuck each other? Yeah, we can.

Still... I remind myself that seducing her would get me closer to where I need to be.

I remind myself that her father brought devastation upon my family with the sole purpose of destroying us.

I remind myself that my loyalty is to the Romanovs. . . my family. And only my family.

I remind myself that if I fuck her, I'm sleeping with the enemy.

CHAPTER EIGHT

"BED," Markov snaps, as if the fact that I'm not currently deep in the throes of REM sleep is a personal affront to him.

"Bed," I agree, shaking my head at him. "Will you relax already? Also, if I'm wearing clothes to bed, so are you."

"I am wearing clothes, woman."

I'm holding my own. "If you don't put a shirt on, I'm stripping."

My cheeks color. No way, no how am I going to strip, but if he calls me on my bluff—

"Fair enough," he grumbles, walks back over to crumpled clothing, and tugs his tee back on. *Argh.* I wanted him to get a clean one since he'll likely—yup. I knew it. As soon as he gets near me, his scent from earlier clings to him.

I scurry under the covers when he gives me a narrow-eyed

look. I'm holding my breath, waiting for the bed to sink under his weight when he joins me.

"I did what you said. Now go to sleep. Early morning comes fast."

I open my mouth to tell him I'm going to sleep because I'm tired and not because he's bossing me around, then think better of it because he's lying right next to me. He's already given me a few warnings about behaving myself. I'm not sure if it's my imagination running wild because I've read too many of a certain kind of novel, but it's probably not smart to talk back in any event.

I'm also really tired and don't need to be told twice.

I close my eyes, letting my mind wander. Of course it settles on all the little things that made my heart beat faster tonight.

The feel of his eyes focused on mine. The way his finger tipped under my chin. The command in his voice and his promise to protect me. The sight of his chiseled inked back —better than the cover of my romance novels. The sound of his voice, all deep and husky with that accent. The warmth of his body behind me. . .

I close my eyes and fall into a deep sleep.

I wake up a few hours later, disoriented, and glance at a tiny alarm clock on the desk. Still a bit longer until I need to wake up. This jet lag is no joke. I toss and turn and stare at the ceiling, then reach for my phone and realize it's plugged in by the desk. I consider getting up but don't want to wake him when the heavy warmth of an arm snakes around my belly, over the bedclothes.

"Go to sleep, Vera," Markov says in a sexy, sleepy voice.

"I'm wide awake."

"Do what they do in the military. Close your eyes and will your mind to stop. Don't allow any more thoughts, then rest."

"I can't stop my *mind*," I protest. What a silly thought.

The sound of his soft, heavy breaths tells me he was able to do that and is already back to sleep.

Okay, then.

I close my eyes. I think *no thoughts,* but a certain large, muscular Russian's face comes straight into my mind's eye. What would it be like to kiss him? What would it be like to be touched by him? What would it be like if...

No. I can't think like this. Nope.

I finally fall into a deep and dreamless sleep until the blare of my alarm clock rouses me. I roll over and stretch before I remember I'm not alone in this bed.

I have plenty of room, though. He isn't here.

Did someone come back in the middle of the night? I push off the covers and walk across the room to shut off my alarm, looking around for Markov. Was there a threat, and he—

I can hear the sound of running water in the bathroom. Okay, he's obviously just in the bathroom, and I didn't hear it before because of the alarm.

Does the man ever sleep?

I'm not going to let him outdo me when it comes to getting ready, not a second time in a row. I laid out my workout clothes the night before, so I quickly strip out of the clothes I slept in, my back to the bathroom, and quickly pull my shorts on when I hear the bathroom door open.

"Stop! Don't come out; I'm getting dressed." My telltale cheeks betray me as always, heating so badly this time I feel it all the way from my hairline to my neck. I can feel his presence just on the other side of this door, standing deadly still as I quickly tug my workout clothes on.

"Alright," I breathe, turning away so he doesn't see my cheeks. "I'm done."

The bathroom door creaks open as I reach down to put my socks on.

"If you don't want me to see you naked, it might be wise not to get dressed in the room we share," he says sarcastically.

"Kinda hard to do when you're hogging the damn bathroom."

I stand up to face him and nearly lose my shit when I see he's only wearing a towel. Good *God*. I spin quickly around so I don't stare at his wall of chest and nearly trip over my own two feet.

He grabs my arm and holds me upright, his face impassive and his lips once more pressed into a thin, severe line. I wonder if I imagined any warmth or hint of humor the day before.

"What did I tell you about your mouth?"

Before he can unnerve me all over again, I pull my arm away from his and head to the bathroom, but he grabs my braid, all tangled and disheveled from sleeping. I stop short.

"I asked you a question, Vera."

"Hey!"

I definitely imagined any warmth.

"Let go of my hair." I hate that the dominant move pulls the rug straight out from under me. I wish I could get a grip on my raging, albeit neglected, libido, but my heart beats faster and my chest is all tight and warm.

Instead of letting go, he holds it a bit tighter and gives another tug. "What did I say?"

I sigh. He's still gripping my hair, and if we're ever going on a run. . .

"You told me to behave," I say in a singsong voice. "I'm sorry. Now let me go so I can pee in peace."

He does, in fact, let me go, but only to give me a parting slap to the ass.

"Hey!"

"Don't tell me you didn't like it," he says, his back turned to me he pulls out clothes to dress into.

God. The *arrogance* of the smug, self-satisfied *prick.*

Why wasn't I more careful with letting him see my reading choices? Now he has it in his head that I want to be dominated.

I go to slam the door to the bathroom for effect but think better of it in case he considers that not behaving. . . or something. And maybe. . . punishes me or something.

Do I want to be dominated?

I stare at myself in the mirror. My hair's a mess, but the half-done braid reminds me of the feel of his fingers in my hair. My cheeks are still pink, and the color creeps all the way down to the neckline of my workout tank. My heart is pounding so hard I can feel it in my ears, and the pressure between my legs after that smack to the ass is undeniable.

Yes. Yes, I definitely want this. *Him.*

Fuck.

I slap toothpaste on my brush and run the water while I sift through my protests, thoughts, and fears in my mind. What if my father finds out?

My father doesn't know the first thing about me. He's never been interested in me before, so why would he start now?

Anyway, who said we had to become a *thing?* It's the modern age. We can. . . flirt.

Maybe even do a ... what do they call that... friends-with-benefits thing, no strings attached.

I rinse off my toothbrush, the cool water not enough to quell the heat rising inside me. *We're supposed to be playing a married couple,* I remind myself. *There should be some chemistry... right?*

"Are you coming out or what? How long does it take to pee?" His gruff, impatient voice invades the silence.

Argh. I'm glad he *isn't* my real-life husband.

"As long as it takes!" I retort, my tone sharper than I intend. *Lame.*

"We have to get moving."

"Oh, Fuck *off,* Markov!" I snap before I can censor myself.

Shit.

I maybe could've handled that better. He isn't exactly the type that will take kindly to me smarting off to him.

When I tentatively open the door, I find him waiting in the doorway, his arms crossed on his chest. His eyes locked on mine, the challenge is clear.

"I heard that, wife." His voice is a low, threatening purr that sends a shiver down my spine.

My heartbeat thunders.

"We don't have time now for me to deal with you, but I'll remember. Do you need coffee or food before we go?" he asks, glancing pointedly at his watch. "Our time is running out."

"After. Let's go."

The early morning air is crisp, a refreshing contrast to the heat that flares between us as we stop outside. The sunlight is brighter than I expected, casting a glow to his tanned skin.

"Wow," I say as we warm up with a casual jog, trying to shake off the tension. "It's so bright already."

"In the summer, the sun rises in Moscow around four a.m.," Markov says, his voice surprisingly gentle. He gestures for me to follow him to the left when we hit a fork in the road. "Sunrise was almost an hour ago."

"Wow," I breathe. "Do you know where we're going?"

"There are city parks suitable for a run, but I favor the parks around the Kremlin. Quieter this time of day."

Ah. So he insisted on early morning so that we could avoid crowds. I can get behind that.

We start to pick up our pace. The soft, diffused light and nearly vacant streets make it calm and peaceful here. I like it.

That said, nature is very much awake. Birds sing, and little critters trot between green bushes, dipping in and out. There's hardly any traffic.

"It's beautiful," I tell him. "Gorgeous."

"Thank you," he says, as if I just paid him a personal compliment. "It's different later in the day, but this time of year is the warmest. We'll have to visit some of the parks, too. We will not run the same route every day, Vera."

Was he picking on me? How does he know I stick to one route all the time? Does he?

"Why?'

"It makes you harder to predict if someone's after you," he says with a shake of his head. "Your guards at home should've told you these things."

"I don't have *guards* at home; I have one guard, and he's old, nearly deaf, and half-asses everything. My father doesn't care. All he cares about is the money in his wallet, how he looks to the public, and his reputation."

Markov doesn't reply but a muscle ticks in his jaw as we slow down near an intersection that has a few shops already open.

"Now are you hungry?" I nod, my stomach churning at this point.

"I would kill for a cup of coffee."

Markov smirks. "I'd kill for a lot less."

I snort, but a part of me can't decide if he's joking or not.

He steers us to a vacant shop with little seats on a paved patio out front and a small menu. My mouth waters at the smell of newly-baked pastries and the rich, warm scent of fresh-brewed coffee.

"I don't have any money with me," I tell him.

He gives me a withering look. "Have you not figured out by now that I'm a very old-fashioned husband, Vera? You won't pay for anything with me. Let's get coffee and food so we can head back and get ready before your first session."

We're both covered in sweat, and my hair's a mess, but no one seems to mind. I predictably choose an Americano to his classic black espresso, and we buy a few traditional sweet buns.

As we leave, Markov looks both ways, up and down, practically in every darkened doorway and behind every bush. I'm not sure why he'd think anyone would follow us here, but if they did, they're invisible.

"Why are you constantly checking to see if anyone's following us?"

"Vera," he grunts.

"I know. I know it's your job, but no one's here. No one's followed us."

"Anyone good at what they do can practically blend into a crowd," he says tightly. "Believe me, I'm very good at it myself."

Finally satisfied we aren't going to be bombed, shot at, or abducted in the near future, we walk back to campus, eating our sweet buns and drinking our coffees. "Tell me about the work you'll do today," he says, sipping his coffee. I'll have just enough time for a quick shower before we meet.

"I'll have to check back to the itinerary to see what's next."

"Can you tell me the gist of it?"

"Of course. How much did you understand of what we discussed last night?"

His brows furrow. "Let's just say I gathered that you were all scientists," he begins. God, he looks so adorable when he gives me that look. It's the only time I'd use the word *adorable* or *cute* about him.

I fill him in in layman's terms as best I can. "So today could be any of those things. A simulation where we're in the middle of a war-torn area with a soldier who has just been brought in with life-threatening injuries. A high-stakes threat where our mock environment's been hit with a biological weapon. Or disaster response to a natural disaster and we have to allocate resources and set up triage areas.

Advanced trauma support training. Our training involves everything from staying calm under intense pressure and trauma to learning how to do things like parachute, building shelter to survive, and mental resiliency."

"Ahhh," he says, nodding. "So that's why you brush your teeth with your left hand."

I'm not sure why it pleases me so much that he actually connected that or freaks me out that he misses nothing. "Right. Doing small things with a non-dominant hand will help you grow resilience. It's similar to the whole ice bath thing."

"Got it." He shrugs. "Well, I can definitely help you with disaster response and trauma support if you need me to feign a few scenarios. Happy to fuck up that asshole American so you can bring him back to life."

"I'm not sure that will be necessary, but thank you for being so helpful," I say as we make it back to campus.

"Stay back when I check things out."

This time, I don't push back or argue. It would be stupid not to go along with him, and a moment later, he gives me the green light.

We get ready quickly, but we're the last ones to arrive. I'm surprised when he actually comes inside with me.

"Irina said I could."

"Oh, really?" Why is she being so amenable? Then a thought crossed my mind. "Markov," I whisper. "Did you threaten her?"

His gaze grows thunderous. "No. Do I need to?"

My heart thumps and I shake my head. "No, please don't." I glance at the time. I can't discuss this any more.

Jake smirks at my damp hair and wrinkled top that didn't travel so well. I kind of rushed in the end, but I figured it would be fine since we'd be covered in a lab coat.

I suddenly hate the way he looks at me, that smug expression on his face, but I quickly forget him when Sophia comes up beside me. "I'm so thankful there's another woman here," she whispers. "We've made many advances in women in STEM, but you know."

I do know. We still are very much in the minority, at least in some places.

"I'm a little jealous you're here with your husband," she says with a smile. "How did you two meet?"

Shit. I forgot what we decided on. I stare at her and wildly try to come up with a way to change the subject. We said we wouldn't say it was school, but that we met. . . online dating!

"Oh, we met through an online dating thing," I finally say. "I avoided them for a long time, but you know. It gets lonely, and those algorithm matches can be spot on."

I can feel Markov behind me, listening to everything I say.

"Oh, I love it," Sophia says. "Takes the drama and guesswork out of the equation!" God, if she had any idea. Markov coughs into his hand. I kick him under the table.

Irina and Morozov walk in, so we both stop talking as they lay out our plans for the day.

"Now," Morozov says, his eyes twinkling. He's totally in his element and loving it. "After basic orientation and the overview of our goals here, we'll outline the modules we'll be studying. We're bypassing our standard introduction since all of you seem to have such great rapport. We don't want to waste time with any of the icebreakers we typically use to warm the team up and will get right to it."

Fine with me. I hate that stuff. I'm ready to get busy.

"Great rapport," Jake scoffs under his breath to me. "Some were accepted because Mommy and Daddy could pay, and the rest got in to satisfy some quota. Not very impressive."

I press my lips together and don't respond.

"And which might you be, Vera?" Jake asks, his tone casual but edged with provocation as he leans closer to the lab table, eyeing the vials of biological agents we've been given to inspect.

I give him a withering look and turn back to the task at hand.

Markov, who has been quietly observing from a short distance, narrows his eyes, sensing the tension. I shake my head at him. Suddenly, Jake, perhaps to demonstrate a misguided point or to taunt me further, begins to gesture animatedly with his hands, dangerously close to the vials.

"Be careful!" I can't help but exclaim as his sleeve brushes against a particularly delicate setup.

But before he can finish, Markov intervenes. With a swift motion, he steadies the vials that Jake's careless movements had nearly toppled. The room goes silent, all eyes suddenly on them.

"Thank you," Irina says. "You must be more cautious. This isn't a place for reckless behavior and those of you at this caliber ought to know that."

With a scowl, Jake gets up from the table and walks away. Markov glances my way, his gaze sharp and protective. My heart beats faster not only from the near-miss but from Markov's look. He's here to ensure my safety in every sense of the word.

Wordlessly, he gets up as well and follows Jake.

Uh oh.

I open my mouth to protest but don't want to cause a scene. My heart, however, hammers rapidly in my chest at the thought of what Markov might be doing.

The rest of the group is occupied with observations, noting things down on their lab sheets, but I'm hyper-focused on Jake and Markov. Markov leans in, washing his hands in the sink while Jake dries his. Jake's ears are beet red, and he looks like a terrified child.

Oh, God.

They come back and Jake walks to the front of the room, says something in Irina's ear, then takes his leave.

"Markov," I hiss. "What did you say to him?"

Markov's eyes darken when he shrugs, but he responds quietly. "Do not worry. I didn't overstep."

"Markov. . ." I give him a pleading look.

Leaning over, he whispers in my ear. "I told him under no uncertain terms what would happen to him if he disrespected my wife again. And then I casually suggested that he wasn't feeling well and could maybe take a bit of a break from this morning's rotation."

My jaw drops even as warmth spreads through me.

He stood up for me.

No one's ever done that before.

The next second, I realize he just threatened a coworker.

"Markov, this is a crucial lab, though. This is where they decide which of us gets chosen for the leadership roles for the rest of the program."

Markov only shrugs. "I know."

"Vera?" Irina says with a smile. "We'd like you to lead our fieldwork."

CHAPTER NINE

Nikko

IT WAS a long but productive day for Vera. She takes a quick rest while I check in at home.

> Aleks: All good on the home front. We've run background checks again on all the participants in the program as you asked, and there's nothing amiss. It doesn't appear there is anyone there out to hurt you or Vera.

> Thank you

I'm surprised to find one from the Ivanov captain, Shevchenko.

> Apologies for the belated reply. There was a delay in the delivery of your text. Please tell us how things have progressed.

Interesting.

> We have a new lock on the door and no further interference that I've noted.

> Would you like us to install video surveillance surrounding your room?

Fuck.

If I say yes, we run the risk of someone discovering that we are currently sharing a bed and living quarters. But if I say no, I limit the amount of protection I can give her. Aleks has drones in place periodically but not much else.

I think about it before I reply and finally come up with what I hope is a good compromise.

> Thank you. I'd like to honor her privacy. Is there a way to set up surveillance immediately outside but not looking into the room?

> Absolutely. Will be in touch.

"Are you going to tell me what led to today?" Vera stands with her hands on her hips.

"You mean why I felt the need to defend you? That's easy enough, though I'd have thought it obvious."

I knew Vera deserved that leadership position. I further knew that the pussy American was doing everything in his power to keep her from succeeding.

Vera might not be too fond of my methods, but I make no apologies.

When she frowns at me, I can't help but notice the fullness of her lips. The way they slant down in a way that's at once pouty while almost being a little girlish.

Now that we're back in the room after a dinner the American had the decency to skip, I want to kiss her so badly I can taste it. There's something about Vera Ivanova that calls to my primal nature.

What does a woman like her want?

I turn my back and unbutton my shirt without looking at her.

I notice when she doesn't move, as if she's frozen in place.

Whether or not we continue to be chaste and play it safe, we can still get fucked over if anyone finds out we're sharing a room and that damn one bed.

Only one of those options sounds remotely appealing to me.

Only one of those options gets me closer to Vera and closer to her father.

I shrug out of the dress shirt, fold it, and deliberately put it on top of the dresser by the door. My back still to her, I ball up my undershirt in my fist and slide it into a hamper.

Next, I reach for my belt buckle. I turn slightly to the side so she doesn't see me looking at her as I very deliberately unfasten it. Her breath catches, and she subtly licks her lips.

Ah. That's what I thought.

Vera has completely submerged herself in the world of erotic romance. She knows exactly what I could do with this belt, and I intend on doing every damn one of them.

I slowly pull it halfway out, then tug the rest out with a little swish.

Vera chokes.

When I look up to her, her gaze challenges mine.

"You've had a long day. You're tired, aren't you?"

Very sighs. "So tired."

"Unfortunately, we have to address something."

She eyes me curiously. "What?"

"I told you there would be consequences earlier, didn't I?" My voice is husky as my need for her grows. My cock aches, and my balls are heavy.

"Wait, what?" Her beautiful eyes widen as she stares at me. "What are you talking about?"

Ha. As if a brilliant woman like her forgot. Nice try.

She's so fucking beautiful and wholesome. Those wide green eyes beckon me to come and rest, like a grassy field under the heat of a summer day. I haven't rested in fucking decades.

"You know exactly what I'm talking about."

"Is that how you're going to play this, Markov?"

Ah, the age-old art of deflecting.

"You were the one who decided I was your husband, and you were the one who thought it wise to be disrespectful to your husband." I wrap the belt around my fist and make a little loop. Snap it.

There's no denying it now. I catch the widening of her pupils, the breathless sound of her breath. The way she swallows hard. Vera Ivanova is turned on. I'm going to give her the slightest little taste of what she's read and no doubt fantasized about.

I shake my head. "I've told you what I expect, Vera."

She opens her mouth as if to say something, but nothing comes out.

"You'll turn around and face that bed. Bend over onto your arms." Doing so will expose her to me, and I'm banking on the fact that the thought likely terrifies and arouses her.

"Markov, what are you doing?" Her voice is all wobbly.

"Teaching my wife to obey her husband."

She stares at me, her eyes wide. "And if I don't. . . do that?" she whispers.

"Then I will forcibly put you over my lap, pin you down, and you will not like the kind of spanking I will deliver. Now, which will it be?"

She's bright pink when she asks in a choked voice, "What if someone hears us?"

"Then they'll learn what happens to disobedient wives, won't they?"

She crosses her arms and shakes her head, a last-ditch effort. "I do not think this is part of our arrangement."

"You're a smart girl, Vera. Brilliant, really. Didn't you think about what would happen if you disobeyed your husband?"

"You're not—" She clamps her mouth shut. She can't say it out loud; if anybody hears her tonight, they'll know she's lying. "This is the modern day."

"You have three more seconds before I come and fetch you." I frown at her. "One."

Her gaze flickers.

"Two." I'm prepared to go get her and do exactly what I promised.

"Fine," she says, jutting her chin out as if she's just made a decision. "I'll give you this, but on my terms."

With one quick motion, she removes her top, revealing nothing but a tiny, barely-there cami. She steps out of her sweats, wearing adorable little white, almost transparent undies. Her small breasts push against the cami, and the chaste undies barely cover her ass.

Damn.

And with that, she flounces over to the bed and bends over. Now, I'm hard as a rock.

She gives me a mocking look over her shoulder. "Does this please you, husband?"

My steps are slow and deliberate as I approach her.

When I reach her, I place my hand on her lower back and can feel her tension. I bend down to her ear and whisper, "Very much. Yes, this pleases me, wife, even if you did so from a place of defiance. I'm only going to give you the smallest chastisement, wife. After all, we're new to this. But I want you to remember what it feels like to have my belt across your ass. I want you to remember what it feels like to be humiliated and punished by your husband. Do you understand me? I want you to remember this the next time you think of disobeying me."

"Oh my God," she chokes out in a rush of words. "Of—of course, husband," she says mockingly. "I hear you."

I slap her panty-clad backside with my hand, and she squeals. A red mark instantly blooms across her butt. Christ, it's beautiful. I lift my belt this time and slap her ass again, not too hard but not lightly. She shoots up onto her toes, clenching the duvet in her fists. Her entire face is red, the heat creeping down her neck, yet she doesn't move. I take a moment to caress her heated ass with my palm. My dick twitches. *Fuck.*

"Good girl. You took that so well, wife. I'm so proud of you. Look what a strong, good woman you are." I bend down and place the gentlest of kisses on one cheek, then the other, before I stand. "One more, and then you get to go to bed with a sore ass. A reminder of what I expect from you in the morning."

I give her another light lick of my belt, just enough to make my point, and drop the belt. I'd bet good money she could take way, way more than what I gave her, likely even craves it, but I want to leave her wanting.

I stare at her and can't help but imagine what it would be like to take her. To be inside her. To feel her hot, tight body around me.

I want to see her back arch when she comes. . .

I rub her sore ass with my palm.

"Good girl. You took that so well. Have you learned your lesson, Vera?"

She nods her head. "I have."

Fuck. My dick presses against my pants so tightly it's painful.

"Good girl. Now tell me. How do you feel after your spanking?"

She pauses, inhaling sharply, her breath ragged. Hiding her face in the covers, she doesn't look at me but mumbles her words through the fabric. "That was the hottest thing I've ever experienced."

Jesus.

Even though I expected this, hearing her actually admit it confirms everything I suspected. It's killing me not to pin her hands to this headboard and show her exactly how a dominant male claims a woman.

Gently, I gather her hair and expose the curve of her neck. I brush it over to one shoulder and press a kiss against her bare skin, whispering into her ear. "If I were to touch you right now, would I find you wet, Vera?" My need to possess her intensifies with every breath she takes.

"Is there a submissive lurking within you, Vera? Do you ever dream of being one of the heroines from those novels you devour? To be completely overtaken?" I draw out each word, my voice a husky whisper. "Imagine surrendering control to a dominant. It's a choice, Vera. Embrace it. Many crave this surrender."

"I'm. . . yes, I'm curious."

Christ.

"Spread your legs," I rasp out.

Without a word, she complies, squeezing her eyes shut, perhaps to deny the reality of her own desires. Yet, I've learned enough about her to know that Vera's solitude doesn't mask her fiery spirit. A woman of her passion deserves a counterpart who worships her ferocity.

Leaning over, I prop myself on one arm and breathe in her scent—spring flowers blended with the crispness of autumn rain. Her pulse throbs under my lips; her sharp gasp fills the silence.

"Tell me exactly how you feel right now."

"So, so turned on, Markov. Damn you," she breathes out in a choked whisper.

I cup her ass, and she gasps. "I just disciplined you for such language, Vera. Was my message not clear?"

She whimpers softly. "You made your point." Her voice is laced with feigned protest and genuine desire.

"Get on your back," I command. The raw urgency to taste her is overwhelming, yet I restrain myself, remembering her innocence. My hands, however, can't resist exploring the fullness of her breasts.

"Touch yourself," I murmur. "Let me see."

Clumsily, she pulls her panties to the side and reaches down to her slick folds just as I release one of her breasts from her bra and lick the peaked nub. Her body jerks, a cry escaping her lips.

Mine.

"You're my wife, Vera," I whisper, caught up in the moment's authenticity. For a second, I forget our pretense, lost in the primal need to claim her.

I move her hand aside, replacing it with mine, feeling her warmth and arousal. Her voice breaks as my finger explores her.

"Markov," she pleads, lost for words as pleasure overwhelms her.

"Mine," I growl, my voice rough. "You chose this path. You were the one who said we were married. You were the one who confessed her longing to be commanded. Don't pretend you don't crave this now."

Her hips rise in response, a silent, primal affirmation of her desires. I tease her relentlessly, drawing her close to the brink then halting. I savor the catch of her breath. Pausing, I hold my breath and hers in the balance.

"*Umolai menya.* Beg me."

Her voice breaks in a desperate plea. "Oh. . . *God.* Please, don't stop, Markov. *Please.*"

"Beg me harder. I want to know you mean it. Convince me."

"Please, keep going. I'll—I'll do anything. I did what you said. You told me you were my husband, isn't this what a husband does? Isn't this what I need? Oh, God! *Please!*"

I indulge her, a small stroke sending her arching off the bed. Her body's silent plea is deafening.

"Will you behave now?"

"Yes, yes, yes! Please!"

"Good girl," I praise, a lazy stroke rewarding her compliance. "That's what I want to see. You please me so much. Such a good, sweet girl you are." I kiss her cheek and stroke her again. "Come on my fingers, Vera. I want to watch you."

I take her mouth with mine as she detonates beneath me. I give one more stroke, easing her through the spasms of pleasure. I continue until her climax washes over her, uncontrolled and raw. She clings to the ecstasy, her cries muffled by my kiss, her pleasure mingling with my being.

She collapses, spent. My fingers linger, savoring the last touch.

Gently, I lay her against the pillows, her eyes hazy, overwhelmed by what she's experienced.

"That was beautiful," I confess softly. "So honest. So free." I brush a kiss on her forehead.

Silence stretches between us.

"Tell me how you're feeling now, Vera?"

She looks at me, her eyes earnest when she murmurs, "Scared, Markov."

I cradle her, stroking her disheveled hair, urging her to share her heart. "Talk to me, Vera."

She pauses before she speaks, drawing in a ragged breath. She buries her face in the covers and won't look at me, but she manages to say, "That was the hottest thing I've ever experienced in my life."

Jesus.

I turn her around to face me and sit on the edge of the bed with her on my lap. I've crossed so far over the line of propriety, there's no turning back now.

My hard-on presses against her heated ass. I stifle a groan before I continue. "What are you afraid of?"

"I didn't know what that would feel like," she whispers. "I'm afraid that if we keep. . . If I. . ."

She tries to look away, but I bring her chin back. Her eyes are back on mine.

"Tell me."

It seems that small spanking I gave her removed her ability to hide from me because she opens her mouth and the truth spills out.

"If my father finds out, he'll kill you."

CHAPTER TEN

Vera

SHARING a room with my fake husband is going to kill me.

I came here to study, not be seduced by the hottest fucking Russian man I've ever met in my life.

But it's the first time I've had the chance to get close to a man – and not just any man, but a sexy, dominant one... maybe, for once in my life, I can live a little. I came here to prove myself capable and worthy of the opportunities I've been given, determined to break free from the confines of my sheltered upbringing. To forge my own destiny. Why should romance be limited to the pages of a fictional book?

"Then we'll have to make sure he doesn't find out," Markov says in that Russian accent that makes my belly dip. Why is he completely unconcerned? It seems he doesn't fear my father at all.

I bite my lip, wrestling with my inner turmoil. I choose my words deliberately, weighing each one before I express it.

"You asked me to trust you. And I definitely want to do that. But I can never live with myself if, because of my choices, I hurt somebody else. I don't want you to be hurt, Markov."

His return gaze makes my heart do a little flip-flop. He cradles my chin in his strong, capable hand. After our first encounter, it was hard to imagine he was capable of such tenderness.

"Let me worry about that. Please. Those books you read? About dominance and submission? The sex, everything that goes on in the bedroom. . . That's only the very beginning. It's about way more than that. In real life, it's about establishing trust. It's about letting things go. You don't need to worry about your father."

I don't know if I can stop, but the next second, my brain short-circuits because he's leaning in. And oh my God, I think he's going to kiss me. I've never had a real kiss with a real man before, just awkward fumbles that left me wanting in the back of the high school auditorium at stupid dances.

"I love that you bite your lower lip when you're deep in thought. I love how naturally graceful and poised you are, even when you're sitting on my knee after getting a spanking." My heart leaps into my throat. Then his lips touch mine, and I'm completely lost to sensation.

I am *floating*. The nerves in my body are teeming with need and arousal. When his lips meet mine, a delicious warmth and awareness spreads through me like molten honey, a sweet fire in my veins. He holds me to him. One arm at my back, cradling me, his other hand grasps my jaw. My hands rest on his strong, powerful shoulders. It takes me a second to realize the moan I'm hearing is mine.

I don't know how long we kiss, but when we finally pull away, gasping, I am as pliable as warmed taffy in his hands. My heart thunders in my chest, and I forget why I protested to begin with. That kiss was everything I wanted.

"We're going to take this slow, Vera," he says, the slightest quirk at the corner of his lips. I don't know if I've seen him smile yet, and I think if I ever do, I might tumble head over heels in love with him. But that slightest little quirk is boyishly charming and warms my heart.

I snort. "Go slow," I repeat. "We barely know each other, and you've already spanked my ass and kissed me. Is that normal?"

His voice is husky. "For a husband? Yes."

Oh, Jesus.

My stomach drops. "Get in bed," he commands. "That alarm is going off at four forty-five, don't forget."

"Are you sure about that? I don't think we need to get up at —" He gives me a firm pat on my ass and then guides me into bed.

"Bed, young lady," he says in that warm, commanding voice that does all sorts of crazy things to me. "Have you already forgotten that you need to obey your husband? *Idi v krovat.* Bed."

Obediently, I roll over and stare at the wall, adrenaline surging through me. I'm not so tired anymore.

"I don't think I can just fall asleep like that. If you're my husband, I need to at least look at you. Can I look at you?"

He climbs in beside me, wearing nothing but a pair of boxers.

"Going to fantasize yourself to sleep?" he teases seductively. "I approve of that."

"Perhaps I will. Will you?"

"No. I'm going to tuck you in and wait until you fall asleep. Then I'll take a quick shower and join you. *Then* I'll get some sleep."

The thought of him standing naked in the shower makes me squirm.

"You can't survive on sleep deprivation. "

"Made it this far. "

A sudden realization makes me groan. "You heard every-thing I said in English when you were pretending, didn't you?"

He nods. "Just call me Jason Bourne."

"Jason Bourne was an assassin," I say with a laugh. Maybe it's my imagination, but the slightest shadow crosses his face.

"He was also skilled," Markov says. "And I'm right here in front of you."

"You're a lot bigger than Jason Bourne. And he's not a small guy. You're impressive. Look at your shoulders. What do you bench press?"

He snorts, which is the closest thing to a laugh I've heard yet from him.

"Now that you've gotten a good chance to look at me, go to bed."

"I really haven't. You have tattoos everywhere. I want to see them."

He picks me up, rolls me over, and sets his hand around my waist. "Tomorrow. Get some sleep."

I stare at the wall like a child who has just been told to go to sleep when it's still light out after feasting on gobs of candy. It's not really fair. "I told you, I can't just fall asleep."

"Fine. Do you want me to tell you a bedtime story?" he teases.

"Um, sure."

He continues in his rough voice, accent thick. "There once was a little girl who was up way past her bedtime. Her daddy told her to go to sleep, but she was a naughty little girl who didn't obey, so her daddy gave her a spanking, tucked her into bed, and she cried herself to sleep. The end."

My cheeks heat.

Daddy. Mmm.

"Very funny. I actually *read* myself bedtime stories, and they're much better than that."

"Go ahead, then. Read your book. Under one condition."

"What's that?"

"If you get to a sexy scene, you have to read it out loud."

"You have no idea what I read."

"Of course I do. You're an intelligent, educated woman. Intelligent, educated women like to read romance."

"How do you figure that?"

"They don't have time for real-life romance."

"Hey! That's presumptuous."

My back is to him, so I can't see his smirk, but I can imagine it. "I'm just teasing you. Intelligent, strong women also like to give their brains a little break. There's no way you could constantly perform at such a high level without fueling your brain. Some women play mindless games on their phones. Some listen to music endlessly. Some watch silly TV shows. You're a reader, so I doubt you're reading academic texts all the time. My guess is romance." He tugs my braid, that's loose by now and half undone. "And the truth is, I saw the title of one of your books and looked it up, so I have an idea of what kind of stories you like."

Oh, God.

I pick up my phone and flick on the reading app. This time, though, it doesn't captivate me as it once did. The hero seems too. . . passive. I've had a taste of a real alpha male, and I crave more. The heroine in this book is also annoyingly dumb, the type that makes you want to scream, "Don't open the basement door!" I prefer someone with a bit more sass, too. And the story itself is all about. . . well, sex. I want *more*, something I can sink my teeth into.

Now that I've had a taste of the real deal, my expectations for my fantasy world are a bit. . . higher.

I skim until I get to a sexy part.

I hold my finger up in the air. "Got it. Are you sleeping yet?"

"I'm dead asleep," he teases.

I roll my eyes and read out loud to him.

"When I return to this room, I expect you on your knees, naked. If you touch yourself, you'll be punished because those orgasms belong to me."

"That's kinda hot," I whisper.

"I agree," he whispers back. "A little predictable and cliché, though."

"Really? Would regular old vanilla sex be better then?"

"If they were in the middle of a restaurant. He makes her stroke herself to the brink of orgasm under the tablecloth. That would be entertaining. Or maybe at a ball game with luxury seats, they're both tucked under a blanket. He edges her throughout the entire game and tells her she can only come if there's a touchdown so her screams blend into the crowd's."

"You've given this some thought."

"Mmm. It isn't that hard."

Great. He's a natural then. I yawn widely. My eyelids are heavy.

"Right, put the book down and get some sleep," he says, pulling the blanket around me. I have to admit, it feels nice for him to take care of me like this. I close my eyes. I'm in a warm cocoon of protection for the first time in my life. I pretend I'm sleeping, regulating my breathing. I want to see what he does when I'm asleep.

After a while, I wonder if he's sleeping, too? But then there's a subtle shift of the covers, and I hear him get out of bed. I sneak a peek as he walks to the bathroom and takes a towel from the shelf.

He did say he was going to shower.

Does he. . . does he touch himself in the shower?

Does he think of me?

I didn't miss the press of his erection against my ass when he laid behind me in bed. I turned him the hell *on*, and I am here for it.

I listen for him in the shower. It might be my way too dirty mind, but I imagine I hear him groan. A short while later, the shower turns off, and he comes out wearing nothing but a towel slung low around his tapered waist. It's dark in here, and he isn't looking my way.

He walks to the dresser and takes out his cell phone. Frowns at it. Then sits at the tiny desk, which is dwarfed by his large frame, and types into the phone, scowling.

What is his world like? What work does he actually do when he's not baby-sitting me? I don't know anything about the man.

His low command startles me. "Go to sleep, Vera."

I close my eyes, sighing, and finally feel the pull of sleep.

I wake up the next morning to the sound of my cell phone

ringing and stare at the screen. Four forty-two a.m. My alarm is going to go off at any minute.

I look beside the bed and find it plugged in. Well. I definitely didn't plug it in. I look around for Markov, but he's nowhere to be found.

"Markov?"

It's a tiny room, and the bathroom's vacant. Where is he?

The cell phone keeps ringing.

"Hey, Mom." I'm hit with a pang of guilt. I texted her when we landed but got so caught up in the hustle of everything that I didn't call her. I do a quick calculation—it's only nine forty-two in the evening the day before for her. It's so strange to be in a different *day* than the person I'm closest to in the entire world.

"Vera! Oh, thank God. I've been calling and texting."

I sit straight up in bed. "Is everything okay?"

"Yes, of course. I just hadn't heard from you and was getting worried."

"Mom, I'm fine," I say. I feel a little guilty. I should've maybe called her last night instead of getting. . . *distracted* by Markov.

God, I miss her, and it hasn't even been that long. Hopefully, it'll get easier. "I was sleeping. Remember the time difference? You'll be getting ready for bed soon, right?"

She sighs on the other end of the line. "I know, I know, I just. . . I felt so awful sending you off with that silent man who doesn't even speak the same language as you. It felt like feeding my child to the wolves."

"I'm not a child, though," I say gently. I look around the room again. "And you'd never guess but he actually very much *does* speak English."

"What!"

I fill her in but leave significant chunks of details out, like my faux marriage. I tell her about the program, getting to meet Dr. Morozov in person, and the other people joining me when the door opens, and Markov comes in, dressed in running gear, scowling at me.

"Let's go."

I sit up and glance at the time. Oof. It's well past the wake-up time.

"Mom, I have to go. I'm going to get a run in before I go to my first session, okay?"

"You're so dedicated and disciplined," she says tearfully. "Yes, yes, of course, sweetheart. Text me some new book titles before you go. I need something to occupy myself with you gone."

"I will, promise." I got my love of reading romance from my mom, so we swap titles all the time. Not sure how she'll feel about my latest obsession, though.

I hang up the call and get out of bed. "Did you plug my phone in? That was really sweet."

Shrugging, he walks over to the bed to tidy the blankets. He lifts the sheets and quickly snaps them into place.

"I did. It was responsible, not sweet. You can't start the day off with a dead phone. Are you going to get dressed, or are you going to stand here and tell me making the bed is sweet?"

"In science, we learn that two apparent contradictions can coexist," I say over my shoulder as I walk to the dresser to grab running shorts and a tee. "The duality is a foundational concept in quantum mechanics. Or take the classic example of Shordinnger's Cat—"

"Vera," he growls. Oh, I love me a good growl.

"Yes?" I ask. I slide out of my pajamas and get dressed in front of him. I don't bother looking over my shoulder. He seduced the fuck out of me last night, so I have no intention of being modest. I smile to myself at the sound of his muffled groan.

"I was going to tell you to stop jabbering on about duality or whatever the fuck it was and get dressed, but apparently, you can do both at the same time. Impressive."

His lips are pressed in a thin line when I turn to face him and pull my sports bra on. "All I was going to say was that someone can be grumpy and sweet at the same time, and you're a classic example."

"Call me sweet again and see how that goes for you," he says as I head to the bathroom to brush my teeth. "And where's your top? You can't go out dressed in shorts and a bra."

I shut the door. "Of course I can. I get hot as hell running."

"I'll douse you with water. Wear a top."

I frown at myself in the mirror while I brush my teeth. I'm not exactly sure how far I'm going to push this whole thing. I am not the type to allow a man to dictate how I dress, but. . . that whole spanking thing last night was *hot*.

I don't know if I'll ever really know how much I like in terms of dominance and submission if I don't give it a go.

"I'm not wearing a top!" I yell, just to see what he'll say. There's no response.

My heart thumps.

When I open the door to the bathroom, I'm not sure what to expect. Markov stands, one of my running tanks in hand.

"I chose the smallest one. I'll carry an extra bottle of water if you overheat and pour it on you. But you are not running on this campus—on my watch—without a top, at least not until I've had a chance to truly survey who's here and who we have to watch." He leans forward and tips a finger under my chin. "My job is to keep you safe, Vera. Don't make my job harder for me, please."

There he goes again. For some reason, his request, combined with that finger under my chin, does a lot more to sway me than his bluster and threats.

I sigh. "Fine, I'll wear the top." I tug it on. "Happy?"

Markov regards me with his arms crossed on his chest. Wearing a sleeveless workout top and shorts, his muscles are on full display.

Lord.

"I'm happy that I managed to cajole you into being smart about things," he mutters, gesturing to the door. "And that attitude still needs to go, wife." I half expect him to swat my ass when I walk past him, but luckily, he's too busy procuring bottles of water.

"Where were you?" I ask as I open the door.

"Just outside the door. I was taking a call from the captain and didn't want to wake you."

"Oh?" I take the bottle of water from him and we begin walking at a good clip, warming up. "Anything important?"

"Oh, yes," he says as we begin to pick up the pace in unison. "You and I have somewhere to be tomorrow evening." He grits his teeth beside me.

"Why?" What the hell?

Markov scowls as he keeps pace beside me. "Your father's arrived in Moscow."

CHAPTER ELEVEN

Nikko

IT'S BEEN A LONG, uneventful few weeks at the clinic. Her father has barely been in touch.

Vera and her team start their day at seven in the morning, scarcely taking breaks for meals. I swear Vera would survive solely on coffee and Diet Coke if I didn't occasionally force some real food into her diet. I can usually persuade her if the food involves grilled cheese, her favorite comfort food.

We've fallen into a comfortable rhythm, almost like a married couple. We start with an early morning run together at dawn, followed by coffee and breakfast. This has become my favorite part of the day. She comes alive during these moments, speaking animatedly with her hands as she shares her passions, hopes, and dreams, with a fervor that is utterly contagious. She tries to get me to talk too, but I prefer to listen.

She lives for this. It's like watching a master artist at work. I stay on the periphery, unless the American douchebag is nearby. I'll have to have another talk with him soon.

Tonight, we have dinner with her father. He's kept to himself. At first, I thought maybe he wouldn't want to see us, and I'd have to pull some strings. I've relied heavily on surveillance and convinced myself it was more important to earn her trust for now.

I briefly considered my options. It's a perfect opportunity to do what I came for, but it's too soon. I wouldn't be able to pull it off without making it obvious who the perpetrator was.

No. Ivanov will live another day.

His arrival complicates things, though. The chances of me being exposed as an imposter increase with every interaction with Ivanov. But I've been assured that the only person who knows me is Ivanov's mistress, and I'm equally assured there's no way he would bring his mistress around Vera.

Still, I tread on a razor-thin line. I remind myself of why I'm here. What my ultimate purpose will be. This is only one more step closer to what has to happen.

"Markov, I don't want to see my father tonight." Vera frowns down at the turkey sandwich in her hand. I've forced her away from today's biological threat simulation to get some food. She's already been working for ten hours straight.

"I know. I don't either. But we have to play the game, Vera."

And I absolutely have to be in the presence of her father.

Combined with video surveillance from my brothers, my personal observations will be telling.

What are his habits? Does he have a daily pattern he follows? Vulnerabilities I could exploit? I need to observe his psychological profile as well. What is his emotional state? Stress levels? How does he respond under pressure? Is he plugged in with any biometric tracking devices? What's his physical condition?

"Ugh. Do we really, though?" she asks in a little voice that almost makes her seem childlike. I half expect her to pout.

"I know you'd rather get back into that hazmat suit and lead your team to find the pathogen so you can set up your mock decontamination stations," I say with a grimace. "But remember, there are no real infected civilians here and you were so successful with the last threat simulation, your professors were practically tripping over themselves to congratulate you."

Her eyes shine at me. "Markov. You've been paying attention."

I shrug. "It's what I do best."

Not the *only* thing I do best, but it's an important skill to cultivate.

"Anyway," I tell her as I reach for a bag of chips and open them up before I hand them to her. "We don't have to stay long. You have an early morning session with your personal trainer before another long day at your clinical." I wink at her.

"And my father doesn't have to know you're my personal

trainer?" she asks, taking the chips from me. "I'm glad they're bringing in some American foods for us."

"A lot is being asked of you," I say as I reach for a sandwich for myself. "The last thing you need to do is try choking down foods that are foreign to your palette after a hard day's work. How's the American asshat today?"

She groans and rolls her eyes. "He's such a goody goody, it makes me sick. When Morozov asked me to explain why I'd chosen a certain protocol, Jake droned on and on about the stupid research he did about decontamination procedures and his experience with the Harvard team. He spent extra hours memorizing protocols. And when Morozov asked me to select the team members based on strengths and weaknesses, Jake made some snide comment about my lack of upper body strength as a woman and how he or Maxim would be better suited for anything requiring physical exertion."

She snorts, but I'm not the slightest bit amused.

"Did he, now?" I ask curiously. I empty my water bottle and crush it in my fist, wishing it was the American's scrawny little suck-up neck.

"Markov," she says, sobering. "You *cannot* intervene. It could put everything at risk."

Not everything.

"Please," she pleads. She stifles a groan. "God, why did I tell you anything?"

"Because it's my job to protect you, and I asked." I lean over and tuck a stray strand of hair behind her ear. "And I'm your husband."

I know it's only fake. I know we're only pretending, but I'd be lying if I said I didn't like how it feels saying that. Vera's two telltale signs—the flush of her cheeks and the way she bites her lip—tell me she's no different. She likes it, too.

"Remember, I asked you to trust me, Vera." I reach for her hand and bring it to my mouth so I can kiss her knuckles. Ah. There's that lip between her teeth again. My cock stirs.

"When do we have to leave to meet with my father? I have to finish this demonstration before we go."

I check my phone and frown. "Dammit. He's moved the time up. We have two hours."

"Two hours!" She leaps from the table. "I can't do that!"

Vera needs a little time to shift from one thing to the next, likely due to the intensity of her focus. I give her a look. She can and will do this, even if she doesn't want to. "In your experience, is your father amenable to you saying you can't meet his demands?" I ask, knowing the answer before she tells me.

With a groan, she shakes her head. "Point made. Fine, alright. I can get ready, but I have to finish up what I'm working on and tell them I need to leave."

Two hours later, we're getting ready to go and meeting the car her father has sent to pick us up. While she was getting ready, I brushed up on the facts I know about Markov, in case her father asks.

Vera looks like a nervous wreck. She's biting her lip nonstop, fidgeting, tapping her foot. I even find her biting a nail, something she never does.

"Why so nervous?" I ask. I open the door to the car and confirm the directions to *Zoloty Kupol,* or "Golden Dome," a renowned restaurant known for its golden accents and panoramic views of the city's skyline, including the famous domes, in the heart of Moscow town. It's a place only for the elite, and reservations are required months in advance.

"It's my father," she says simply. "Our relationship is complicated."

I shut the door and make sure her seatbelt's fastened. She doesn't even protest as I check the locks. Good. She's catching on.

"Yes. It's your father. He'll be self-serving and self-focused as always, only wants to hear what will make him look good, and is here more for show than to actually visit with either of us." I tip my head to the side. "Yes?"

"Yes," she sighs. "Did you look this place up? Have you been there before?"

I shake my head. "I looked at the specs and blueprints so I know where the exits are, but I haven't been there, no."

I also know the best place for cell reception and where we can sit where the lighting is dim, mitigating any possibility of anyone identifying me.

"It's," she makes air quotes, "'unmatched in opulence and sophistication, and well-known for its unparalleled fusion of traditional and contemporary Russian cuisine, culinary techniques, and an outstanding wine menu that rivals the best in the world." Rolling her eyes, she paraphrases. "In regular person speak, that means we'll pay ten times what we'd pay a street vendor for something that's half the size and healthier, so it won't taste anywhere near as good."

I know her a bit better by now, and I happen to know that while Vera loves good food, she is more focused on her books and studies than anything. She'd just as soon eat something from the school dining hall to get back to work. It isn't the uppity food that's concerning her.

"What's really bothering you?"

Our driver picks up speed, heading into the city. She looks at him, then me, and jerks her chin at my phone. She doesn't want to be overheard.

> Us. It's us that's worrying me. We have… energy together. What if he picks up on it?

> How soon you forget that I can feign indifference and coolness quite well.

When she still doesn't look convinced, I try again.

> Relax, Vera. This will work out. Trust me. Your father's way too into himself to care about us.

> And what if that's exactly what's bothering me?

I look up in surprise to see her wiping a stray tear from her cheek.

Goddammit.

She's spent a life being ignored by a man who came in and out of her life, drawing close to a woman her father betrayed and mistreated. Of course she doesn't want to be in his presence any more than I do.

I'm having dinner with the man responsible for my younger brother Lev getting his ass beat and put in the hospital and almost causing the death of my sister-in-law. He's an evil son of a bitch.

I put my phone down and reach for her hand.

"At least we have this one consolation. We don't have to pay for the overpriced *stroganina* and wine."

My phone buzzes with a text. I glance at it, and my blood runs cold.

> Aleks: His Moscow mistress is in the nearby vicinity. If she makes an appearance, you're fucked. You'll have to make a sudden disappearance.

And leave Vera alone with that son of a bitch? Not on your life.

I scowl at the phone, viscerally aware of Vera's eyes on me. My mind is racing with the possibilities of what I need to do. There's no fucking way that jerk is so self-focused he'd bring his mistress to meet his daughter, not when he's still married to her goddamn mother.

My phone vibrates again.

Aria was able to get an aerial view. The mistress is on site but that's only because he's staying at the hotel that's adjacent to the restaurant. She's in a spa getting some kind of facial peel procedure, which Aria says will take a long enough time you don't have to worry about her showing.

I blow out a breath, almost as concerned for Vera having to meet the woman than my own identity being leached. Aleksandr's texts continue.

Word is that he has three of his closest confidantes nearby. They likely won't join you for dinner, but my concern is that one of them might recognize you. Be careful.

"We're here," Vera says. Her hand is cold in mine when I take it. It's the last time I'll be able to touch her until this is all over. "Remember, we're nothing to each other."

There's a hollow echo of sadness in her tone.

"Only for a time, Vera." I see a familiar face out the window. "Let's go. Your father's arrived."

CHAPTER TWELVE

Vera

"WELL, LA-DE-DA," I say with a groan.

The moment the car turns down the street leading to the restaurant, the air seems to almost shimmer around us. There are so many luxury cars and uniformed valets lined outside the restaurant, I feel like I'm at an exhibition for the world's most expensive cars. The entrance is flanked by more uniformed valets who look more suitable as royal courtiers than restaurant staff. The restaurant's claim to fame is being *golden*, so there are decorative gold leaves on the ground in front of us, on the lettering on the door, and accented on the uniforms of staff. God. Leave it to my father to pick a restaurant that's more about social status than genuine connection. *Ugh.*

I'm dressed in a little black dress, the *only* elegant dress I brought because every girl needs an LBD and I didn't know when I'd need something formal. I dressed it up with a pair of gold hoops and gold heels, and I even did my eye makeup for once. After the display of golden opulence here, I sort of wished I'd worn silver jewelry.

Markov looks exceptionally hot in his suit, and it will feel nice walking in beside him, even if we have to pretend we aren't a couple.

I haven't told Markov much about my father, but he knows plenty and will see soon enough. My father is a man always looking to make an impression. I'm only his daughter inasmuch as I benefit him, just like my mother. And because I'm loyal to her, he means nothing to me.

Taller than me and polished and refined, if you didn't know my father, you'd think he was an absolute charmer. His hair and beard are laced with silver, he's impeccably dressed, and when he smiles, the flash of perfectly straight white teeth nearly blinds me. The smile doesn't reach his eyes, though. They never have.

Markov opens the door for me, nods to my father, then quickly turns to offer me his hand to help me out of the car. It will be the only time he touches me this evening, and I savor the seconds we're connected before he releases me.

My father doesn't recognize Markov. I'm guessing they haven't met yet. But when he sees me exit, he grins broadly, his eyes shining at me. I can't help it—for one weak moment, I wish it was genuine. I wish he really did want to see me. I wish he cared.

But I quickly push that thought away because I know the truth.

"Hello, Father." I give him a small, tight smile, which he doesn't even see because he's too busy looking around, more concerned with being seen by whatever social circle he's in than engaging with his daughter.

"How are you?" he asks, kissing both cheeks before reaching to shake Markov's hand. A wave of cloying, expensive cologne consumes me. My stomach roils.

"And you're Markov," he states. "I've heard so much about you."

Markov scowls at him, even though he shakes his hand. "Pleased to meet you, sir." I silently fist-bump him. He is absolutely not going to play a part to please my father.

"And how is everything going at your. . . your program?" my father asks.

"Markov, join us." It's unusual for a bodyguard to join us for dinner, so I'm not sure what my father's planning.

"Oh, things are going well. I've been working alongside Professor Morozov. He's world-renowned for his leading research on the advances made against biological threats. We actually had a simulation today."

"Oh good, good," my father says placatingly. He hasn't heard a word I said.

I wink at Markov behind my father's back as he arranges for us to have a seat inside.

"We were able to extract DNA from monkeys to cross-breed them with the African elephant with much success. We'll be able to market our new breed to upcoming entrepreneurs within three years. They'll be able to climb high trees while maintaining the status as the largest land animal on earth."

"Is that right?" my father asks, following the waitress toward our table, a circular one at the way back, clearly reserved for VIP guests only. "Fascinating."

He's still not listening to a damn thing I say. *Ugh*. I grit my teeth and go on, making it more ridiculous.

"Mmm," I say. "Quite. They'll subsist on a diet that would be far too pricy for the average consumer, but perhaps some of the elite would find a way." I give him a huge smile. Under the table, Markov pinches my thigh to remind me to behave. I turn and look at him while my father peruses the wine menu and shake my head at him. He narrows his eyes and makes a subtle swinging motion with his palm. Good. I hope he spanks me tonight. Might calm me down after all this nonsense.

"So proud of you, Vera. You always were exceptionally brilliant." He looks up and winks widely at Markov. "For a woman, am I right? Do what you can, love, before you have to take maternity leave."

He laughs loudly at his own joke, but I'm pleased to see Markov actually looks horrified. He quickly schools his features, though. "Actually, sir, I don't believe brilliance is confined to gender. In the short time I've witnessed Vera's accomplishments, I have to say her abilities are at a level and intensity that outshines all her peers. She's earned that scholarship." He smiles, and it sort of chills me. He says something to my father in Russian that I don't understand, then decidedly ignores the glare I give him for freezing me out of the conversation.

My father smiles and looks thoughtful, then nods and

responds in Russian. What the hell? I plunk my menu down.

Another warning squeeze of my knee has me immediately wet. *Ugh.* He can't turn me on in here. It's completely inappropriate.

As my father scans the restaurant, I sneak a glance at Markov, who is staring hard at his phone, deeply concentrating, it seems.

"I don't mean to insult you, Vera," my father says with what appears to be genuine kindness. I know better. "I just don't know why you're putting so much time and effort into your studies when you know the expectations of marrying and settling down are likely your lot in life."

My cheeks color. I hate how easily I give myself away by blushing, but I've never managed to figure out how not to.

"In the modern age, women do both, Father."

My father snorts, but Markov speaks up. "In my family, we have two women who are unparalleled with their skills. One is exceptionally brilliant with cyber security, while the other's a marksman like no other."

"I hear you're quite skilled yourself with a weapon?" my father asks. "I'd like to see that sometime."

A waiter appears out of nowhere and brings my father a bottle of wine. He makes a big show of tasting it and pouring it into wine glasses. Still, I take the glass gratefully.

The two of them continue their conversation in Russian for a few moments until Markov looks at me. "Vera doesn't speak Russian yet," he says. "We should continue in English."

My father gives me a look of disdain. "That's her mother's fault," he says, his cheeks flushed already from the effects of the wine and likely something more. He took it as a matter of personal injury that my mother wouldn't have him back after he cheated on her my entire childhood. She stayed with him, but I knew she had no choice. A woman does not divorce her Bratva husband, especially one whose entire world revolves around his self-image.

I decide instead of discussing my own work, which he's disinterested in any way, to steer the conversation back to my father's favorite topic of conversation—him. "Tell me what brings you to Moscow this time, Father."

He sits up straighter and nods to Markov. "I had business with Markov's aunt. She unfortunately couldn't join us for dinner this evening due to a previous engagement and sends her well wishes to you, Vera. She says she hopes to meet you in the near future."

I stare at my father, uncomprehending at first. How is he so cavalier about his infidelity?

"Who is she?" I ask, my voice dangerously low. "A young little something you picked up on one of your latest travels to a foreign land? Someone who didn't know you were married with children?"

My father laughs too loudly and snaps his fingers at the waitress. I flinch at the obvious rudeness. "Child," he says with a laugh. "Vera, my love, look at you. You're a full-grown woman. An adult. I have no children. You're my daughter, yes, but a man of my stature and age has the privilege of associating with whomever he chooses."

I saw how the infidelity wore my mother down. I witnessed how he would gallivant around the world with his mistress of the week, but should she ever do the same, her punishment would be severe and swift. There was the double-standard as a Bratva wife; don't expect fidelity from your husband, but a woman was expected to bear the ring and name of one man for life, no matter how philandering he might be.

"Please," I say in a soft voice, not wanting to draw attention to us. "You do what you must, but there's no need for me to meet whoever she is. Whether you like it or not, I'm faithful to my mother."

I down the rest of my wine. My father's face colors and his fingers tighten around his wine glass.

"I'll have you remember you're my daughter, Vera Ivanova," he says in that chilling voice that, even now, never fails to send an unwanted shiver down the back of my neck. It was the voice he used before he broke things or lashed out.

He wouldn't do that here, would he?

"I know exactly who I am," I counter, leaning closer to him. "I'll ask that you do the same."

My father reaches a hand out for me, but Markov intercepts him.

"Sir, this is neither the time nor place for a show of power," he says in that quiet way of his. Since he spoke in English, the words were for my ears as well. "If our presence has upset you, I'm happy to escort Vera back to her apartment, and you can give my aunt my best wishes."

My father stares at Markov's hand on his wrist and seems to come to his senses. Markov is younger and stronger than my father, but my father outranks him. However, Markov has a bargaining chip. His aunt is my father's lover. Markov has the ability to pull some strings.

My father smiles and nods. "Yes, yes, of course," he says, as if he wasn't just on the verge of hurting me or making an absolute fool of himself. Markov releases my father before he places a reassuring hand on my thigh. I squirm uncomfortably because I know if my father saw his hand under the table, no amount of wish to save face would save Markov.

I veer the conversation back to my father's pursuits. He talks at length about the subject, going on and on about infrastructure, cost-effective investing strategies, and political alliances that would benefit international relations while I strategically remove all the onions off my salad. Though I'm bored to tears, I can tell Markov listens keenly.

"Fascinating," I say, giving my father the same energy of bullshit disinterest he gave me, but it's completely lost on him and only serves to encourage him to blather on. Markov's eyes twinkle at me, though, and he gives me that almost quirk of the lips. He's getting kissed thoroughly for that when we're alone *after* he tells me what they discussed in Russian.

I'm grateful when the rest of our food arrives and happily busy myself with the house special: a smoked starlet, a prized Russian fish, served with caviar cream and roasted root vegetables and potato medley, thinly sliced and crispy, sprinkled with sea salt. Alongside the vegetables is an arrangement of edible flowers. Markov digs into a steak the size of Manhattan with gusto.

The longer our dinner takes, the more my father drinks. I don't remember him drinking so heavily, but I've hardly seen him in recent years. It seems Moscow brings out the 'best' in him.

"If you'll excuse me," my father says. "I must take this call. I'll return shortly."

He steps away from the table, and I become aware of the three men in suits sitting at a table adjacent to ours, their eyes on our table. One of them rises and approaches.

"Shevchenko," one says, extending a hand to Markov. "We've exchanged texts. I won't stay long but wanted to make your acquaintance in person. Thank you for your regular updates and dedication to your work." He bows his head and takes his leave.

My heartbeat quickens. I was only moments away from having a private conversation with Markov. Letting our masks come down for a moment while my father was away from the table. How could I completely forget that my father always brought with him a small group of guards?

Markov looks down at his phone, his fingers flying over the keys. He seems preoccupied, but I'm not sure why. I don't think he likes being here any more than I do.

Finally, before my father returns, he places his phone down on the table and leans closer to me. "Listen to me, Vera."

Now, this is the real Markov. The one I know behind closed doors. The one that holds me when we climb into bed at night. Who pays attention when I talk about my studies and experiences. And the one who makes my heart turn in my chest with a mere look.

"Mmm?" I sip my wine, my hand slightly trembling.

"He's nothing to you," he says in a whisper of a voice. He might as well be telling me about when we're going to leave and going over our schedule for the following day. "He's never been. I can see how disappointed you are in him, and it's only natural. He has no idea who you are, but I will always tell you with confidence. It's his loss."

He doesn't wait for a reply but goes back to his phone, detached once again, as my father joins us.

I swallow the lump in my throat and take another sip of wine.

"Your aunt says you haven't been in touch with her, Markov."

"I am so sorry," Markov replies. "Vera's schedule has me quite occupied as I assist her, and I've recently switched to a new phone. My contacts are still in the process of syncing. Please have her get in touch, and I will respond promptly. Also, express my gratitude to her for this opportunity she's given me." He shares a knowing glance with me while my father is preoccupied with the waitress, asking for the dessert menu. "Being back in the city has been a profound experience."

His reference to the city must be about Moscow...right? Surely, he's referring to the geographical and cultural significance of being here. It seems too daring for him to subtly thank my father for being involved with. . . me?

Profound experience.

I give him a warning glare just as my father turns back to us. He eyes Markov coldly, which takes me by surprise. For most of the dinner, he's actually been trying to get Markov on his side, like part of some twisted brotherhood thing.

"Family is the most vital of assets," he says soberly. "You'd be wise to remember that. Your aunt is an exceptional woman, Markov."

I flatten my lips. I have no desire to hear him wax eloquent on his mistress's many virtues any longer, even if she is related to Markov. No matter how hard I try, no matter how I distance myself mentally from my father, I can't help the genuine disappointment that wells in my heart at his cold and selfish attitude. I'm frustrated that I still, even now, seek the tiniest modicum of his approval. I'd have hoped I'd know better than that by now.

I put a hand to my head. "While this has been lovely, I seem to have developed a headache. I'm so sorry," I lie to my father. "I'm going to decline dessert and head back to the campus."

"Of course," my father says, folding the dessert menu. He picks up his phone and smiles, obviously taken by whatever conversation he's reading. "Your aunt says hello, Markov. She wants to know if you've spoken to your mother recently."

Markov stands and smiles. "I'm ordering a ride for Vera. My

aunt's always checking in on me and my mother. Tell her nice try."

With that cryptic message, he's gone.

I feel bereft without his presence. I had an ally when he was here. I give myself a mental shake. I'm an adult. A week ago, I didn't need Markov, and I definitely don't need him now.

I have a sudden realization, as my father continues his texting conversation, oblivious to my presence, that this is a turning point for me.

I've left home. I've struck out on my own. My father has made his motives and intentions clear as day.

I don't need my father's support. I don't need my father's love.

I've chosen my path, and he's chosen his.

He rises when Markov joins us again and gives me a perfunctory kiss on both cheeks.

"Thank you for indulging an old man," he says with an almost wistfulness. "Markov, take good care of my daughter."

He shakes Markov's hand firmly.

Keeping up with those appearances is hard, old man.

"Of course, sir." He gives me a knowing look my father doesn't catch. "Taking care of your daughter is exactly why I'm here."

Once more, I imagine something like regret flashing across his features, but when I look again, his face is impassive as always. I get the distinct feeling that Markov is hiding something.

I've had a lot of wine, though. I chalk it up to my imagination.

Someone reaches for Markov's shoulder. "Nikko?"

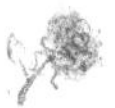

CHAPTER THIRTEEN

Nikko

FUCK.

I vaguely recognize the woman's voice behind me, and she could fuck up everything. Vera stares at me, her eyes wide in surprise.

I turn, my face impassive. "Excuse me?" I ask in Russian. "Can I help you?"

It's an older woman with gray hair twisted in a loose bun. Her blue eyes are kind, her face soft.

"Nikko Romanov," the woman says. "You were in my class in grade school. Did you forget me?"

"I'm sorry," I tell her apologetically. "My name is Markov, not Nikko. I am told I look like someone else."

"Oh." Her face falls, and I feel like a total douchebag. *Shit.* But if anyone finds out my real identity, all will be lost.

"You do look so much like him," she says, giving me a curious look. She doesn't buy it. "Well. That's too bad. I quite liked Nikko and would've loved a chance to catch up with him. Have a good night."

She turns and is gone.

"Who was that?" Vera asks. "And why did she call you Nikko?"

I shrug as we walk toward the car and don't reply. Adrenaline surges through me, and I want to punch something. "She mistook me for someone named Nikko. Someone she taught." I give her a forced smile. "Grade school for me would've been over twenty years ago."

Vera snorts as she gets into the car. "I forget how old you are."

Oh, I look very fucking similar. I close the door with a bang. I have to change the subject.

The doors are tinted, and we're alone. We're so close our knees touch in the warm, dark interior. I reach my hand as if to caress her but lace my fingers through her hair and give it a sharp pull. "Are you calling me old?"

Her eyes go wide for a fraction of a second before she licks her lips and smirks at me. "No," she says with a hint of mockery in her tone. "Never... *Grandpa.*"

I tighten my grip and bring my mouth to her ear. "Do I need to take you over my knee?"

My gaze lingers on her neck. Her pulse is beating rapidly when she swallows. "You do," she says softly. "I really think you do." I pull her head back slightly to expose her neck and shoulder, where I place a mix of soft and demanding kisses. She stifles a moan, and I drag my teeth along her collarbone and bite.

She gasps, but I hold her in place with my hand on her nape. "No. Not yet." I wait until she submits, her body softening toward me before I release her hair and tenderly cradle her chin. Warmth spreads across my chest with the urge to protect her, even though I know I must seduce her. But I'm left pondering. When does the act of seduction become true affection?

"You've had too much to drink, Vera."

"And you had nothing. I noticed you didn't touch a drop." Our whispered words in the dark, hidden back of the car linger in the air.

"I used to. Used to smoke weed and drink myself under the table. But no more."

She runs the tip of her finger over my shoulder, barely touching me. "Why not?"

"Because I've learned that I like to be in control."

"Really?" she says with a little laugh. The vibrant green of her eyes seems to intensify. "*Shocking.*"

I shake my head and make a little tsking sound. "Careful, young lady. You've already earned yourself one spanking."

When she tries to look away, I bring her gaze back to mine. "When we get back to that room, you're going to strip for me. I want to see your beautiful, naked body. I want to see every inch of you." I bend closer and whisper in her ear. "I want to paint your ass red before I taste you. You'll be my dessert tonight."

"Oh God," she says with a groan. "You can't do that."

I rest my hand on her thigh and tighten my grip. "I can and will. You know you've been imagining this."

"Imagining what?" She barely manages to whisper.

"*Everything*. What it would be like to draped over my lap while I spank you. To surrender all control to me. To feel the blend of arousal and pain before I lay you out and lick your pussy. My hot, wet tongue eating you out. Don't lie to me, Vera, or I'll have to punish you."

"And what if I have?" she whispers as I drag my thumb along the very top of one nipple. I give it a squeeze, and she hisses in a breath. "What then?"

"Then we'll have to see where fantasy meets reality. There's only one way to find out what you really like."

"What's that?" She stifles a moan when I lift her top and drag one finger along the swell of her breast before I tease the hardened nipple.

"Try *everything*."

Her eyes flutter shut. "Markov, why—why do I—why do I feel you'd be a total expert at that?"

Because it's the only kind of sex that interests me.

The car cruises to a stop. We're back.

Late night has settled over the campus. Though the undergrads are in full-on party mode, the private area where we stay is quieter. There's too much on the line for these students to fuck around.

I'm going to make damn sure it's safe before we go in.

I tip the driver, and he leaves. Vera stands behind me. "I'll go first. They were supposed to install those locks while we were gone. I got the set of new keys. Let me check."

"And if they didn't?"

"Tomorrow, I take matters into my own hands."

Vera winks lasciviously at me. "You do that, big boy."

I stifle a snort and open the door.

The locks have been changed. They're definitely more secure. There's no evidence anything's been moved or that anyone's been in here. Perfect.

I waste no time removing my tie, my eyes on her. I shrug out of my suit coat while she watches, unabashedly taking me in.

"You're so strong," she whispers, reaching out to squeeze my biceps through my dress shirt. "So powerful. And the way you were with my father. . . God, Markov, you were amazing to watch."

I reach for her and lift her up. I cup her ass, and her legs go around me. We've cuddled and kissed so far, but I've kept things innocent.

No more. I want this woman.

I kiss her until she moans, until she's pliant and supple as I walk toward the bed. I slide her down the length of my body. "I want you to bend over that bed. *Now.*"

I turn her around and guide her over the edge of the bed. The sight of her perfect, heart-shaped ass and her willing submission makes me hard as fuck. I maneuver the buckle of my belt out and draw it through the loops. The sound of leather through fabric makes her squirm.

"What are you doing?" she asks. When I don't answer, she gets a little nervous. "Markov?"

"You want a taste of dominance. We start here, Vera. I give the commands, and you obey."

A wise man once told me that women are slow cookers and men are frying pans in the bedroom. Women often need a long, slow build-up to more. They need to feel safe. Emotionally secure. They need to trust.

"Look how gorgeous you are. Fucking stunning."

"Markov..."

I tap my folded belt to her ass, a prelude. Her whole body jumps as if expecting much more. I tap her again and again, light taps over her clothing to tease and build expectation. My voice is low and controlled between light smacks of the belt.

"Is this what you want? Have you fantasized about this?"

She hesitates for a moment before nodding. "I've definitely fantasized about this."

I give her another smack of the belt, a bit harder this time. Warming her up.

"You want to lose control. You want me to take over."

"Yes. Fuck, *yes*."

I snap the belt a bit harder. "Watch that language."

She gives me a sidelong glance, and I can tell she's halfway between telling me off and leaning into this. Allowing herself to submit in a way she never has before. I lean closer and fist her hair. "The correct response is *yes, sir*."

Vera blinks wide eyes. Swallows. Licks her lips. A myriad of expressions crosses her face before she nods and whispers, "And if I say *no, sir?*"

A surge of adrenaline courses through me. A challenge. She wants to challenge me, and I'm fucking here for it.

"Then I'll need to punish you. I'll show you what happens to naughty girls who run their mouths." I snap my belt hard across her ass, and she comes up on her toes. I spank her again, harder this time, and she squeals and squirms. Again, I bring the belt down. Now that she's warmed up, she'll be able to take more. I want to bring her to a place of no return.

"Tell me what your answer is, Vera. Let's hear it, *Kotyonok*."

"Ooh. What does that mean?"

"Kitten. I want to hear my little kitten purr."

She smiles, her eyes close, and I slap my belt across her ass again. I drop it to the floor and lift her skirt around her waist. Her ass is bright pink and stunning. I press myself against her, loving the way my hardened length feels against her hot, punished ass.

"Did you learn your lesson, Vera? Will you be a good girl now?"

"Mmmm," she says, squirming against me. I palm her ass and she draws in a breath.

"Is that a *yes, sir* or a *no, sir?*"

"Yes, sir," she says on a moan. "Yes, sir, I'll do whatever you say."

"Good girl." I bend and kiss her neck, still red from my earlier bite. I lick the reddened flesh, slide her dress up over her head, and toss it to the edge of the bed. Her rumpled undergarments are next, leaving only her simple white bra.

"Up on the bed." I give her ass a firm pat. "I want to taste you."

"Markov," she begins, shaking her head. "I don't know about that."

"You said you'd do anything I said. Don't push me, little kitten, or I'll have no choice but to keep disciplining you."

She bites her lip. I move up to the headboard and lift her up so her body's straddling mine. I kiss her while cupping her breast. My cock aches to be inside her, but I know my patience will pay off. I will not take advantage of her.

She trembles as she places her knees on either side of my face. I kiss the inside of her thigh, where the sweet, warm evidence of her arousal coats her thighs. I lazily lick her inner thigh and groan. She's going to taste better than I ever imagined.

CHAPTER FOURTEEN

Vera

THE EFFECTS of the wine have long since worn off, so I blame his utterly perfect dominance for the way I feel like I'm going to float away. I've never wanted to please a man before, but there's something about the way he is that makes me like putty in his hands.

My body hovers over his, my hands trembling while I support my weight on my wrists. It's not so much a hard position to hold as it's utterly, irrevocably *vulnerable.*

I mewl at the first swipe of his tongue on my clit. I grin at the sound of his groan.

"Fucking candy," he mutters, his voice muffled against me. "You're addictive."

While I kneel over him, he reaches a finger to my nipple and gives a little teasing squeeze. A pulse of arousal surges through me, and I'm completely engulfed in flames. How does he do that?

The sensation of his tongue over my clit at the same time he tweaks my nipples makes me weak. I can't help but totally surrender to him. The more he touches me, the stronger my need to climax overwhelms me.

"Markov," I say, begging, even though I don't know what I'm begging for. I can hardly form a thought. It's so intimate, so personal, I'm bared to him. There's nowhere to hide. . . *anything.*

"You want me to stop?" he asks, his voice muffled between my thighs, his tongue hovering right over where I desperately need him to go.

"Noooo," I moan. "Please. Oh, God, oh my God—"

"Beg me. Say *please, Daddy.*"

I blink, shocked, as waves of arousal drown me. My cheeks heat, and before I can think, he claps his heavy hand on my ass.

"Do it."

I open my mouth, but nothing comes out. I feel choked, desperate, and I feel like—

Slap.

Another hard smack of his palm takes all thought out of my mind, right along with my breath.

"Please, Daddy. Please let me come. Daddy. . ."

His growl of pleasure and approval fills me with head-to-toe bliss just seconds before the rest of my body catches up. He suckles my clit between his lips, and I lose my *mind.*

Euphoria explodes through me, overtaking every nerve in my body. I'm screaming, helpless to stop. I don't care who hears or what they think. I'm powerless over the ecstasy taking over my body like I'm a woman possessed.

"Thank me," he growls against my thigh. "Thank me while you come."

"Thank you," I mewl as another wave of ecstasy crashes through my veins. "Thank you. Thank you. . . *Daddy*," I whisper and sob as I come against his tongue with abandon.

Seconds, minutes, *years* pass while I'm totally encompassed in scorching hot pleasure. I finally slump to the side as he guides my hips over to the side. I can't move. My limbs are immobile. I've been paralyzed with pleasure.

"Come here," he says.

"Can't. . . move," I manage to whisper. I can't even open my eyes.

"Good," he says approvingly. "Then I did my job right." With effortless ease, he lifts my body and slides me onto his chest before threading his fingers through my hair. I feel the length of his cock against my belly.

"Markov. . . you can't just do that for me and leave yourself, you know."

"I won't," he whispers. "But we're not ready to take it to the next level."

Aren't we, though? I trust him.

"There's no turning back if we go there, Vera," he whispers. "No turning back."

It sounds as if he might be speaking from personal experience.

"But I—I want to know. Please, Markov."

He cups the back of my head, his tone fierce when he says. "You want to give yourself to me? Are you a virgin, Vera?"

I swallow and nod. I was sheltered and alone, of course I am.

He makes a strangled sound, like a muffled, masculine groan. "That's a gift you should never give lightly, Vera. It's yours to give, and you can only give it once."

I nod, my decision made. "But I want it to be *you*."

Who else would give me his undeniable protection? Who else would cherish me? Who else would make sure I had everything I needed, from food in my belly to a fully-charged cell phone? Who knows what I've grown up with and what's left me wanting as a grown woman?

Who else has seen me, all of me, and accepted me as I fully am?

"Come, Vera," he whispers, the rumble of a voice in my ear making me shiver. I love the sound of his voice. I love it more when he calls me by name.

"You're drunk on sex," he says. "I can't take your virginity when you're drunk on sex."

At that, I've had it. I push myself up to my elbow and stare at him. "You're talking to a woman who made it into the most prestigious program in all of Russia. You're talking to a woman raised in the bratva, who's seen and heard terrible things and still, here I am." I look him straight in the eye. "You're not talking to a girl, Markov. You're talking to a woman who knows what she wants. . . and I want *you*."

Before I can process what's happening, I'm on my back beneath his weight, and it feels *so damn good*. I'm still all pliable and warm after he made me come, and even now, my body aches for more.

With one deft movement, my wrists are in his hands.

"I don't fuck casually," he warns.

"I know." Anything less would betray his character and integrity.

It's why I want him. Why *I need* him.

"This is your first time," he says, as if checking.

I nod and swallow. Confirming. He knows it is, but it's like he needs one final check to have my consent.

"This is my first time, and I want it to be with you."

"It will hurt, at least at first," he says gently.

I rest my hand on his cheek. "Markov. Are you. . . trembling?"

I'm shocked that the strongest, most fearless man I've ever met seems scared at what we're about to do.

He nods and licks his lips. Swallows. Tightens his grip on my wrists. "It's only because I've never wanted something so badly in my life," he says hoarsely.

I hold his gaze. "Take what's yours. I'd help you in, but you're holding my wrists."

His stern face breaks into a grin, an actual *grin*. In seconds, he's pushed down his boxers with his free hand and taken out his hard length. I swallow, my breath catching. I'm so eager to have him in me.

"Please," I whisper. I want him to know how badly I want him.

The warm head of his cock teases my slick entrance. I'm holding my breath, and he's holding my gaze. Slowly, firmly, never wavering while he looks at me, Markov enters me.

I'm so full and stretched, but he's so gentle it barely registers as pain. He's trembling from the effort of holding back.

His eyes roll back, and he curses out loud. "Fuck, you're so goddamn tight and hot. *Jesus,* Vera, your hot little cunt's like a goddamn masterpiece."

I wrap my legs around his waist, my heart surging in my chest. My need for him pounds in my veins. Finally, he thrusts.

I hold my breath, pleasure mixed with pain as he eases nearly all the way out before he comes back in, his cock filling me. Again, he thrusts, this time a tiny bit more forceful. Again, pleasure-pain consumes me, and my moans join his until he builds a rhythm that takes over all thought and replaces it with utter bliss.

Every thrust brings me closer to another surge of pleasure, and I hardly know what to expect.

The tightness around my wrists intensifies as he thrusts again, this time harder than before. I whimper.

"Did I hurt you?" he asks, his forehead crinkled in concern.

"No, God, no, don't stop," I beg. "Please. . . please, Daddy, take me."

"You're perfect," he whispers in my ear. "Perfect, Vera. Thank you. I'll never forget what you gave me."

Thrust after thrust, he builds a steady rhythm of perfect bliss, carrying me and sending me higher and higher. I wanted to be as close to him as humanly possible, and this, this right here, is the only way.

He curses in my ear as he spills inside me, and my own climax, this one sweeter and fuller and somehow more perfect, overtakes me at the same time. We ride the high of ecstasy until he falls beside me and utters something in Russian.

And while I run my hand silently down the length of his muscled, inked back slicked with dampness, I realize. . . it's the first time in my life I feel like a *woman*.

"Markov," I say quietly. Thoughtfully.

"Mmmm?" he asks, his head buried on my chest. It makes him almost look boyish.

"What just happened?"

CHAPTER FIFTEEN

Vera

"YOU GAVE me the greatest gift a woman can give."

"My virginity?"

"Your trust. Your openness. Your vulnerability. And yeah, baby. Your virginity."

He kisses my cheek.

I giggle at the memory of what I just did. "I called you *Daddy*." I smack his shoulder. "You made me."

"I did," he says with a satisfied chuckle. "And you *liked* it. I knew you would."

Of course I did. It was all kinds of taboo and hot.

"I never called my own father *Daddy*. I barely called him anything. Why did that not feel wrong?"

He grins. "Because you're kinky as fuck, sweetheart. And

you like what I give to you—protection. Nurturing. A safe place."

Mmm. Yes. All of that.

"My mind is trained to find the *why* behind things and I—I need to stop that sometimes."

He smiles. "You do. Sometimes, we don't need to know the reasons behind why we do what we do. Why we love what we love. Why we love *who* we love."

Love.

He went there. He totally fucking went there, but we're still obviously talking on hypothetical terms. Still. . .

We're lying in bed. It's inky dark outside, and the window is cracked just enough to let us hear the tell-tale sign of late-night crickets. It's a marvel to me that in a place where humans can't understand differences in language, the late night sounds of crickets are a universal language.

"That's amazing," I whisper. I feel split wide open. Exposed but in the best possible way. Bared. And the effect is making me quite contemplative.

"What is?"

"I don't understand a word of Russian, and there are people here who don't speak English. But the language of the crickets has no barriers. They all speak the same. What if humans never had such limitations?"

"We'd kill each other," he quips. "Sometimes a language barrier is the only thing keeping people from fighting."

"True," I say with a smirk. "When I was little, my sister and I invented this language to speak to each other. It was fun."

"Cute. My brothers and I did something similar. We had hand signals, and we thought we were something else."

He buries his face in my hair and inhales.

"You like that?"

"I do. You smell so damn good. I feel like I'm in the middle of a field in spring, surrounded by violets."

"I guess that expensive shit's worth it, then."

He inhales again, deeper. "Indeed. When my brothers and I did our hand signals, my father thought we were mocking him, so he put a swift end to that."

"Dammit. Those strict Russian fathers. How many brothers do you have?"

He doesn't answer at first. It's a simple enough question. Why the hesitation?

"I have five brothers and one sister," he says. "And you?"

"Wow. One older sister. So that's a lot of brothers."

"Mmm hmm," he says. "But I don't want to talk about my brothers in bed." He leans over and nips my ear lobe. I squeal.

"I'm not that tired, though. I like these late-night convos." I stick my toes out from under the blanket because I'm over-heating. He helps me by tugging the rest of the blanket off when my toe gets stuck.

"I didn't say we had to go to sleep. We can keep talking."

I love the feel of his warm, strong body beneath mine. I lift my leg and crook my knee so I'm sort of straddling him. It's as cozy in this small, utilitarian room as it would be in a much larger room with a crackling fire and the soft glow of lights.

"Tell me about you and your siblings. I want to hear." I cozy up to him. Having a large, bustling family and getting into mischief with siblings is one of my fantasies.

"I didn't have much of a relationship with mine. My sister was sent away to some kind of Russian boarding school."

"Why were you the only one at home?"

"My mother put her foot down. I was the baby, the youngest. She begged my father to let me stay home with her, and by then, he had a mistress and only wanted to keep my mother pacified."

"Ahh."

I lean toward him and intertwine my fingers with his. "I've wondered what it was like coming from a large family. Did you know your aunt growing up?"

He shakes his head. "No. Her getting me a job with your father was a way of getting in my family's good graces again."

"Interesting. Making up for lost time?"

"Exactly. I spent much more time with my siblings than anyone else. My father was often away for work, and my mother was a bit overwhelmed with so many of us at home. My older brother and I took charge frequently."

"No wonder you're so bossy," I tease.

He only lifts a shoulder. "It comes naturally, perhaps. My father had a saying. 'The older brother is the father's right hand.' The older ones are often expected to take on many of the responsibilities and leadership roles within the family."

"Can you tell me what that was like?"

Markov's eyes soften, a hint of nostalgia flickering across his features. He shifts slightly, turning more towards me, his voice deep and thoughtful. "It wasn't easy, Vera. I had to be both a brother and sometimes a father figure. It meant a lot of responsibility, and discipline was a big part of it. My father had rigid expectations."

I love hearing this human side of him. I love how he talks with such love for his family. I want to meet them.

"Could you share a story from those days? Something that really sticks out to you."

He chuckles, the sound low and resonant, then pauses, searching his memories. "Alright, there was this one time," he begins, his gaze drifting off as he recounts the tale. "My younger sister had this wild spirit, always getting into trouble. One day, she decided to climb the largest tree in our yard, the one my mother forbade her to touch. I caught her just as she was about to reach the first huge branch that hung over the ground with nothing beneath it."

I gasped. I could just imagine a mischievous little girl defying her mother and hoping to prove to herself she could do it.

His hands gesture vividly as he speaks, painting the picture for me. "What did you do?"

"I could have scolded her and made her come down and face a punishment. But we had enough of that with my family. Instead, I climbed up there with her and positioned myself between her and the ground in case she fell. She didn't, though. My mother called her her little monkey. I asked her why she disobeyed Mom and why she had to do something that thrilled her."

I hang on his every word. I love hearing him share these stories with me. "What did she say?" I ask, my voice a whisper. I can almost see him with that same straight-laced look about him, though maybe a boyish softness still clinging to him.

He smiles. "We made a deal. She promised to come to me if she felt the urge for an adventure, and I'd find a safe way to do it together. It was a moment of understanding, of connecting with her not just as her older brother in charge, but someone who cared about her."

I have a realization. Markov would make a good father.

I reach out and gently brush his arm. "That's. . . really beautiful, Markov. You showed her love and guidance, not just discipline. It's no wonder you're so dedicated now. You're definitely a natural-born leader—bossy but in the best possible way." I kiss the underside of his jaw, rough with a hint of stubble.

"I'll take that as a compliment."

"It makes sense to me that you'd be attracted to a certain. . . flavor in the bedroom."

"Yes. I like to be in control."

"Mmm."

"And you, Vera. Tell me. If you could have one thing in your future, what would it be? You've lived a sheltered life. Do you want to explore? See the world? What is it you want?"

I sigh. As a romance lover, I've thought about this. I've lived so many lives, caught in the pages of my books, that I've spent more time than I care to admit thinking about what my perfect future would look like.

"No. . ." I say slowly. Will it sound silly? "I really want. . . a place I call my own. Four children and two dogs, a home close enough to a city so that we don't have to drive forever to go shopping, but it's far enough away that you can hear the crickets at night and see the stars overhead. One of those comforting places, you know? With a porch and maybe a swing and. . . I want to be able to see the sunset from my porch." I flush a little. "That probably sounds so cliché and boring, doesn't it?"

"*Nyet,*" he says firmly. "It sounds idyllic."

My heart squeezes.

"Now, I want to know more." He gives me that look that makes me feel like I'm the only person on the face of the earth. Markov's superpower is his ability to focus with unwavering attention.

"Mmm? Go on. More questions."

"Why do you crave submitting?" he asks quietly, his gaze respectful as always but probing. I love that when Markov is with me, I am the utter focus of his attention. I love that he listens, truly actually *hears* me, not just what I say but what I don't. He's intense, and sometimes I feel like being near him is like staring at the sun. I have to look away because the brightness might blind me. But it's also his intensity that I love about him. His attention makes me feel valued.

I pause before I answer. Why *do* I crave submitting? It's so much more than the fact that it turns me on, which it definitely does. It's deeper than that, though.

"I don't actually crave submitting in general. I like to read about it, yes, because it's hot. It's a fantasy. But I'm...not really sure where fantasy and reality meet."

He brushes my hair off my forehead and bends down to kiss it. My eyes flutter closed at the warmth that trickles over me. I swallow and continue. "You're here to protect me. I'm learning to trust you."

This time, his responding kiss is to the top of my cheek. I smile shyly.

"With you, I. . . it's not just hot. It doesn't just turn me on. There's so much more to it than that. It's. . . liberating." My tone grows thoughtful as I think it over. "I've poured myself into my studies. I've worked so hard for so long. It's a relief to trust someone else completely for once." I shrug. "Not to mention it's erotic as hell."

"Mmm," he says. "Agreed. So it's about finding strength in vulnerability."

"Yes, that's it. I feel like if I can trust you. . . really, truly trust you and allow myself to give myself over to you. . . you can take me to places I have only dreamed of before."

"There's a lot to be learned from some power play, isn't there?"

My next question begs to be asked, even though I cringe at the thought of hearing his answer. "Have you. . . has there ever been another woman you've been with like. . . this, Markov?"

His immediate response makes my mouth dry. "No one, Vera. There has never been another woman like you, and there will never be another one after you. *Never.*"

Oh, God. Hello, intensity.

"If you think—"

The blare of an alarm on his phone makes both of us freeze. Markov jumps out of bed first, grabs a pair of sweats, and tosses me mine. "Get dressed."

I watch as he glides a gun to the small of his back with ease. It's a stark and brutal reminder for me to not get too comfortable. I can't ever forget who he truly is.

As we hurriedly dress, he receives a text on his phone. "Motherfucker," he grunts, his eyes growing dangerously black.

My heart thumps. "What?"

He stares at his phone for a moment and quickly types something out. "I was alerted by outside security. They can send remote drones, but it might be too late."

"Then. . . what other option is there?"

Still calm, he scowls at the ceiling and the heating vents, his eyes scanning the entirety of the room as if he has x-ray vision.

I can hardly breathe as the tension in the room thickens. I know that look on Markov's face by now. His jaw set, his flinty gaze going from one corner of the room to the next. I feel the urge to look away so I don't see the cold, calculating side of him that unnerves me.

"You crawl to safety. Underground. Are you afraid of confined areas?"

I shake my head. Heights, yes, but confined areas, I'm cool with. "I scoured the place when we first got here and found a maintenance tunnel underneath the building."

"A *maintenance* tunnel? What?"

He nods, quickly grabbing a few things from the bedside table. "Move, Vera." He pauses long enough to reach one rough hand to my jaw. "Are you alright?"

I nod. "Of course I am," I lie. My heart threatens to leap out of my chest, and I feel like I'm going to be sick.

"The tunnel is linked to the old utilities systems. It won't be comfortable, but we'll be safe down there."

I breathe a sigh of relief, and he gives me a curious look.

"I was afraid you'd make me go ahead of you and, like, scout things out or whatever. And I don't want to go without you."

He shakes his head. "No way am I sending you ahead without me. We go together, or we stay here together. There's no other choice."

I stare at him for long moments before I reach my hands to the back of his head and pull him fiercely toward me. I kiss him, a silent vow that we're in this together.

"Let's go."

He takes my hand, and we hurry toward the back of the room just before an explosion sounds in the tunnel.

CHAPTER SIXTEEN

Nikko

IT TAKES a minute after an explosion for everything to settle. I reach my hand out to Vera and feel her warm, reassuring presence beside me. I run my hand along her arm until I feel for her hand, but I pause long enough to check her reassuring pulse beneath my fingers.

"Are you alright?" she asks. She's asking *me* if I'm alright? No one ever asks me if I'm alright.

"I'm fine." My words sound hoarse in the darkness. "You?"

"Good, yeah. I mean, it's cramped in here, but I'm alright." It's dark and confined but built large enough for a maintenance crew, so we'll be fine. "Do you know where this leads to?"

"Yeah, the end of this tunnel reaches the community room in the main building. Only a handful of rooms are accessible through the tunnel, but anyone who came into that room could get in here." I check my gun. "The longer we wait in here, the greater the chance that whoever did that will find us. Stay here. I'll be right back."

I push ahead of her when she grabs my arm. "No! I'm going with you."

"You absolutely are not," I snap. "You stay here where it's—"

"Safe?" she scoffs. "Yeah, right. What if someone found a way in? What if that someone hurts *you*? You might be the one who knows how to shoot a gun, but I'm the one who knows how to stop you from bleeding out if you get shot."

"I can handle myself," I say through gritted teeth, but she has a point.

"Markov," she fumes.

I don't have time to fight her, goddamn it. I blow out a frustrated breath, pull her to me, and grab a fistful of her hair. "This isn't over. We'll have a talk later about the importance of doing what I fucking say in an emergency."

I hear her swallow before I feel her hand on my chest. I can barely make out the whites of her eyes in the darkness. "Fine, we'll do that. And then we can talk about the importance of educated decisions under duress."

Goddamn, this woman.

"Now, are we going to stand around here and argue, or are we going to see what the hell just happened?"

I curse under my breath, take her hand, and push ahead, muttering to myself at the meager light from my flashlight. The end of the tunnel lightens as we get closer to the entry by the community room.

"When did you have time to find this?"

"That first afternoon we got here and you were sleeping."

"You really jumped straight in with both feet, didn't you?"

I did, goddamn it, and I'm not so sure if that was smart in retrospect. The thought of her getting hurt—the thought of not being able to protect her. . . *Fuck.*

At the end of the tunnel, I push her behind me. "You stay the fuck right there, and do *not* push me right now, woman."

"Fine, fine," she says. "But if someone hurts you—"

"You'll let me handle it."

When she doesn't respond, I suspect she's made up her mind but isn't going to argue with me right now. With another low growl, I turn around and hold her by both arms as if to forcibly remind her to stay *put*.

I draw my gun and head into the community room.

It's empty. I move ahead cautiously, checking every corner, but there's no place for anyone to hide under the bright overhead lights. It's a standard office-type room you'd find anywhere with collapsible tables, a coffee maker, and a threadbare couch.

I move quickly. When under attack, the worst thing to do is hide and wait for your attackers to find you. I open the door.

"Markov!"

Irina stands outside with Morozov. I quickly tuck my gun away, but if either of them saw it, they don't give any indication.

"What's going on?"

Irina heads to me, dressed in loungewear, while Morozov is wearing a robe.

"It appears there was an explosion in a nearby lab," Morozov says, peering at his phone. "We've called in an emergency, and we're waiting for them to arrive now. Never fear; all is fine, though. We just need to be sure no contaminants were leaked and that whatever caused the explosion won't detonate again."

I don't buy it. I heard it *here,* not in a lab. Or were there explosions in both places as a cover?

"I definitely heard one outside of the lab."

"Mmm, did you?" Irina asks. "We will have to investigate."

Jake and the silent blond man join us.

"Ah. Quick thinking," Irina says. "Thankfully it looks like no one was injured."

"Yes," I say, still disbelieving. "I'll be right back."

I head back inside and get Vera, who's standing at the entrance to the community room, her arms crossed over her chest, glaring at me.

"They say there was an explosion in the lab."

She shakes her head. "That's bullshit. We were there. It was way too close to our room to be explained as an explosion in the lab."

"Right." Something's definitely amiss.

"Am I allowed to come in now?" she asks petulantly, rolling her eyes at me.

We're alone in here but may not be for long. I reach her in three long strides and hold her chin in my hand. Her fiery gaze meets mine, and she doesn't back down.

"Behave yourself, little girl."

"Markov," she says, even as her eyes widen. "This is not the time or place —"

I lean in and put my mouth to her ear. "To make sure you stay safe? The fuck it isn't."

"Well, no, I mean to start like. . . flirting with me," she says in a whisper.

I pinch her chin and speak more harshly. "I am *not* flirting."

The door behind us opens, and we pull away.

I hate this. I hate that I'm concerned for her safety, but my hands are tied. I hate that the two of us have to hide who we are and what we want. I hate that I've had to lie to her. I hate that there can't and never will be anything between us but what we have here because of who we are.

Morozov and Irina enter, and the American starts running his mouth off.

"The security system and alarm system are so outdated—"

"It was nearby," Vera says. "I heard it."

He gives her a withering look and rolls his eyes before he catches me staring at him. He doesn't even bother to hide his horror as his cheeks flush bright red, and he mutters something about needing rest and seeing them all in the morning.

I don't trust this scrawny asshole.

As he exits, so do I. "Be right back."

"Markov—" I shut the door before Vera can protest.

"Hey."

Jake stops short, a look of terror in his eyes. "I didn't say anything to her. You can't give me shit about anything. I didn't say a word." He draws himself to his full height, still a full head shorter than I am. "And anyway, you can't touch me."

Oh, really?

I take a step toward him. "Can't I? I told you to leave her alone. I told you to make sure you—"

"Didn't blab about who you two really are to everyone else? Right."

Though he still looks scared, a smug look fills his face when I clamp my lips together. What does this stupid asshole know?

"I heard you talking," he says, his trembling voice betraying his nerves. "And where are your rings? You aren't married. No one believes you are."

I take another step closer to him. "We aren't? So you know the truth, then?"

He wilts and doesn't reply. He doesn't know shit.

"What's the truth, Jake? Go ahead. What is it you want to share with everyone?"

"You're not her husband," he says, but less sure this time.

I take another step toward him so the toes of our shoes are touching. "Listen to me. Who we are or who we aren't doesn't impact you at all, does it? You earned your place here and so did she." I lean closer to him. "Morozov joked about a bodyguard, didn't he? Let's just say he wasn't far from the truth."

Jake's eyes widen.

"I'm here because that woman is worth more than you can imagine. Her life is of great value and her family of great importance." I tip my head to the side. "You do know what the purpose of a bodyguard is, don't you?"

"Of course," he flusters, and I can tell by the look in his eyes he's dying to know who she is.

"So that means that I *do*, indeed, take her safety very, very seriously. But more than that, *Jake*." I reach over, and he flinches away. I flick a speck of dust off his shirt. "I also take her well-being very seriously. Are we clear? I want her happy, *Jake*. Very happy. So don't rock that boat again."

It seems he can't really hold back who he is for long. The flash in his eyes tells me he's not only jealous.

"Who is she?"

I grab him by the shirt as the door behind us opens.

"Markov." Vera stands behind us. "Put him down," she says in a low voice, the way someone might gently coax an angry dog to release its prey. "He didn't hurt me. He didn't hurt anyone."

"*Yet,*" I growl, but I still toss the guy down. He stumbles and falls to one knee but jumps back on his feet, eyes darting between us. "I'm just trying to protect the integrity of our program."

"We all have secrets, *Markov,*" he says, my name a mockery on his lips as if he knows it isn't my real name. "I've got evidence, and if you don't stop interfering, I'll use it against you." He waves it in the air and shakes his head. "About you and that self-important bitch who bought her way—"

My fist connects with his jaw, and before he can react, I lift him and slam him against the wall. I pound the wall beside him, bloodying my knuckles in an effort to keep myself from killing him. "Don't you fucking name call. And you do not fucking threaten her." My voice is a low growl.

Vera's voice cries out as she grabs my arm. "Markov! Stop! Enough!" I blink as if coming out of a haze and realize the American is bloodied and his shirt is torn. The bastard got lucky. He's trying to catch his breath when I let him go abruptly.

The door opens, and Irina steps out. "Gentlemen. What's going on here?"

To my surprise, Jake shakes his head and swipes at his cheek. "I tripped," he says. "Markov picked me up."

He turns, and Irina must not see the blood on his cheek. "I'm going back to bed before tomorrow's lab."

I watch him storm off, Vera breathing rapidly next to me, but Irina only smiles. "I wouldn't have blamed you if you'd decided it was time to teach him some respect, Markov. Honestly, he's so full of himself and incredibly rude to the others." She shakes her head and winks. "Not that I condone violence, but. . ." Her voice trails off as Morozov joins us.

"Now, let's all get some rest before a big day tomorrow, shall we?"

They turn to leave, and I stare after them, stunned at Irina's reaction. It isn't what I expected. Does she know more than she's letting on? Was her observation and recommendation another attempt to flirt with me?

"Markov," Vera says in a voice just above a whisper as we head back to our room, side by side. "Did she basically. . . tell you it was okay to beat up Jake?"

I frown. "Sounds like she's had enough of his antics."

"It's unprofessional."

"As is his behavior toward you and the others in the program."

"You can do no wrong in her eyes."

"She honestly has flirted with me a few times."

Vera stands still. When I look down at her, her eyes are wide in shock. "Um, *what*? Did you say she's flirted with you?"

I nod. "Nothing exceptionally untoward. And I don't know if you've noticed her sidling up to me when you're all working on your labs. She hasn't crossed a line, but I feel almost like the teacher's pet. . . and I'm not even a pet."

Vera snorts. "You're definitely not that. Listen, you know how I feel about you interfering with things. I asked you not to hurt Jake. I asked you not to let anyone else know who you are," she says in a whisper of a voice. "You can't just beat up any loser who looks the wrong way at me, Markov. You *can't*."

I shrug. "I warned him fairly. I gave him plenty of chances. He crossed a line."

She groans and shakes her head. "What does he know?"

"Nothing. He's got nothing. You know you didn't buy your way into this program. Your father didn't interfere. And if he knows you're part of the Ivanov family, let him tell them. You stand on your own credentials, Vera."

There's a brief pause before she reaches her hand to me. "Markov. . ."

"Mmm?"

"Why do you have a different phone?"

CHAPTER SEVENTEEN

Vera

MARKOV LOOKS down at his phone, though he has that look again—the one he got right before he decked Jake. I'm not afraid he's going to lash out at me; I'd like to think I know him too well for that by now. But something. . . something's made him angry.

"I had this phone when I arrived. I have two. You can see them if you'd like. One is older, but the contacts didn't sync correctly, so I carry both."

I'm not quite sure I believe him, but what reason would he have to lie?

"Oh."

Tonight has shown me again the reality of who we are. The truth crashes into my thoughts like thunder.

It isn't right. It isn't fair. But it never was.

I've given myself to a man who can never be who I need him to be. I have fallen in love with a man who'll always abide by his own code of ethics, everything and everyone else be damned.

I need to sleep. We both need to.

I'm bone-weary when we get back and don't give Markov a hard time when he sweeps the room. Checks the door. Checks his phone and sends a text. Checks his weapon and makes sure it's loaded before placing it on the dresser.

"Come to bed, Markov," I say gently. My eyes feel scratchy when I blink, but when he joins me, I draw in a gasp.

"Your hands," I whisper. "They're a mess."

He scowls down at his bruised and bloodied knuckles and shrugs. "It's fine."

"We can at least wash them," I say, pushing out of bed and getting a washcloth from the bathroom. I wet it with warm, soapy water and rejoin him. "I don't have much in the line of first aid with me. . ."

"I don't need it. I'm only humoring you."

I give him a serious look. "Protection is your job, and I've humored you. But this is *mine*. Medical, remember? First aid? This is my jam. Don't take this away from me."

He grunts and reluctantly nods. "Go on."

I kneel in front of him so I can get a better look. I take his large, calloused palm in both of my hands and peer at the damage. He could use antiseptic but we're lacking a fully stocked first aid kit. Instead, I clean the blood and sweat from both hands and find that the wounds are only superficial.

"Told you I was fine," he grunts.

I nod, placing his hands down and going to put both of mine on his knees to push up to standing, but something stops me.

I'm. . . kneeling before him. This feels intimate.

Submissive.

The utterly possessive look in his eyes tells me he feels it, too.

"You have an important day tomorrow, Vera," he says in a way that's very. . . *Daddy.*

I nod.

"You're on the verge of a breakthrough, aren't you?"

My chest swells. He knows. He's been following along while I chatter on and on about the challenges we've faced. "Yeah," I say softly. We've been studying specifically how certain plants indigenous to remote areas are unaffected by a biological threat with widespread pathogens. If we learn how to harness this knowledge, it could change so much. . .

"I believe in you. I know you can do this." His eyes heat, and the tone of his voice tells me he feels what I do, too. "I like this vantage point. What about you, Vera? Do you?"

I do. I so do. Slowly, I nod because I don't trust my voice, and I'm confused about why this feels so nice. I'm a strong, independent woman who gets shit done. I got here of my own volition and on my own merit. Why do I melt into a puddle when I'm *kneeling* in front of him?

Slowly, he cups my face with his large hand. I swallow when he drags the pad of his thumb along my lower lip.

"I'll have to remember this. Now, you need some rest so you're ready for tomorrow."

I want to pout, but I feel my body aching for rest.

"Tomorrow, we'll discuss that little fit you had in the community room."

I open my mouth to protest as my heartbeat thunders in my ears. "Markov—"

One sharp shake of his head tells me this isn't the time we'll discuss anything. "Now you need sleep. We both do. You have to work tomorrow. And when your work is over. . . we'll have a talk."

I can't help but wonder if that talk will involve me over his knee. Why does a small part of me hope that it does while the rest of me balks? This is way more complicated than I anticipated.

It isn't complicated sliding into bed, though. I close my eyes and feel the softness of the mattress and the warmth of Markov beside me."Rest, Vera."

I close my eyes, resting easy in the knowledge that he absolutely has this under control.

THE NEXT DAY, Jake doesn't show up to the clinical. He's *not* missed, though, and even Irina isn't bothered by it. She doesn't say much, likely because she aims to be professional, but at the end of the day, she says, "It was nice to see the rest of you have more of a chance to. . . participate."

Sophia and I worked hard side by side cataloguing specimens while Maxim and Liam studied test tubes. It wasn't until we were a full twelve hours into it and Professor Morozov ordered us dinner that I finally, *finally* made the breakthrough. Markov was just outside the door, taking a call.

"Markov. Oh my God. Markov," I say, my voice wobbly. My eyes are somehow a bit misty, and I'm so overcome with emotion at what we've finally done. "You won't believe it." I sniff hard. He shoves his phone in his pocket and takes both of my hands in his, all ears.

"Yes? What is it, love?"

He plays the part of a doting husband so damn well. *Too* well.

I swallow and lick my lips. "I figured it out. I finally found a way. It's absolutely groundbreaking." I'm trembling with the enormity of what I discovered. "You know how if you plant marigold flowers around a flower bed, it serves as a natural barrier to pests and insects and even woodland creatures like deer?"

He shrugs and shakes his head. "I did not, but go on."

I can't help but giggle a little. He really is outside his sphere of knowledge and is totally comfortable with owning it. And

I love that. I *love* that he isn't threatened or intimidated by me.

"We can develop crops with a similar approach. Natural deterrents to biological threats or air-borne illnesses. It's basically like building a *bubble* around certain areas that would be otherwise compromised and endangered. This is. . . this is *huge.*" I swallow against the rising lump in my throat. "I mean, we knew this, but what we developed in the lab today has the potential of increasing our speed of application by like *tenfold.* We're only in the beginning stages, but. . . but *we did it.*"

I squeal when he lifts me straight off the ground and tosses me in the air before he catches me and spins around right there in the open. Some onlookers chuckle.

"Amazing, Vera. I'm so damn proud of you. I knew you could do it. I *knew* you could."

I nod, still a bit tearful. "I know," I say, swiping at my eyes. "I know you did, which is why I'm an emotional basket case right now."

No one has ever believed in me the way he does. Even my mother, who adores me to pieces and is always my biggest cheerleader, often lets her own fears get in the way. "Now, don't get ahead of yourself," she'd say, or "Let's take one thing at a time." But I pushed past the cautionary words and fears. They seem far away now, unable to hold me back.

He pulls me into a big hug, so warm and reassuring I want to stay here forever. I breathe in his familiar masculine scent and let myself sink into the strength of his embrace. "And I'd bet it's no coincidence that you didn't have to wade through the arrogance of a certain American to get there, mmm?"

I giggle against his chest.

"Um, can you put me down now so I can save face?"

"Of course," he says, immediately complying while he whispers in my ear. "I'll give you that out here. But when we're alone, little girl. . . *you're Daddy's.*"

Gah. Is swallowing your own tongue a thing? Because I'm choking on literally nothing.

"Are you needed back at the lab?"

"Not today," I tell him. "Morozov dismissed us."

"Excellent. Why don't we go back and you can call your mother and tell her the news?"

"Yeah," I say softly. "I'd like that."

Could the man be any more perfect? Of *course* he knew the next person I had to tell was Mom.

Perfection. Science tells us it doesn't exist, that it's only a figment of our imagination and yet my romance-lover's heart dares to hope.

Back in the room, I let Markov check everything to make sure we're safe and half-expect he'll find something. "Coast is clear."

I hear footsteps behind me and look over my shoulder to see Jake scurrying past us. His hands are shoved in his pockets, and his head is down; he doesn't even look my way.

I wonder if Jake will pose a problem anymore. I suspect not.

"Did you find out anything about the picture of the front of the room?" I ask Markov.

He shakes his head. "No. We haven't been able to identify a source."

"Ah."

I close the door behind me and remember what he told me last night. I remember his promise.

I swallow hard.

When your work is over. . . we'll have a talk.

My work is over. . . what will that talk entail, and why does my heart threaten to leap out of my chest?

"Here," Markov says, handing me my phone. "Before you and I pick up where we left off, call your mother."

Gah. Whyyyyy did he do that to me?

"Markov," I choke out.

"What?"

"Why did you say that before I called my mother?"

A corner of his lips quirks up, and he shrugs. "Because I know exactly how you'll respond, and I want you to remember who you belong to."

"Even when I'm on the phone with my *mother?*"

"Especially when you're on the phone with your mother. Your mother will praise you and tell you what an accomplished woman you are. And while that praise is well deserved, you were the one who told me you like the idea of putting things down for a while. That you don't *always* want to be the strong, powerful, in-charge woman."

I swallow. "Right." I dial my mother. It'll be lunchtime back home. Nostalgia hits me in the chest with a wave of homesickness.

She answers on the first ring.

"Vera?"

"Mom! How are you?"

"Oh, it is *so* good to hear your voice. I know you're busy, but I miss you so much. Thankfully, Markov's been keeping me updated, so I don't have to bug you too much." She laughs.

I stare at Markov. "Markov's been keeping you updated?"

What?

"Oh, yes. He texts me every day just to tell me how things are going. He said you were on the verge of a breakthrough. Something to do with. . . I could only follow so much. . . using crops or something to prevent. . . something."

I smile and shake my head at him. "Yes, exactly, and Mom, it's big news." My voice gets a little husky again because this is so monumental for me. "*We did it.* We figured it out."

Her whoop is so loud in my ear I have to hold the phone at a distance until she settles down. Markov and I grin at each other.

"Oh, Vera, *I knew* you could do it. *Knew* it! Markov did, too. He said he had total faith that you would persist until you figured it out."

I swallow. "He. . . did? Oh."

For the first time in my life. . . I have a little circle of support. I'm not even sure how to handle the surge of emotion.

"Tell me everything," Mom says. I'm grateful for the chance to pull myself into facts and out of the emotions that threaten to choke me.

I tell her everything, and while she probably only understands about twenty percent of what I say, as usual, she's attentive and curious.

"Oh, Vera," she says. "Your grandma and I are so, so proud of you. You're going places, sweetheart. You watch and see."

Heh. I try not to think about the fact that the next place I'm going is probably right over Markov's lap.

Double gah.

"Now, I want you to tell me about *other* things."

I look up at Markov, who's sitting on the edge of the bed, his strong, sturdy hands braced on his thighs. "Mmm?"

"You and Markov. How is our Jason Bourne?"

I look Markov straight in the eye while I respond. "He's bossy as hell. Kind of old-fashioned, too. Thinks he knows everything. And he won't even let me walk in our room—I mean my room—without checking to see if it's safe first."

My cheeks heat. I'm thankful my mom is thousands of miles away and can't see how beet-red I am. If she caught that little blunder, she doesn't let on.

"Of course he is. Men like him would be, you know. They always would be."

I wish Markov wasn't here right now. I'd want to talk to her. . . honestly. Woman to woman. About everything.

Mom, why am I capable and independent but crave his dominance?

How can I justify being a woman in modern-day and still allow him to tell me what to do?

How do I make peace with what my body wants and what my mind knows is right?

And most of all. . .

How can I love a man who's forbidden for me?

But I don't. I don't ask her any of these things and just assure her that I'm fine.

I assure her Markov is.

I tell her I love her and that I can't wait to come home.

"Stay close to him, sweetheart. Your father has made many mistakes in his life, you know I believe that, but appointing Markov as your bodyguard was one of his better decisions. And on that note, Vera. . . you and I need to talk."

Why do those words never fail to incite fear in me?

"What is it? Is everything okay?"

"Yes, yes, don't worry. It's just that your father called. He said that there's a benefit in Moscow this weekend, and he wants you to attend. Now, I know how you feel about him—"

"No, Mom. We had dinner with him recently, and it was a

disaster. Ugh. I hated being around him. He is so full of himself! Besides, I don't have time to go to a benefit."

I feel guilty hearing her sigh on the other end of the phone.

"I know, Vera. I know, I really do."

"Then why make me go?" I feel like an angsty teen. "It's too much. Why does he insist I go to these things?"

"Because he's trying to mend bridges. He thinks if you see him with his peers, you'll think more highly of him. Because you're his *daughter*, Vera."

I hate that my father puts my mother in this position. She must hate him more than I do, but she knows she's stuck being married to a powerful man of the Bratva. She knows he keeps mistresses and has long since broken their vows to one another. He's done all of this and still makes her do his bidding because he can, the power-hungry asshole. Without him, she'd be penniless and homeless and blacklisted from everyone she knows. It's shitty, and it isn't fair.

"It isn't just all that, Mom. It's also because he wants to parade me around and make himself look better. He has no interest in who I am as his daughter. None! My perspective won't change just because he's playing the part of philanthropist for a night."

Markov shifts on the bed. When I look over, he taps his wrist as if to remind me to wrap this up. My pulse races.

"Having Markov with you might make things a bit more bearable, no?"

That's. . . debatable.

Finally, I agree with a sigh. I can't make life harder for my mother because I protest on principle. I have hoops to jump through, and this is one of them. "Yes. I can go. I'll do it, Mom."

"Thank you, sweetheart. I know this isn't easy for you."

We talk for a little while longer, and I have to admit, I keep the conversation going a little because I'm a little. . . nervous. . . about what happens next.

I finally hang up the phone and turn to face him.

"What did she ask you to do? You weren't happy about something. What's going on?"

I sigh and shake my head. "There's some *benefit* thing my father wants me to go to, and he wants me to go with *you*. I don't want to go. I mean. . . your aunt is the one who's with him in Moscow, right? *Ugh.*" I can't even think about the fact that Markov has a connection to one of the many women my father cheats on my mother with.

"Ahh. And when's that?" He's once more wearing his poker face, but he doesn't exactly look thrilled at the idea of what we have to do.

"I know, you hate socializing. You'd rather stay here, where things are, at least for now, predictable and safe."

"Mmm. Yes. And why didn't your father tell you he wishes you to attend this. . . what did you call it? Benefit?"

"Ugh, because this is what he *does*." I stifle the need to whine. "If he suspects I'm not going to want to do something that he *wants* me to do, he gets my mom to ask me instead because I can't say no to her."

"I see. When is it?"

"This weekend. And Markov, if he thinks he can parade his mistress around in front of me. . . I don't care if she's your aunt or not. That's just not right."

"Indeed," he says with a sober nod. "In any event, we will deal with the details of the upcoming benefit. But in the meantime, we'll deal with the issue at hand."

I turn away and bite my lip. "About that."

"Mmm," he says soberly, reaching for me so his hands grip my hips. "I told you we'd talk about things, didn't I?"

"Yes, but. . ."

"No buts. Come here, Vera. We'll have this conversation now. With you over my lap."

"Markov!" I protest as he tugs me over his knee. He doesn't do anything, only rests his large hand on my ass.

"Now," he continues. "Let's talk."

The blood rushes to my face even as my body heats. I'm instantly aroused. It feels as if all the blood in my entire body has rushed between my thighs.

"You disobeyed Daddy, didn't you, Vera?"

Why does it feel so wrong yet so. . . why do I love hearing him *say* that?

"Um. I maybe did."

I gasp when he brings his palm across my ass. A flare of arousal stokes my pulse. I stifle a whimper.

"There's no maybe about it, is there?"

"Welll. . . I had good reason," I begin, and he brings his palm across my ass a second time.

"Let's hear that reason," he says. "Though I can guarantee that you will *always* answer for disobeying me."

"I—I—" It feels as if my brain's short-circuiting.

Do I want this?

Yes, I do.

But. . . Daddy?

Gah, hawwwwt.

I can hardly even think straight.

I'm a grown woman!

A grown woman who loves being called little girl. . . by him.

But he's going to spank me, and he's talking about all sorts of things like. . . obedience.

Hawwt.

Gah!

"I was scared for you. I didn't want you hurt. And I—" Okay, here comes the brutal honesty. "I don't know what I think about you telling me what to do."

I brace myself for another hard spank and hiss in a breath when he cups my ass in his hand instead. "Good answers, Vera. Those were very honest." I feel the warmth of his chest at my back when he brings his mouth to my ear. "Daddy likes it when you tell him the truth."

Oh. Dear. *God.*

Why is that so fucking *hot?*

I could get into this. . . With just a little more persuasion, I could. . . totally get into this.

"Good little girls who do as they're told get rewarded," he says warmly, the tone of his voice melting me into a big old pile.

Oh, do they?

What might. . . that look like?

With deft fingers, he unfastens my skirt and tugs it down over my heated ass. *Oooh.*

I'm hardly breathing as he parts my legs and sinks one blunt finger between my folds.

"Oh God," I whimper. I'm so swollen, so wet, so intensely turned on I feel like I'm on the edge of coming already. "That's so—my God—how did you know?"

"Know that a spanking from Daddy turned you on?"

Not just that, I want to tell him. My God, it's *everything.* The spanking, being over his lap, the whole *Daddy* thing.

"I didn't know. I theorized. See, I'm a scientist, too, baby, just like you. I had a hypothesis, and I tested it. And it looks like I've made my own breakthrough."

He circles my clit with his warm, rough fingers and my hips jerk of their own accord.

"You're a naughty little girl who likes this. You come alive when Daddy disciplines you. You crave more of this, more of me. This is probably what you fantasize about when you touch yourself, isn't it? Tell me the truth, Vera."

I nod. I have been fantasizing about the dirty things Markov could do to me the second I met him because he oh-so-easily replaced my collection of Jason Bourne fantasies.

"Tell me what you imagine when you touch yourself."

"I don't—-"

He spanks my ass, hard. *Shit*, that hurts like hell over naked skin.

Why do I want him to do that again?

"Don't lie to Daddy, Vera."

How does he know I'm lying?

I squirm uncomfortably on his lap. "Well, yes. I imagine you tying me up. I imagine. . . this. Being over your lap. I imagine you lecturing me before you spank me. I imagine. . . like. . . maybe you. . . using things on me."

"That's a good girl," he says in that voice that makes me melt. "Like what?"

"Like. . . that time you used your belt. Or maybe. . . I don't know, something like. . . to keep my wrists together. I. . . I've only read about these things, and I don't know what I like or want."

I breathe out and complete the melting process. I'm literally boneless now.

"But are you willing to find out?"

CHAPTER EIGHTEEN

Nikko

I NEVER IMAGINED Vera would come alive like this.

"Yes. Yes, Daddy," she says. She can't even look at me when she says it, and she's doing that adorable thing where her cheeks get all bright red. But the woman's as aroused as she's ever been, and I've barely touched her.

Fuck.

"Open your legs," I say in a growl. Her obedience is the most erotic aphrodisiac I ever could've imagined. My dick is painfully hard when she obeys immediately.

But she still needs to learn her lesson.

I spank her pretty, perfect little naked ass. "What do you say, Vera?"

"Y-yes, Daddy," she breathes as she parts her legs.

I stroke her until her back arches.

"Beg Daddy for your climax, baby. Beg me."

"Please," she begs in a choked whisper. "Please, Daddy."

I stroke her clit until she comes, her back arching and her voice a jumbled chorus of whimpers and pleas. She's still coming when I lift her onto the bed.

"Touch yourself. Keep going, baby. Keep touching yourself."

I unfasten my belt as she obeys me, her lips parted as she comes so fucking hard. I fasten it in a loop around her wrists and secure them before I lean back on the bed and position her over my mouth. I savor every lick, the taste of her scorched into my memory like a brand. And when she comes on my mouth, I savor the way she moans in pleasure until she falls beside me, her eyes fluttering closed.

"Good girl," I whisper, leaning over her. "That's a good girl. But we're not done here, Vera. You'll learn to obey Daddy. That was your reward for taking your first punishment like such a good girl."

"My—my first, Daddy?" Her eyes are half-lidded staring up at me.

I nod. "It's my job to make sure you know that will never happen again. Ever." I tip my hand under her chin. "Will it, baby?"

"No, Daddy," she breathes.

I lay her on the bed beside me as she stares at me, curiosity mingling with arousal in her gaze. I spread her legs and taste her clit again.

"Daddy!" her hips jerk. "I'm so sensitive! I just—oh, God, Markov!"

I lick her clit again, lazily stroking and tasting while I unfasten my pants and take out my dick. I groan into her wet, hot, sweet pussy. She protests but doesn't try to stop me as I nip the swollen bud before I stroke her with my tongue again.

"Oh my God," she breathes. "Dear *God.*"

My cock swells in my fist while I fist it, eating her sweet pussy like it's the world's finest goddamn delicacy.

Maybe it is.

"Please," she whimpers, shaking her head. "It's too much. Too—I can't take this," she whispers.

I lift my mouth from her pussy just as her hips jerk with the first spasm of her climax.

"Will you obey me, Vera? Will you trust me to protect you?"

"Of course I will," she promises, even though I suspect she'd promise damn near anything right now. My dick throbs, and I moan against her folds.

"Good girl. Such a good girl. Come on Daddy's tongue, Vera."

She screams with her second climax. I release my swollen cock and flip her onto her belly. Her wrists, still bound, brace on the bed in front of her as I part her legs and stroke the entrance of her pussy with the head of my cock.

"Markov," she whimpers. "I want you in me."

My forehead falls to her still-clothed back, damp and hot. I love the feel of her around me when I enter her. I'm slow at first because she's still new to this, and I don't want to hurt her. But when she meets me thrust for thrust, I pick up the intensity. She likes a mix of pain and pleasure together.

Noted.

I slam into her, claiming her body with mine. I relish the sound of her moans and the tight, tight feel of her pussy around me like a goddamn glove. Fucking *perfection.*

I come, my hot seed lashing into her just seconds before her own release consumes her. I bend and bite her neck, needing to taste her, to consume her.

Finally, we come down from our high, and I kiss the red part where I bit her neck. Vera looks like she's sleeping.

"Are you alright?" I ask.

"Mmm," she whispers. "I can't move, but other than that. . . yeah, I'm good." She opens one eye with effort. "You?"

"I'm perfect, baby. I didn't take it easy on you." I kiss her cheek. "Did I hurt you, Vera? Are you hurt anywhere?"

"Hurt?" she asks, half-grinning at me. "Markov, you bit my neck, fucked me so hard I felt like you were going to split me open, *spanked* me, but it was. . . ." Her voice trails off. "I am a woman with a strong vocabulary, but words fail me. *Fail* me."

I brush her damp hair off her forehead and kiss her cheek. "You're so brave," I tell her honestly. "So damn brave. To trust me like that. . . " I trail off because I'm surprised to find I'm choked up.

This goddamn upcoming benefit could destroy everything. If Markov's aunt or anyone who knew him shows. . . my cover will be blown. I'll have to make my move.

It will be time.

But we've had so little time together.

How can someone forbidden be so damn perfect for me?

CHAPTER NINETEEN

Vera

MARKOV LIES BESIDE ME. He runs his fingers through my hair, combing it from my face.

"I'm so proud of you," he says. He's just cleaned me with a warm washcloth and is tucking me into bed. "You handled that like you were meant for it."

"Meant for it?" I ask. My words sound slurred. "Or meant for *you?*"

As soon as I say it, I regret it. His eyes shutter, and his face grows flinty, almost as hard as he did when we first met.

"I shouldn't have—I'm sorry I—"

"Don't you dare apologize," he says with a sigh, shaking his head. "I'm not upset with you. Come here, baby. That couldn't be further from the truth."

He pulls me onto his chest and holds me. I listen to the

beating of his heart and close my eyes. I've never felt so safe in my life.

I've read about things like this before. How men like him can be dominant yet nurturing. . .

I never knew I craved a blend like that. . . until him. I never knew I *needed* something like this. . . until him.

"You need to eat, Vera."

"I don't want to move," I tell him, not opening my eyes.

He waits for a beat, just holding me, before he continues. "It's important that you get food after something that intense. You work hard. We'll go on a run again in the morning, but we have to get something to eat, even something simple."

I smile in the dim light of dusk when my eyes fly open.

"Oh God. That window's open. Oh my *God*. I thought it was closed."

He leaps out of bed, and for one brief minute, Markov looks as terrified as I am. It scares me. I don't know if I've ever seen him scared before.

"Shit. How could I have been so careless? I closed the other shades and didn't realize this one was still open. *Fuck*."

Even though there's a slim sliver of light at the bottom of the shade, it's too risky. Anyone could've seen us, and if anyone in my family ever caught wind of what we were doing. . . I can't even imagine what would happen. The punishment for me would be severe, but for Markov. . .

My belly churns with anxiety. What are we going to do?

"Stay here. I'm going to investigate." I sit up and clasp the blanket to me as he turns around and pins me in place with his glare. "My job is to protect you, Vera Ivanova. You do not leave this room."

He turns and is gone.

I stare at the window and see his large form move past the window. My mind reels with the possibility of what could happen. Even if no one in the Ivanov Bratva saw us. . . even if there was no evidence of the two of us together. . . he just dominated me. What if another student or one of the professors caught wind? Would I ever be able to live that down?

But right now, our safety is a bigger concern, especially after everything we've been through.

I'm still trembling and boneless from our lovemaking.

Will life with Markov ever be normal? Does he even want a woman like me? I've been sheltered my whole life. I don't know anything about what it's like to be. . . *normal*.

What have I gotten myself into?

The door opens, and Markov steps inside, his face impassive and flinty as usual.

"Irina passed by a few moments ago, but she was on the other side of the campus and only waved to me. There's no way she saw anything."

I feel my eyes flutter closed as I sink back on the pillow.

"Okay, alright. So we did this thing as an undergrad in one of my emergency preparation classes. We had to envision the worst-case scenario and then imagine ourselves walking through it." I blow out a breath. "Let's do that."

Markov shakes his head and sits on the edge of the bed. "Worst case scenario? The worst-case scenario is someone sees us together and makes me leave your side. The worst-case scenario is your father knows we're an item and tears us apart." He shakes his head. "I don't give a shit about what he'd do to me, but if he takes me away from you. . . if I can't protect you anymore. . ."

I reach a hand to touch his arm. I can feel the tenseness of his muscles. "Markov. . ."

"You want me to walk myself through it?" he continues. "Yeah, I can do that, Vera. It would be ending anyone that got in my way so I could get back to you. To make sure you were safe and no one hurt you."

I swallow the lump in my throat. "The worst case for me would be losing you. If you got hurt, Markov. . . if they took you away from me. . . I don't know what I would do."

He half-laughs while cringing. "We need a plan, Vera."

"Can our plan involve running away where no one will ever find us? Change identities and try out witness protection? I'll leave everything, Markov."

"*Nyet.*" He shakes his head, his Russian coming out in full force. "*Ty etogo ne sdelayesh.* You will not do that. You worked too long and too hard for you to give it all up for *me*. I won't allow it, Vera."

"I don't care," I say, feeling like a stubborn child. "Those all mattered to me more before I realized what matters to me *most*, Markov."

"Vera—"

"Listen to me," I say, tears shimmering in my eyes. "I'll call my father. I'll explain everything. I'll tell him how you've taken care of me, how good you are to me. He has to understand. Surely, I can make him see reason—"

"*Vera.*" He grasps both of my hands in his. They're warm and rough. . . like him. "You don't really know me. You know the man I am here. You know the role I play here. But I've done wicked, terrible things." He leans forward. "*Unforgivable* things, Vera. If you knew what I've done. If you really knew who I *am*. . ." his voice trails off in a ragged whisper. "You'd never forgive me."

I blink, a lone, fat tear rolling down my cheek. "I know you aren't the classic definition of a good man, Markov. I *know* that." I sniff. "I'm a smart girl, remember? And those were your words, not mine. Life is complicated. We can make this work. We *can*."

He pulls me to his chest in a grip so tight I can hardly breathe before he releases me, both hands on either side of my face, his gaze burning into mine.

"Life is complicated. Yes," he says with a nod.

"We can do this," I whisper. But even as I say it, I can feel the futility of my words.

He slams his mouth onto mine, and all thoughts come to a screeching halt. I can hardly remember what we were arguing about. I can hardly remember how we got here or where we go from here. When his tongue tangles with mine, I taste the salty essence of my tears.

We pull away, press our foreheads together, and entwine our fingers. Hold each other. Hold this space of fear mingled with love and of past misdeeds mingled with grace.

Can I forgive him for the atrocities he's committed? How much do I really, truly know him?

"You are right," he whispers as he licks his lips. "Whatever comes. . . whatever happens. . . We take grave risks, but it's nothing we can't handle."

Why do his words seem hollow?

Why do I question his sincerity?

Where, truly, do we go from here?

"Let me make a call," he whispers. "Let me see if surveillance saw anything. We don't have to make a decision right now other than whether or not we'll go to tonight's team dinner."

"Right. Yes."

I watch as he takes a phone out of his drawer and texts, scowling at it, before I push myself out of bed and find something to change into. The window's closed now, as it should've been in the first place.

I step into a pair of jeans and tug on a fitted top. Even though he's on the phone, he crooks a finger at me.

I walk over to him, and he grins at me—one of those wide, toothy grins that splits his whole face into two, as rare as a solar eclipse and as bright as the midday sun in summer. I kiss his prickly jaw.

"You're so damn beautiful," he says. "We're going to make this work, Vera." The deep timbre of his voice somehow seems foreboding when he says, "No matter what."

CHAPTER TWENTY

Nikko

> Aleks, tell me if there was anyone outside our door between the hours of 18:30-19:40. It's crucial.

> I see no one in the nearby vicinity at that hour, just the program director Irina walking by at 19:40. Why? What's going on?

I tell my brothers everything. We have no secrets from one another. But I have no idea how to tell him. . . this. I cannot betray my family, yet I cannot betray the woman that I love.

And yes, I'll admit that, if only to myself. I love Vera Ivanova. Against all better judgment and knowledge in my head, I've fallen in love with this fierce, intense, brilliant, beautiful woman. So I do what's become a habit by now: I tell him a half-truth.

> The window was open and I suspected our privacy was invaded. After the last fiasco, I feared the worst

> All clear brother. Our sources tell us that her father is still in town. Your thoughts on your timing?

I draw in a breath and release it.

> It is time.

I shove my phone in my pocket and release my grip on Vera. She lifts her head from my shoulder.

"Did I do a good job, Daddy?"

I kiss her forehead. "Such a good job, baby girl. Let's get dinner."

Though Irina walked by, nothing seemed off. She'd smiled widely, as usual, and reminded me that dinner was approaching. She asked if we'd join them, and when I said yes, she said she'd see us there.

Still, I feel torn. I have to protect Vera, no matter the cost, even if that means hurting her in the process.

I have to.

We walk hand in hand to the dining hall and are joined by the American at the door. He only gives us a curt nod and walks in ahead of us. Maxim, normally silent and aloof, smiles at Vera. "That was incredible. Did you tell Markov about your breakthrough today?"

"She did," I say warmly, wrapping my arm around her shoulders. "I couldn't be prouder. This is why we're here."

"This is why we're *all* here," Professor Morozov says as he enters and joins us. "Today was a landmark day and calls for a celebration."

He removes a bottle of chilled wine from his lab coat and opens it.

"I half expected him to serve it in beakers," Vera says in my ear. I stifle a snort.

"That's terrible."

"Oh, honey. I've seen worse in a lab, believe you me."

Here, in these small interludes of normalcy, it almost feels like we could actually make this work. That Vera and I could be a normal couple, unhindered by the restraints and demands of family.

Still, I can't shake the feeling that something is terribly off. Aleks says no one saw anything Irina is acting normally, and Vera's fellow students are buoyed by their findings today and proud of her. Even Jake begrudgingly toasts her and admits he's impressed with the progress they've made.

"In honor of today, we'll take this weekend fully off," Morozov suggests at the end of the meal. "You've all worked so hard, some of you even getting a run in before the sun rises."

His eyes twinkle at us.

Vera looks at him in surprise. "You've seen us?"

"Oh, yes," he says with a wink. "An old man misses nothing."

"You two are dedicated," Sophia says. "I crash at night and don't even think of moving until it's practically time for our next clinical."

"Aye," Liam says. "The days are long and taxing. I'm thankful for a weekend off."

"As am I," Irina says. "I actually have to step off campus for a bit to attend a benefit this weekend."

Vera is shit at masking her facial expressions. She looks absolutely terrified.

"Do you?" I ask, reaching for the bottle of wine to refill our glasses. "We do, too, with Vera's family. Which will you be attending?"

"Oh, I don't remember the name," she says, shaking her head. "Someplace near Ostankinsky District. . ."

I breathe out a sigh of relief and give Vera's leg a reassuring squeeze under the table and a shake of my head. The Ostankinksy District is in the northernmost part of Moscow, nowhere near where we'll be going.

"Will you two need us to arrange transportation?" Morozov asks.

I shake my head. "Thank you, no. I've already done so."

Irina smiles. "I think going forward, our students might benefit from having supportive partners with them, don't you think?" she asks Morozov. "It's such an added bonus."

They all laugh as dessert comes out, but I'm not comforted by any of this.

Today, our necks were bared to our enemy.

I have a job to do. A mission to complete. But I can't allow Vera to be hurt on the sidelines.

My time has come.

CHAPTER TWENTY-ONE

Vera

THE NEXT FEW days pass without incident. Though we're only at the very beginning stages of what we've discovered, it's monumental.

I have to admit that's all in the periphery of my focus, though. I came here to focus on my studies, but the prevailing concerns about me and Markov have taken precedence.

"You look troubled."

It's Friday night, the day before the benefit, and Markov is kneeling beside me, doing what's become routine for us: braiding my hair. He does it every night before bed. I'm loathe to admit that I don't actually *need* him to braid my hair. It doesn't tangle much when I sleep and is easy to fix in the morning. What I need, though, is the feel of his strong, masculine fingers on my scalp. The slight tug when he gives it an inevitable tweak.

I won't lie. . . I'm nervous as hell about tomorrow.

"You're as skittish as a little kitten, Vera," Markov says, bending to kiss my shoulder before tweaking my braid. My God, I love all of it. The intimacy of this moment, the warm feel of his mouth on my bare skin. The solid wall of his presence behind me. The way my name sounds on his lips. "Tell me what's going on."

"Oh, you know," I say with a sigh. "The benefit and all. I'm just nervous about my father. Even if you and I didn't have this. . . going on between us. . . I'd still be nervous."

Markov turns me around to face him and frames my face with his hands.

This. This is what I love.

My eyes water as I peer into his intense gaze and see a well of love he hasn't even yet voiced to me.

"Vera Ivanova," he says earnestly. "You said it yourself that this will work out. We have to take this one step at a time. For now, you need rest." When he bends and kisses me, I can almost believe it will be as simple as that—trust, love, and a kiss that makes it all better.

With a sigh, I crawl into bed. "That's right, baby girl," he whispers in my ear as he spoons me from behind. His warm body wraps around mine. "Put your mind to rest and get some sleep."

But I can't. Soon, Markov is breathing more deeply behind me while my mind spins and spins. I can't get my fears out of my mind.

I make a decision. I push out of bed and walk over to where my phone is plugged in. I look over and Markov is still asleep.

I call Mom.

"Vera! How are you, darling?"

"I'm good, Mom. A little nervous about that stupid benefit, but it will be fine. There's. . ." my heart beats so quickly that I'm a little shaky, "something I have to ask you."

"Mmm? What is it?"

I draw in a breath and let it out slowly, gathering my courage. "Do you love Dad anymore?"

There's silence on the other end of the line before she answers. "What makes you ask, Vera?"

"I—I just need to know. Please," I whisper.

"Sweetheart, your father and I never loved each other to begin with. Our marriage was one of convenience, not love. And while others in that arrangement have learned to love one another despite the difficulties they faced. . . that was never us. I could not love a man who was self-serving and unfaithful. And while I'll give credit where credit is due— your father's taken good financial care of us and allowed me to raise you the way I saw fit—no, Vera. I do not love your father and never have."

I nod. That will make what I have to do so much easier.

"Thank you, Mom. I love you."

"Are you alright?"

No, I'm not alright. I'm in love with a man who's forbidden for me, and I have no idea if he feels the same way. How will I navigate this without both of us being destroyed?

"I'm fine," I tell her. I don't ever remember lying to my mother before.

I hang up the call and immediately place a second. My father answers after five rings.

"Vera! What a pleasant surprise. I didn't expect your call." Of course he didn't expect my call. I have never, ever called my father. I hear the sounds of clinking glasses, music, and laughter behind him. He's partying, as usual.

"Father, we have to talk before tomorrow's event."

I feel Markov's eyes on me. I'm not sure at what point he woke up.

"Ah, good, your mother's told you I requested your presence then."

"She did. I'll be there. Can we talk, though?"

"Of course, Vera. Anything for my daughter," he says too loudly, likely making sure that whoever he's with hears him.

Gag me.

"I want you to know that you don't have to hide. . . whoever it is that you're seeing." It pains me to say it, but I press on. "I've been thinking about it. I know that officially, you and Mom are still married, and I. . . while I'm thankful that you've respected me enough to keep her distanced from me, it's alright if she's with you tomorrow."

My father doesn't speak for a moment. "This is a big step, Vera. I'm honestly taken a bit aback by your selflessness."

Well, that hurts, but he's done worse. Also, it isn't selfless.

"It's just that. . . I want you to know that I know sometimes situations aren't perfect. Sometimes, people fall in love with someone they shouldn't, and it's important to give each other grace. Don't you agree?"

My cheeks are too hot, my heartbeat too fast when I say it in a rush of words. My father, however, is quick to agree.

"Yes, of course. Very wise of you, Vera. Very wise indeed. Thank you for that. She won't be attending tomorrow because she has a prior engagement, but thank you for this."

I nod. "I understand."

"Now, I must get back to my friends here, but I look forward to seeing you."

We disconnect the call. I plug my phone in and place it back on the desk before I look up at Markov. He stares at me in the darkness. Immobile.

"Don't be angry with me," I begin. "I—I needed to take a preemptive step."

We don't speak for a few long moments.

"That was very brave of you," he finally says. "Very brave. Thank you, Vera. You inspire me."

I cross the room to him and crawl under the sheets. He lifts the blanket and welcomes me closer. I snuggle up to his chest and allow myself this guilty pleasure. Being safe and secure in the arms of the man I love yet can never have.

I want to protect him. I want to protect *us*.

"Is my aunt coming?" he asks. It surprises me because I didn't expect he'd want to see her.

"No, unfortunately, she won't be able to attend."

I don't know if I imagine it, but he seems to relax a little.

"Ah. Now that you've gotten that behind you, get some sleep, baby girl." He helps me roll over and gives me a firm smack to the ass.

I close my eyes and relish this moment, and finally, I fall asleep. I dream of dark forests, hidden places, and long tunnels that never, ever end.

The next day passes quickly with our early morning run and leisurely coffee downtown. Markov seems to be on his phone more than usual, which is a bit unnerving, but when I press, he admits he's going over security for tonight. Fair enough.

Soon, it's time to get ready. I was planning on wearing the same dress I wore for dinner out with my dad, but Sophia told me she has a dress with her that I can borrow. She's smaller than I am, so the little red dress is so tight on me I can't fit a bra on underneath. It hugs every curve and makes my breasts somehow look bigger, and at first, I'm not sure it's decent. . . then Markov's reaction when he sees me is absolutely worth it.

"Where the fuck did you get that?" he says with a growl as he prowls my way.

"Oh, this little thing?" I ask, tossing my hair. It sticks to my lip gloss, and I nearly stumble on my heel. This is why I'll never be a model.

"Vera," he says warningly. "Where the fuck did you get that thing?"

"From Sophia!" I protest. "It's *her* dress, not mine."

"But *you're* wearing it," he says. When he reaches for me, he wraps his hand over my throat and gently pushes me against the wall. His body presses up against mine, caging me in.

"You may wear that dress, baby girl," he whispers in my ear, his fingers tightening. My pulse spikes at the feel of his heavy hand on my naked skin, right at my pulse. "Under one condition."

"Mmm? What's that?" I ask in a throaty whisper, a bit afraid of what that condition might be.

With firm movements, he yanks the dress up to my belly and tears my thong right off me. It's a thin, lacy little thing that fairly crumples in his grip. "There," he whispers, lifting my panties to his nose. He inhales.

"Markov!" I say in a strangled gasp.

His eyes closed as he inhales the scent of my arousal.

"These are mine now."

My cheeks burn as he pockets my panties. It feels all kinds of wrong to be going to this benefit with no bra or panties, in a dress that hugs my curves, but the possessive look in his eyes makes it worth it.

"Turn around and place your hands on that wall."

Obediently, I do what he says. I won't disobey him, not now. I can't. At this point, every fiber of my being purrs at his command.

I brace myself at the clink of a belt buckle behind me. "Let's remind who you belong to out there dressed like this."

I close my eyes and hear him tuck the buckle in his palm right before he swings the looped leather across my ass. I hiss in a breath as the searing pain blossoms into arousal. A second lash, followed by another, has me up on my toes as he whispers, "You'll wear these stripes when you go there. You'll feel the marks of my belt."

Bending down, he bites my ass cheek. I squeal, but the firm clap of his hand across my ass makes me squeeze my lips together.

"And if at any point we get separated, remember who you belong to, *wife*."

"Mmm," I agree. "And if at any point we get separated, *you* take those panties out and remember who *you* belong to."

I grin at the deep sound of his pleased chuckle when his phone beeps.

"Our ride is here."

We're quiet on the ride over. I'm sitting right up close to him, still hot as hell after his display.

I hope we can handle this like we handled dinner. Arrive, do our duty, take off. No harm done.

"Ugh," I say, shaking my head when the car comes to a stop. "We're jumping straight into the fire."

My father stands at the entrance while other couples enter, dressed impeccably and surrounded by his guards.

Markov's heavy hand rests at the small of my back. "You'll do fine, baby." He kisses my cheek. I squeeze his hand and take a deep breath.

I am not letting this man go.

No matter *what*.

My father stares when Markov and I exit the vehicle, looking me over with scrutiny. "Vera," he says, kissing my cheek. "Did your mother pick that dress? Markov, I'd like you to join us. There's no need for you to keep your distance."

I stiffen, but Markov moves right in with stride, reaching for my father's hand and shaking it firmly. "I told her she looks beautiful," he says with a smile. "Did you hear about what she did this week? Their amazing discovery will be posted in every medical journal from here to America. Let's go in, and Vera can tell you all about it."

I give him a small smile in return.

Though my father's far from interested in me discussing what I did this week, he's impressed that the work will garner attention from powerful people.

"Excellent," he says as he turns his back to me. "Let's get a drink. Oh, and I have a surprise for you, Markov."

Markov and I share a look. There can't be any good that comes from starting a conversation like that. When we reach the bar, he lifts a large bottle of Beluga Gold Line, a premium vodka. Even implacable Markov looks impressed. "Excellent," he says approvingly. "Thank you."

We make small talk, and Markov helps me navigate it all with perfect ease. He remains somewhat aloof, maintaining his position as a bodyguard while interjecting praise when my father makes rude or dismissive comments. My father probably never imagined that the guard he hired would protect me from *him*.

"Excuse me," I say at one point, ready for a break from him. "I need to use the ladies' room."

"Of course." My father points in the general direction of where to go. Markov steps beside me. "I'll accompany her. Anything I can get you on my return, sir?"

"Nothing, thank you, Markov."

"My God," I whisper to Markov as we walk toward the restrooms. "He's insufferable. How can you handle it?"

He shrugs. "I pretend people like him are overgrown children in need of a nap." When I laugh, he smiles back. "It really helps."

I snort. "I bet."

The darkened hallway is vacant when I return. Markov stands in the shadows. It's risky, the two of us being alone. Close like this. He leans in and whispers in my ear, "Do you still feel my stripes, Vera?"

"Mmmm," I whisper in his. "Do you still feel my panties in your pocket?"

Markov stifles a groan and squeezes my ass.

"Don't!" I hiss. "Please."

"Fair enough. But when we get back to our room, you're mine, Vera."

"Can we go now?"

"Almost."

My father isn't where we left him.

"That's strange. Where did he go?" I ask Markov. My heart begins to race. If he was outside that restroom and I didn't see him. . . if he followed us. . . .

"There," Markov says. "Over by the exit."

"Markov! Vera."

"Father, we're going to head back now. I'm just so tired."

"You do have to stay one more minute," he says. "Do you remember our conversation last night?"

"Mmm. I do."

"I've thought about what you said, and I—I'd like you to come to my room and have a drink."

Markov goes stiff beside my father. I suddenly feel the need to run, and I'm not sure why.

"Maybe another time," I tell my father, shaking my head.

"Come now. Come back to the hotel room with me. We'll have a drink," my father says. "Please. The suite is big enough for all of us."

All of us? Not including his guards, there are only three of us. And those guards will be stationed outside.

"Vera said she'd rather go home," Markov says. "But thank you for the invitation, sir."

My father's gaze grows stony. "I paid for that ride you took over here. Your plane flight here." He jerks his chin at Markov. "*His* salary. The least you could do is say thank you and come with me. You should know better as one of my paid men, Markov."

CHAPTER TWENTY-TWO

Nikko

I HAVE no choice but to go with him. Her father has mostly played nice at this point, but he no longer will if we don't obey him.

I'm torn between allegiance to my family, to the oath of loyalty I've sworn and why I'm here. . . and protecting Vera.

I can't let her get hurt, no matter what.

"One drink, sir, please. Understand we mean no disrespect, but you've asked me to protect Vera, and she's asked to go home. Surely, you understand after the hard work she's done this week."

Ivanov nods, his gaze hazy. He's already stone-cold drunk.

That will make my job much easier.

I've been in touch with Aleks at home who's given me the specs and location of all of his guards. If we get him alone in his room, and I can isolate Vera. . .

I can keep her safe. I know I can. But if I kill her father. . . what will it do to her?

Her father prattles on and on, name-dropping people he knows. Vera is tight-lipped and distant but plays the part with her responses. He's given us no choice. A confrontation with him will not end well. We'll have to comply so we don't give him a reason to pull rank.

I can send her home. . . ahead of me. I'm not just a close-range assassin but a skilled sniper. I could kill her father, and she never has to know it's me.

And then say goodbye to the only woman I've ever loved.

Khristos.

I carry the heavy bottle of vodka he gave me as a gift as we exit the elevator on the top floor, where he's rented his suite. Vera looks at me, her eyes wide and afraid. I'm not sure why. I give her the smallest of smiles behind her father's back.

I love you.

I'd given up hope in happy endings and "one true love."

With Vera, though, I thought I found it. If we weren't who we are. . . if our families weren't sworn enemies. . .

"And a local artist here in Moscow was kind enough to give us his latest highly acclaimed painting." When neither of us responds, her father adds, "It's valued at over three million dollars."

"Wow," Vera says, her brows rising. "And he just gave it to you?"

Even now, it surprises me how innocent she is. One does not "give" a priceless piece of art to a powerful *pakhan* out of the goodness of one's heart.

"Yes," her father says, his lips curving upward in a way that makes my skin crawl. "People always give me what I want, Vera."

"Mmm," she says drily, albeit politely. "I remember."

A small cavalcade of guards stands outside his room, flanking either side of the door. They are familiar to me, as they accompanied him to dinner when we first met.

"Has she arrived?"

"Yes, sir," one of the men replies.

Vera and I share a look.

Has who arrived?

"I told you I had a surprise for you, Markov," Petr says, turning to me with bleary eyes and a smile. "I wouldn't just give you a bottle of vodka, now, would I? Come. Your aunt awaits us."

He opens the door.

CHAPTER TWENTY-THREE

Vera

HIS AUNT. God. The thought of meeting my father's mistress churns my stomach, yet here I am, having boldly declared that "people love who they shouldn't," possibly alerting my father to my relationship with Markov. But really, what was I expecting? My father has always played by his own rules, always prioritizing his desires over the needs of others. He wouldn't even permit us to skip a drink and a visit to his suite, let alone forgive his bodyguard for falling in love with his daughter.

As we enter the suite, Markov's stiffness beside me is palpable. I try to muster some courage, but honestly, I just want this meeting over. We can meet her, then escape back to our lives.

The suite is a testament to opulence, unsurprising given my father's penchant for displaying luxury and power. The iconic silhouette of the Kremlin frames the backdrop of several interconnected rooms—a private office, a dining area, a sitting room, and a bedroom, all dominated by heavy, imposing leather furniture.

"Now, now, don't be shy," my father coaxes. At his beckoning, I notice a woman perched on the edge of a massive leather chair, her back to us. At the sound of his voice, she stands.

I gasp, my hand flying to cover my mouth. Beside me, Markov freezes.

"Vera, Markov, so nice to see you," Irina greets us, her dark gray gown complementing her sleek silver hair. Her smile is warm and disarming.

I'm struck mute, my mouth agape. How? Why? What does this mean?

Markov's gaze hardens, and he steps protectively between me and Irina. My father retreats to the bar, his back to us, oblivious to the tension. As I move my gaze between Markov and Irina, it becomes evident—one of them is lying. Possibly both. They clearly aren't related; they met for the first time upon our arrival. . . or had they?

The tension escalates. Thankfully, my father is preoccupied as he pours himself a glass of wine and offers one to Markov and me. Markov gives me a stern look and subtly shakes his head: *Don't drink it.*

My father takes a hearty swig of his wine and addresses us. "Vera, it's because of Markov's aunt that you have the finest bodyguard available." It's possibly the only truthful thing he has ever said.

"I wasn't aware that your. . . girlfriend was working with

us," I manage to say with a strained smile. "Why didn't you inform us, Irina?"

My father looks confused. "You know her?"

His response is interrupted by a loud knock. "Yes, yes, who is it?"

"Sir, there's an urgent matter."

"It better be, interrupting me like this." My father frowns and strides over. Meanwhile, Irina's smile remains unfazed.

He has a hurried discussion at the door, their voices a mix of urgency and concern, before he turns back to us. "Excuse me. My apologies, I must see to something briefly," he says, his expression etched with worry.

Irina rushes to him. "What is it, Petr? Can I assist with anything?" she asks.

"No, no, just stay with my daughter until I return." He closes the door behind him, and Irina locks it.

Silence engulfs us, heavy with unvoiced questions. Markov remains tense, his eyes locked on Irina, who still wears her cryptic smile.

"Vera," Irina begins, her tone now softer, contrasting sharply with her earlier formal greeting. "There's much you don't know about your father, about me, and the real reason Markov is here."

I glance at Markov, searching his face for any sign of denial, but find none. His jaw is clenched; his gaze never strays from Irina as if trying to solve an intricate riddle.

"Start talking, Irina," Markov demands, his voice low and threatening. "Enough with the charades. Who are you really, and why are you here?"

Irina exhales, her poised demeanor slipping momentarily as she gestures toward a cozy sitting area by the fireplace. "Let's sit. It's time we cleared the air. I could ask you the same, couldn't I?"

"Firstly, Vera, your father and I were more than just old acquaintances, as you've been led to believe," she reveals, taking a sip of her drink. "Go ahead, take a sip. I assure you, it's not poisoned."

I ignore the drink, my heart hammering in my chest as I turn to Markov, whose stern expression has not softened. His eyes remain cautious.

"Don't trust her, Vera," he says.

"And Markov," Irina continues, turning her attention to him, "is not merely a visitor and certainly not my nephew. You see, Vera, I hired an assassin. It was easy enough to seduce your father and convince him I had a nephew in need of a job. My aim was to eliminate you, as you are the only obstacle between me and my goals."

The word 'assassin' echoes in my mind, drowning out all other thoughts.

There are things you don't know about me, Vera. Things that, if known, you could never forgive.

"Ironically, I had no clue who Markov really was but knew he was not the man I hired. I wanted to see his end game. I wanted to see how I could manipulate the situation to get what I needed. So, I waited. I couldn't just kill you outright; it had to appear accidental."

I stare at Markov, whose narrowed eyes remain intently focused on Irina. His hand is hidden in his pocket. What is he concealing? He can't simply kill my father's mistress without consequence.

"Petr was called out just now because one of his men has been found dead. That will keep him busy while we decide our next move. Get rid of her, Markov," she directs, nodding at me. "Then you and I can dominate the Ivanov empire. It's as simple as. . ." She snaps her fingers.

"Never," Markov asserts firmly. "You will not harm her!"

"Oh, dear," Irina sighs, feigning disappointment. "I'll have to move to another plan."

My world tilts on its axis. What is happening? Who are these people?

They both deceived me. Everything has been a lie.

"You used her." Markov seizes Irina, swiftly disarming her. He shakes her violently.

"Markov!" I shout, even though I doubt that's his real name. "Stop!"

"She just confessed that she wants you dead," he growls, lifting her off the ground by her neck. She struggles vainly against his grip. Suddenly, there's a pounding at the door, and I hear my father's voice.

The door bursts open, and my father rushes in, flanked by his guards. "What is the meaning of this?" he thunders.

Markov releases Irina, positioning her in front of him with a gun to her temple. I stare, disbelieving.

"Petr," she pleads. "Petr, help me!"

My father stares at Markov, realization dawning. "You would kill your own aunt?"

"They aren't related, Father," I say in a choked voice.

My father stares. "Who are you?"

Markov stands resolute, the most commanding presence in the room. Despite my heartache, I can't help but feel a surge of pride in him.

"She deceived and betrayed you," he declares. "She intended to murder your daughter, but now, the truth must be revealed." He fixes his gaze on my father. "Tell your men to stand down, or I will kill her."

My father glares at Markov but gives the order.

Markov continues. "My name is Nikko Romanov. I am here on behalf of the Romanov family, your rivals from America. You attacked my brother and attempted to poison his wife. I came to seek justice. Tell the truth, Ivanov, or your mistress dies."

My father's face drains of color. "Romanov," he whispers, recognition and fear bleeding into his voice.

"The truth!" Markov thunders. I gasp.

"I never ordered such a thing," my father protests, shaking his head. "Yes, there were tensions, but I never sanctioned violence against your brother."

Markov's eyes narrow, his suspicion evident. "Yet you acknowledge the incident I refer to."

The room spins, the revelation overwhelming me. Spots cloud my vision.

Markov presses the gun to Irina's head. "Now you. Confess your role."

"I orchestrated the attack," she admits. "It was simple enough. I used his phone to coordinate it, and his foolish men followed blindly."

"Why? Why would you do this?" my father demands.

"Because they were a threat to you, and it's *my* intent to take over the Ivanov family. You're so powerful, Petr. So, so powerful. Can't you see how we could rule together?"

I finally speak up. "She said the same damn thing to Markov when you weren't here," I seethe.

My father stares. "Markov. Please. Release her. Allow me and my men to take care of her. Send my deepest apologies to your family for what the Ivanovs have done."

Markov stares. Shakes his head. I don't believe my father any more than he does.

He looks back at me, and in his eyes, I see what I longed for —a plea for forgiveness and a pledge that the two of us matter. I choke back a sob.

Markov's voice booms through the room, every word loaded with the weight of years of enmity. "Your life is forfeit for what was done, for what your men have done, even if not directly on our behalf," he says, standing tall and unyielding before my father. "There is only one way forward. Only one way to bring peace between the Romanovs and Ivanovs and put it all to rest. No more hiding. No more betrayal. We face this like men."

My father nods, but I think he'd give Markov—or whoever he is—anything right now.

"Release her, Markov, and our families can form an alliance."

Markov stares and seems to think this over. "We're in agreement, then. We'll honor a time-honored tradition that brings families together. Give me your daughter, Ivanov."

My father casts a knowing glance between Markov and me. His eyes linger on my tear-streaked face. Silence engulfs the room, tension thickening the air with old grievances.

"My daughter?"

"Give her to me. Give me Vera, and we will end the feud between our families."

I stare, disbelieving.

"Take her," he says, his voice resolute. My blood turns to ice. "If this is what it takes to end our families' feud, to prevent further loss, so be it."

Mutterings from the Ivanovs' corner swell like an impending storm. Disbelief and anger ripple through them, yet their leader raises a hand, commanding silence.

"No!" Irina struggles within Markov's firm grip. "Petr, you promised me!"

"You betrayed me," my father booms, stepping toward her. He reaches out, wrenching her from Markov's hold. I flinch as he raises his hand to strike her, but she seizes her opportunity. With a swift knee to my father's groin, she breaks free, reaching into her dress to draw a concealed gun.

"You will not hold me back!" she screams, her voice a mixture of fury and desperation. "After everything I did for you. After everything you've promised me!" She aims the gun and pulls the trigger. "You're a lying cheat! How dare you!"

My father's guards react instantly, weapons drawn, but it's too late. A gunshot rings out.

"Father!" I scream. "No!"

But it's too late. His body hits the floor and blood pours from him. Her bullet struck her target: straight between his eyes.

As Irina pivots, her gun now aimed at me, Markov acts. With no hesitation, he leaps in front of me, intercepting the bullet meant for me. His body slams into mine as we hit the floor together.

"Nooooo!" I cry out in horror.

Too late, one of the guards fires, striking Irina. She falls, her threat ending with a thud against the floor.

My medical training kicks in amid the chaos. Authority surges through me as I rise to my feet, facing the guards.

"You!" I command, pointing sharply. I'm taking no risks. "Make sure she's secured immediately! My father is injured, and I am his daughter. Do what I say!"

My father is more than injured. Even I know that.

But I can save Markov. *I have to.*

This is my moment. This is what I know. I'm trained to handle intense, high-stakes medical situations under pressure.

The guards snap to attention, hesitating only a moment before moving to comply with my commands. They quickly observe the still body of Irina, ensuring she poses no further threat, while others rush to my father's side, checking for signs of life that I already fear are absent.

I kneel beside Markov, my hands trembling as I assess his wound. I blink back tears and push every thought aside. I have to focus on saving him.

I can do this.

Blood blooms across his shirt, a stark red against the white fabric. His eyes meet mine, filled with pain yet revealing so much strength. "It's okay, Vera," he whispers, his voice strained. "I'll be fine. You are the one who has to remain safe. Now that Irina and your father no longer pose a threat, I'll have to trust his guards. . ."

"Shhh," I whisper. One of my tears drops to his shirt, a dark circle spreading alongside the blood.

Ignoring the tears that blur my vision, I press my hand firmly against his wound, trying to staunch the bleeding. Around us, the room is a flurry of activity—guards shouting, the distant sound of sirens approaching, the heavy footsteps of medical personnel arriving. Someone here at the hotel's made some calls.

"Stay with me," I whisper. "Let me see how badly you're hurt."

I tear open his shirt and assess the wound with a frown. I need to assess the wound—*location, size, and type. Prevent the loss of blood.*

Please be only a graze. . . please be only a graze. . .

"It looks like a flesh wound," I whisper, frowning at the sight of his blood on my hands. I'm shaking, but stay calm. "Potential superficial muscle injury but we'll only know with further testing. It hasn't hit any major arteries, and you've lost a lot of blood, but you're a big guy—"

"Vera." Markov holds my hand, blood making our grip slippery. "Go with your father. I'll be taken into custody by the rest of his men. Even if my injury is minor, my life is forfeit for treason."

I break out in a cold sweat. Markov isn't...Markov. What does that mean for us? What does that mean for *him?*

His life is forfeit, yet...he saved my life.

It's then that I realize we're surrounded by my father's men, EMTs putting my father and Irina on stretchers. I watch in shock as they pull a sheet over her body.

I look at the men who stand above Markov. "He kept me safe. That bullet was meant for *me.*"

"We have our rules, Ms. Ivanov."

I blink back tears.

"You can't take him. You can't!"

I'm pulled away from Markov by strong hands, everything passing in a blur. I struggle and scream and rail against them, but I'm overpowered. I can't stop them. I watch in helpless agony as the emergency team takes my father but the Ivanov men take Markov.

A sob catches in my throat when I see my father taken away.

Despite everything, he's still my father. I never allowed myself to believe that his end would be so abrupt, so violent.

As they wheel my father away, I stand on the threshold of the now eerily quiet room. The weight of leadership in the wake of tragedy settles on my shoulders.

A uniformed officer speaks to me in Russian. I didn't even know they'd arrived. When he realizes I don't understand him, he gets a younger female officer to translate.

"Your father was a friend. As the daughter of Petr Ivanov, you've been exonerated from questioning," she says. He knew people, he must have. I swallow hard. "Is there someone you can call?"

I do the only thing a strong, independent woman whose world has been shattered does.

I call my mother.

CHAPTER TWENTY-FOUR

Vera

MY MOM IS TAKING a red-eye flight to Moscow and will arrive late this morning. The officers take pity on me and find me another room in another hotel. I insist on firsthand communication from my father's men.

I text Sophia that there's been a situation: her dress was ruined, but I'll pay for it, and can she please somehow arrange for my clothes to be brought to the hotel? To her credit, she asks nothing and drops clothes off. There will be rumors. . . and I hope we can sort through them all.

Markov isn't Markov.

Did a part of me, deep down inside, know that, though?

I want to reach out to him somehow. I want to find out if he's okay.

I want to shake him and scream at him for lying to me and

ask him what part of our relationship was *real*. What part mattered to him.

But I don't.

I drink one of the little bottles of wine in the hotel fridge and finally go to bed. I have more questions than answers, so it's no surprise I sleep fitfully.

I wake up to my phone ringing and answer in bleary-eyed confusion. "Hello?"

"Vera. It's Professor Morozov. May I come and see you?"

"Of course." I sit up in bed. What will he think of me? Of what happened? Does he know about Irina?

"I'll be there in fifteen minutes."

"See you then," I say and give him my location.

I open a bottle of water and down it before freshening up. I was too tired last night to shower, but now that I'm here, the hot water triggers my pent-up emotions. I lean against the shower wall and weep.

I don't have the luxury of an ugly cry, though, and have to force myself to get ready. I slide into a pair of yoga pants and a tank top minutes before I get a call from the front desk.

"Let him up, please."

There's a knock at the door.

I look through the peephole and can almost hear Markov telling me not to let anyone in and to be wary. I shouldn't be surprised, but it still takes me off guard to see men stationed on either side of my door, flanking Professor Morozov.

I open the door, trembling. I don't know what to expect. I don't trust anyone anymore.

The professor looks tired and older than he normally does.

"Come in," I say. My guards look questioningly at me. "He's a friend."

Morozov says something to them in Russian, and one of them nods.

I close the door behind us.

"How are you?" he asks. A part of me wants to come apart and tell him everything that happened. I long for someone to trust right now.

He's someone I trusted. But so was Markov. And so was Irina. I swallow hard and keep my shit together.

"I'm fine," I say, my voice husky. "How much do you know about what has happened?"

I gesture to one of the chairs beside the desk. He sits and folds his hands.

"Some. The authorities at the college told me that Irina was killed. We looked into the matter, and I spoke to the police last evening. I wanted to give you some time to rest, but I also needed to speak with you. How are you?"

"I'm sad. A little. . . bewildered. I never expected any of this. I thought I could trust. . . both of them. Markov and Irina. "

"Vera, I feel like I owe you an apology. I was the one who hired Irina at the strong suggestion of one of my peers, who I now know was bribed. I didn't know her before this, but her credentials checked out. I should have listened to my gut. My intuition told me something was afoul and that she wasn't to be trusted when I had never heard her name. And," he shakes his head, "while I cannot name every single expert in the field, I typically know those of her supposed rank. So when I didn't. . ."

He shakes his head. "But that is no matter. She's gone now, and I'm so sorry to hear what you've been put through."

I shake my head. "I thought I was accepted into this program based on my own merit, and it pains me to know that—"

"Vera Ivanova," Morozov interrupts. "I was the one who accepted you into this program, and you have not only shown me that I made the right decision, but you have proven that you're capable of so much more than I could have imagined. After the fiasco with Irina, we are going to have to dissolve the program."

I swallow. "Of course."

"Will you do the honor of telling me your side of the story? I want to know I have the full picture."

I draw in a breath and promise to do my best, even though there are parts of it that I'm still confused about. Parts I'm not sure I want to repeat.

"Yes, sir. Of course. I was told that I was accepted into this program. Vera Ivanova is my real name, and I am the daughter of Petr Ivanov, the head of the Russian Bratva here in Moscow and in America. In my home in New York, I was shielded from all these things. I knew nothing about what was happening except that my father was a high-ranking official. My mother kept me away from it all. This is why I don't even know Russian," I say with a sad smile.

"And has your mother been apprised of the situation?" Morozov asks quietly.

I nod. "Yes, sir. She's on her way here."

He knows. "Excellent. I look forward to meeting her. With your permission, of course. "

"I would like that."

"Please, continue," he says in his gentle way. "I interrupted you."

"The day I was to leave, my mother told me that I would be accompanied by a bodyguard. I didn't know anything about this, and I was horrified at the thought of someone here knowing that I had a bodyguard. That I was anyone of importance. I just wanted to be. . . me." My voice catches. "I wanted to know that I belonged here and wanted to prove my worth based on my own diligence to my studies."

He knows sagely, then shakes his head. "And to think I joked about him being a bodyguard. I mean. . . he looks like one. I'm sorry. So you pretended that he was your husband?"

I nod. "Which probably wasn't the wisest thing. Probably would've been smarter to be honest because look what dishonesty has produced. . ."

"You pretending to be married to Markov was the least of our worries, Vera. I understand why you did what you did, and I don't blame you. Now, what else can you tell me?"

I might as well tell him the whole truth now. "I fell in love with Markov. At least with who I thought he was. Even though I knew our families would never allow us to be together. Even though I knew that he would never be someone I could be with." My emotions rise to the surface despite my efforts to keep them down. "He really, truly did protect me. "

"I know. He really was very sincerely proud of you and made that known. And then what happened?"

"Irina was trying to get to my father and needed me out of the way. At least that is what I've gathered. . . But it appears she took the scenic route. She said she hired an assassin, and when she saw that Markov wasn't the man that she hired, she assumed he was here for the same reason and wanted to see how it would play out. She didn't want to lose her tenure at the college, I'm guessing, or to show her cards to anyone unnecessarily. But I do know that he was shot yesterday by a bullet that was meant for me." I swallow hard. "She shot my father. And my father didn't make it." My voice cracks. I did not have a good relationship with my father, but he was still my father.

"I'm so sorry for what you've been through, and I under-stand why you've made the decisions that you have."

"Thank you."

"Is there any support I can offer you? You were caught in the crosshairs of warfare, it seems."

I shake my head. "Thank you, but no. When my mother arrives, we will decide how to proceed from here." There will be a funeral mass. A shift in leadership. Me figuring out where I go and what I do.

Morozov looks sorrowful. "Vera, I'm not going to press you to make another decision now, but I would like you to think of one thing. As I said, don't answer me now. But after all this settles, if you decide to go back to America, I understand. However, I'd like to invite you to be my partner in our next adventure. We are going to have to dissolve the studies program here at the college, but if the two of us pool our resources, I'm confident that we could make incredible strides."

I'm being asked to partner with Morozov? Even though my heart is heavy, I still need to stifle a squeal. "I will think about it, "I say as politely as I can.

I wish Markov was here. I wish Markov was. . . Markov. I wish I could tell him.

I need to see if he's alright.

CHAPTER TWENTY-FIVE

Nikko

THE IVANOVS KEEP me in a holding cell. It's not the most comfortable situation I've been in, but I expected worse after my confession. I wake to find the Ivanov captain sitting across from me.

"Even though you're on trial for treason, we have our reasons for what we've done. You've only suffered superficial wounds, and I will instruct them to give you pain relievers. It's time to go to your trial."

My head is pounding as I rise, but I'm alive.

I'm alive.

"Is Vera alright?" is all I ask.

He nods. "She spent the night safe in a hotel room, protected by my best men. Her mother is arriving today."

I exhale.

I'm led to what looks like a large study. It's an intimate setting for a trial, but it seems fitting. When I arrive, I see Vera and her mother. I hold her gaze. I want to tell her I love her. I want to ask her if she's okay. I want to tell her I'm proud of her and how well she handled everything.

"Nikko Romanov, you stand trial for treason against the Ivanov family. Your case is a complicated one, and we will give you an opportunity to speak," the Ivanov captain begins. "First, the crimes against you."

They read everything in Russian. When I look over to Vera, I expect to see a look of betrayal in her eyes, but she looks terrified. Frozen in place. I want to tell her that everything will be okay.

But when they ask her to speak, she's nothing but intelligent and graceful, the woman that I have fallen head over heels in love with.

She stands. "As one of the heirs to the Ivanov throne, I am grateful for an opportunity to speak. I will speak in English. Do you need a translator?"

The captain shakes his head.

"EXCELLENT. Then from here on out, we will proceed in English."

My heart swells with pride..

"I appreciate that you're giving Nikko Romanov a trial. Before I give my side of the story, I want him to tell us all what his intentions were." She holds my gaze across the study, her voice never wavering. "I want to hear the truth straight from him."

I nod and push past any discomfort I feel in my body and heart. I love this woman, and I want to save her more than I want to save my own life.

"As you know, my name is Nikko Romanov. I pretended to be Vera Ivanova's bodyguard. I never hurt her. Not once." I look her in her eyes. Something flickers. It may be the only thing I say today that isn't the complete truth. I know my lies hurt her and made her feel betrayed, even if I kept her physically safe.

"I kept her safe during several tense situations. We likely know that the attacks were orchestrated by Irina herself, who wanted Vera out of the picture. I did not know about Irina. I did not know that she was the one who called the hits on my family. All I knew was that I would keep my promise to my family."

I stare across the room at her. She holds my gaze unblinking. "During my time with Vera, I fell in love. I love Vera Ivanova with all my heart, and I know that that may be a crime to you, but in my defense, I would absolutely lay down my life for her."

Her mother's jaw drops, and she stares at me. Vera's eyes water.

"That is all I have to say. Nothing but the truth."

Vera doesn't speak as the men talk amongst themselves until she finally interrupts. "I said *English*."

They sit up straighter, and one of them nods. "We were

only saying that what he told us corroborates what we've found out about him."

Vera clears her throat. "My mother arrived here an hour ago, and we've only been able to speak briefly with one another. She reminded me of something that I will bring to your attention. Here's a clearer version:

"Our family believes that honoring the wishes of a dying leader is a sacred duty, bringing good fortune. Though superstitions aren't everything, fulfilling this duty remains paramount."The leader nods, listening to her. I hold my breath.

"My father's death creates a void in the leadership of Ivanov Bratva that will only be filled by a solid connection to another powerful group. With your leader gone and potential instability looming, the Romanov skills and connections may be too valuable a resource to lose. It is my opinion that our family's best interest is to ally with them." She swallows. "Through my marriage to Nikko Romanov."

They could take me away now and execute me, and I'd die a happy man. In the short time I got to know her, my world was made brighter. More vivid. She is my everything.

Zofia Ivanov stands. "And on that note, I have something to say." All eyes go to Vera's mother. She stands with grace and holds her head high, much like my own mother back at home.

My heart aches to go home. To be reunited with my family.

Zofia clears her throat. "This family is ruled by hierarchy—it always has and it always will be. Killing Nikko Romanov will ensure war with our family and theirs. Instead of further blood-shed, I urge you to make the decision that will ensure our family is *strengthened.*" She bows her head. "That is all I have to say."

She sits back down. Vera leans over and hugs her.

I sit stoically as the high-ranking members of the Ivanov Bratva discuss my future. I prepare myself mentally for the possibility of execution and remind myself of the words of Marcus Aurelius that Kolya, my family mentor, drilled into us at a young age. *"You could leave life right now. Let that determine what you do and say and think."*

Kolya told us we should wake every day knowing it could be our last.

I draw in a breath and ask myself. . . could I live with the choices that I've made if this were my last day on earth?

Yes. Yes, I could. I did all that I've done out of love and loyalty to my family, and in the course of doing so, I fell in love with a woman I'm prepared to die for. I will not plead for my life. I will not beg for mercy. I will not apologize for who I am.

After a few minutes of discussion, the Ivanov leadership reconvenes.

"We will consider sparing your life, Romanov, but our mercy comes at a steep price. You will personally oversee the negotiations for this alliance between our families. Fail to secure a treaty that benefits both the Ivanov and Romanov families, and it won't just be your life at stake. We will retaliate against everyone you hold dear."

I hold my breath, the gravity of the threat weighing heavily.

I've been granted an opportunity I won't take lightly. I clench my fists. "I accept," I reply. "I will not fail you."

He nods. "I will not speak poorly of my deceased leader, but I will say this. You have the potential to lead our family to much greater strength here in Moscow. We would never defy the wishes of a dying leader. Doing so would bring curses upon our family. We acquit you of all charges with the knowledge that you will bring our family the strength and solidification of allies and resources that will make joining you worthwhile. Are we in agreement?"

We shake hands.

"Agreed."

The leader nods to Vera. "With your permission, we would like to expedite this as soon as possible."

CHAPTER TWENTY-SIX

Vera

THE NEXT TWENTY-FOUR hours pass in a whirlwind.

I'm so thankful that my mother's with me.

I want to be alone with Nikko as we have so much to talk about and so much to share.

I want to tell him I forgive him. I want to tell him I love him.

His testimony at that trial. . . And the results.

I don't know how a woman like me, who has a higher level of education, can't wrap her brain around the simplest of things. But I can't quite comprehend the fact that we're getting *married*. I never imagined that I would end up in an arranged marriage. But also. . . engaged to the man I love.

Is he really the man that I love? *Yes.* Yes, my God, I love Markov. . . No. *Nikko.* I don't care what his name is or who his family is; I love this fierce, strong, selfless man who would lay down his life for me.

"Are you okay?" my mother says in my ear. Nikko's mother, Ekaterina Romanov, has set us up in a beautiful guest room on her estate. We only just arrived an hour ago, and while I'm tired from travel, I'm energized with what will happen in the days ahead. I am eager to put all of this behind us. Eager to be united to Nikko without false pretenses.

The insistence of leaders that we get married soon worked well for me because it meant I could leave Moscow. Professor Morozov and I will resume our studies together, away from the college that's riddled with memories. But we won't begin for another month, which means I get to spend time in America.

"I'm so glad you're with me," I tell my mother. "Mom, there's been so much. . ." My voice catches. I will not cry. Not when I have to be the strong daughter of the Ivanovs. There are only us women now.

"The family will take good care of you," my mom says, squeezing my hand. She's right. So far, we've only met two of the Romanovs: Ekaterina, the Romanov matriarch, and her beautiful, blonde daughter, Polina, Nikko's sister. She was the one who got stuck in the tree, I know it. Those late-night stories we shared with each other were real. I know that now, too.

I don't have a way to get in touch with him, but I know he's coming soon.

My mother and I are just about finished getting ready when there's a knock at the door. "Come in," my mother says.

A woman stands at the door. She's beautiful with light brown hair that hangs all the way down her back in gentle beach waves, bright brown eyes, and a few freckles across her upturned nose.

"My name is Harper," she says brightly. "I'm married to Aleksandr Romanov, Nikko's older brother. I came here to speak with you if I could?"

I stand and shake her hand.

"I'm Vera."

"So nice to meet you. You'll get to know everyone soon. We have a large family, and now that some of us are having children, it's only getting bigger," she says with a little laugh. "My marriage to Aleksandr was also arranged. I know that our circumstances are very different, but I wanted to let you know that I know what it's like to be in this position. And I know Nikko well. He'll take good care of you."

I nod. While I appreciate the sentiment, I don't need her to tell me that.

"I'm here so I can offer to help get ready for the wedding, if that's okay with you? I'm good at hair and makeup and things like that."

I nod. "Yes, please. I would love that. I'm not a super fancy person. I just want something simple? I don't even know if we have time. . ."

She waves her hand in the air. "We have connections. We're friends with the Rossi family, and their sisters own a boutique. We can get you anything you want, and there's plenty of time. I mean, you definitely have more time than I did."

I remember Nikko talking about the women in his family. I think a lot of what he told me actually was based on his family.

"Wait, I heard about you guys. Aria is the cyber hacker, his sister is a nurse, and that means that you must be. . . like really skilled with a gun?"

She grins. "That's me."

"Wow," I breathe. "And you just so happen to also know about makeup and look like you just stepped out of a magazine?"

"Okay, now! I love you, and we just met," she says. "Now let's take a look at this catalog I brought and pick out a nice expensive dress!"

We're all laughing now. There's another knock at the door, and Polina enters. She's tall and willowy with beautiful blonde hair that's almost white, and bright blue eyes that shine like stars in the night sky. It's interesting to me that the Romanovs don't really look like each other, but they're a tight group. I can tell. I'm curious to see what Nikko is like with them.

"Polina, I have a question for you," I say, biting my lip.

"Yes?" she says, smiling. "Oh, is that a bridal catalog? My favorite!" She gets excited like a little kid when she picks up the glossy pages.

"Was there a time when you were little and you climbed a tree and Nikko found you?"

"Oh my God, I can't believe he told you that story," she

exclaims. "Though his reaction to that did solidify him as my favorite brother. Did he tell you about me?"

I smile. "Not that much. But that was a funny story."

We flip through the bridal magazine, and I select the simplest yet most beautiful gown. It's sleeveless and made of lace but still modest. I don't want something overly sexy. The last time I wore something like that, things ended disastrously.

I chose a simple veil, as I suspect I'll need it for the Russian Orthodox traditions that include wearing a gold crown at one point.

After we finalize wedding details, we go downstairs and join the rest of the family. I look around and there's still no Nikko. My heart sinks.

"Your home is beautiful," my mother says to Ekaterina. Like my mother, Ekaterina Romanov has silver hair and holds herself regally, like a queen, with laugh lines around her eyes and a warm, beautiful smile. She hugs me warmly and says in my ear, "I'm so sorry about the circumstances that brought you here, but I couldn't be more thrilled to have another daughter. Welcome, Vera. I've heard so much about you, and I can't wait to learn more." She kisses both my cheeks, and I blink back tears. It feels like my emotions have been on edge for the past forty-eight hours, and I can hardly contain myself. Everything feels magnified by a thousand.

"Thank you," I tell her. "While I wouldn't have chosen this, I'm going to make the most of it. And I have to say, your son took very, very good care of me—even if he was pretending to be someone else."

"I would expect nothing less from him," she says. "He is loyal to the absolute core." Then, with a twinkle in her eye, she adds, "Speaking of my son, I hear he's about to arrive. My sons have decided to enact some of our old Russian traditions for old times' sake. This is the first time in our family, you see, that a Russian is marrying another Russian."

Oh, that's right. Aria is American, and Harper is Italian-American, from what I've heard. This is the first time we have two Russian families, which means we have to pull out all the Russian tradition stops in superstition. "Now, maybe some brief introductions?" I look around at all of the people. I am so overwhelmed, but I try to remember what Harper said.

"Mom, we don't have time," Polina says. "Nikko's at the door and we're about to demand his ransom. He's locked out."

My mother squeezes my hand and smiles. "Oh God, that brings back so many fun memories," she says.

He's here.

Right outside the door.

My heart beats faster. I swallow the lump in my throat and hold my head high.

Russian tradition says that the groom has to pay a ransom, but in many cases, the ransom is completely different from what you'd expect. Something other than money or payment in order to gain access to his wife. And this all takes place before the wedding.

What will they demand from him?

Another knock sounds at the door, louder than the first.

If I'm to believe what they say... that's my future husband.

My heart leaps in my throat, my pulse erratic and racing. I have missed him so much. I feel I can hardly breathe from the need to feel his strong arms around me again. To feel his hands in mine. To hear his deep, reassuring voice once more. We've been through so much...

I look around quickly to see who's here.

The only woman I haven't met yet is Aria. She has glasses perched on the edge of her nose and wild hair tucked into a bun at the nape of her neck, but some strands have escaped, curling around her face. She gives me a wink and stands by a man with golden skin who holds himself with authority. I'm assuming he's her husband, Mikhail, the head of the family.

"Is that Nikko Romanov on the other side of the door?" Polina asks loudly to be heard through the doorway.

"It is," he growls. Polina giggles.

"This is the first time in our generation a Russian is marrying a Russian, Nikko Romanov. Therefore, you must uphold all the Russian traditions."

"Jesus," we hear him curse on the other side of the door. Laughter ripples through the room.

"First, we demand a ransom. You've spent time with your future wife, a luxury many of us haven't had. To earn your way in, you must answer our questions."

"Well?" he responds.

Polina crosses her arms and winks at me. "How does she take her coffee?"

"Two creams, two sugars, no flavors. Hot and strong," he replies.

"Hot, dark, and sweet, just like her men," my mom whispers in my ear.

"Mom!" I say, my cheeks flushing with embarrassment.

Polina glances at me for confirmation. I give her two thumbs up, feeling the heat on my face. "Ding, ding, ding!" she says. "First ransom paid. Now for the second question. What can you tell me about her hopes and dreams? Be specific, Mr. Romanov."

"She dreams of working alongside Professor Morozov in Moscow. She wants to bring affordable healthcare to the masses, with a focus on medical science. She'd like to have four children, two dogs, and a home close enough to the city for easy shopping but far enough away to avoid traffic noise. She wants a front porch that overlooks the sunset."

Even though we haven't known each other for long, he has been remarkably attentive. In this brief period, we've shared moments of profound intimacy and unveiled our deepest secrets. I found myself compelled to trust him, thrust into a situation where I had no other option, and he rose to the occasion with unwavering support and understanding.

As he speaks, my vision blurs with unshed tears, a testament to the emotions swirling within me. The room around us seems to have fallen into a hushed silence, every eye fixed on this moment, amplifying the weight of his words. I swallow hard, attempting to ease the knot tightening in my throat, but the effort feels futile against the overwhelming surge of feelings.

I draw in a deep breath, hoping to steady myself, as he continues to speak, his voice a steady anchor in the emotional storm brewing around us.

"She's a speed reader; she reads at least five times as fast as me but types so slowly because she uses just her index fingers. She has to dictate her thoughts because her mind races. She devours romance novels between reading academic literature as a form of stress relief. Last year, she read over two hundred romance books and is on track to break that record this year."

Murmurs of approval and surprise spread through the room. I shrug. "Accurate," I say. "Very accurate."

"Her love languages are acts of service and words of affirmation. She loves it when people do things for her but needs a bit of praise now and then. She enjoys Diet Coke but hates onions. Her comfort food is grilled cheese. She did fine in Russia, but she'd give anything for sourdough bread and American cheese."

I nod. "Also accurate."

"She's close with her mother, who is her best friend," he continues. "She gets up early but stays up too late because she's always reading and doesn't get enough sleep. She can't hold her liquor, and she loses herself in her studies. She needs someone to remind her to rest, eat, and take care of herself."

Polina looks at me, her eyes shining. "How did he do?"

I dab my eyes, hoping they don't notice that he's brought me to tears. Nikko Romanov loves me. And he knows me. He's going to give me all those things: the love languages, the grilled cheese, the home with kids and dogs and sunsets.

"I think he's more than paid his ransom," I say with a grin. "Can you let him in?"

They open the door, and he's standing there, silhouetted against a sunset. My tall, serious man.

He looks at me like I'm the only person on the planet, with that intense gaze that makes everything else fade away.

He crosses the room to me, rests his hand on the side of my face, bends down, and kisses me in front of everyone.

The salt of my tears mingles with our kiss. The tightness in my chest loosens, and I feel like I can breathe again.

Life is complex. We make decisions that we don't always have to justify. And sometimes, we make decisions that look like they are so wrong. But this—this is what love is. Forgiveness in the face of failing. Willingness to pick up the pieces. Understanding each other. Effort to come back together.

"Well done, son," Ekaterina says. And I'm not sure if she's praising him for answering all the questions correctly, for doing his job well, or maybe all of the above. He releases me and turns to her. "You've met my future wife?"

She nods.

He holds me to him and kisses my forehead. "Then you have met my world."

CHAPTER TWENTY-SEVEN

Nikko

WE SIT NEXT to each other in the grand ballroom that my mother has decorated. She's pulled out all the stops, but she had to. The setting must reflect the power and wealth of the Romanov family as we unite with the Ivanovs. A rehearsal dinner is an American tradition, but we are in America, and this is our chance for the families to meet, the night before the wedding.

"Have you met everyone?" I ask Vera. My future wife. I haven't let her go since we've reunited.

Vera shakes her head. "I've met Polina, Katerina, and Harper," she says, smiling. "I assume that's Aria because she's the only other woman I haven't met, and I've heard so much about her," she says with a smile, pointing in fact to Aria. "The man next to her must be Mikhail, and let's see. . . You've mentioned your brothers, but you need to introduce me to them."

"Ollie's the one with the green eyes and leather jacket, sitting apart from everyone. I'll be working with him as the liaison between the Ivanovs and Romanovs. He specializes in international relations. My other brothers. . ." I jerk my head toward the other side of the table, where my other brothers sit.

"That's Viktor." Viktor, a hulking, muscular man with a shaved head and a scar running down one cheek, lifts a hand. He gives Vera one of his rare smiles.

"Harper's husband is Aleksandr." I point to Aleks – a tall, well-built man with bright blue eyes.

"And Mikhail, our fearless leader," I say, gesturing to the man with the golden skin and decided air of authority. "The *Pakhan* of the Romanov brotherhood."

"Finally, our youngest brother Lev." Lev, the one who was hurt and almost died at the hands of the Ivanovs. He has a well-defined, athletic build, short dark hair, and deep blue eyes. Lev keeps to himself, likely not as keen to join forces with the men who hurt him. I can't blame him.

"You'll meet my mentor, Kolya, soon. He couldn't join us today. And the children are around here somewhere," I finish. I've missed them.

The wine flows, and food is passed around, but there's a subtle tension in the room. My mother and Zofia are getting along fine, but Mikhail sits brooding, watching everything, as it's his job as the patriarch of the family to keep everything in order. Finally, at the end of the meal, he speaks up.

"I'd like a word, please," he says. "There are a few who don't know me. I speak frankly, and everything I'm about to say is for the benefit of both families. We can't pretend certain events haven't happened, but we need to ensure we're all on the same page."

Vera's mother nods.

"If you'd like, you can record this or conference them in."

"It's too late for that," her mother replies, "but thank you. May I record you?"

Mikhail agrees.

Everyone is on their best behavior, but we still need to address the underlying tension.

Mikhail begins. "We all know that Nikko was on a mission. He was directed to go by me. I had him pretend to be Markov for a good reason. We learned that the late Petr Ivanov had called for the execution of Harper Bianchi— Harper Romanov—and nearly killed my pregnant wife in the process."

My mother pales.

"Furthermore, under more of his orders, my younger brother Lev was attacked and almost killed."

Everyone sits in silence as Mikhail speaks.

"We must address the alliance we're forming tomorrow, the need to solidify ranks, and the reality that our combined forces will be powerful. But justice must be served. We know that Nikko was ready to lay down his life. While we'd like to think we're beyond an eye-for-an-eye mentality, that's not always the case."

I speak up. "We clarified with Petr Ivanov before his untimely death that the attacks against us were not his orders."

"I understand," her mother says. "But it was our family who attacked you. And I've already thought this through." Vera looks at her in surprise, not quite as in tune with politics as her mother. "We're willing and able to discuss how our families will make amends for all that has happened."

Mikhail pauses for a moment, sitting up straighter. "Then Nikko, I will depend on you to report back. It's essential to have a working relationship with the Ivanov hierarchy. Am I clear?"

"Yes, sir. Of course."

"Excellent." Mikhail sits down. "Let's eat."

Neither Vera nor I are very hungry. We've been apart and need time alone. Though it's Russian tradition for a bride and groom to spend the night apart, I'm going to insist on seeing my future wife alone.

"Take a walk with me, Vera?"

CHAPTER TWENTY-EIGHT

Vera

WE WALK hand in hand outside the family home, the skyline casting a faint pink glow on falling dusk around us. Nikko walks at my side so that he's between me and the street. Just like he did in Moscow.

"Vera," he begins at the same time I say, "Nikko?"

It feels strange saying his real name, but a part of me rejoices. We need to start over. To begin again. What better than with a new name, a new location, a new family?

My heart is in my throat when he turns to me, and I see the toll this has all taken on him. The lines around his mouth and eyes and the weight on his shoulders make him look tired and belabored. I want to smooth out those lines. Sit on his lap and tell him I still love him. That I understand. He was torn between loyalty and honor and chose what he thought best. But I don't tell him any of that.

When I open my mouth to speak. . . he kisses me.

My eyes flutter closed at the feel of his mouth on mine. I sigh, allowing myself to finally actually *breathe.*

My breath catches when he tangles his fingers in my hair. I sigh and melt into him, into the warmth of his embrace and his claiming mouth on mine. I moan when his tongue licks mine. I move closer. The next thing I know, his hands are under my ass, my legs are wrapped around him, and he's carrying us to a wrought-iron bench beside a leafy bush.

Sitting down, he positions me to straddle his lap and pulls back slightly. Our foreheads touch. His voice cracks when he begs for forgiveness. "Vera, please. I want to tell you I'm sorry. I am so, so sorry for lying to you."

"You thought my family was responsible for attacking yours, and to a degree, you were right. You have a sworn duty and loyalty to your family. And while you had a plan. . . you didn't act on it, Mar—" He isn't Markov. That's gonna take some time.

"I never thought I would be able to forgive someone for lying to me, but. . . you took a bullet for me. And by most standards, I'd think. . . I—" My voice gets all choked up. For some reason, just being this close to him and seeing the earnest expression in his eyes brings everything to the surface. Everything. My father's gone. Irina betrayed us. Markov isn't Markov. We're going to be married tomorrow. I open my mouth to speak, but I can't. I'm choking on emotions in a way I didn't even with my mother, my best friend.

"Nikko. . . " I whisper. "Nikko Romanov." It feels right saying his real name. When I blink, a fat tear rolls down my cheek. I need to release these pent-up feelings before I explode.

I watch his Adam's apple bob up and down when he swallows, his own emotions choking him. "Yes. And I promise you, Vera. I meant every word I said about how much I love you. I meant every word I said about wanting to protect you. And now that we'll be married, those circumstances are behind us. My love, there will never be so much as the glimmer of a lie between us again."

When he cups my face in his hands in that familiar, possessive way of his, he captures my gaze. In that moment, the world dissolves around us, leaving nothing but the space we occupy. It's just us, and in this fleeting instant, that's all that matters.

Us.

"I love you, Vera," he says, his voice thick with emotion, resonating with the depth of his feelings. "I love you more than anyone in the world. And tomorrow, it will be my honor to proclaim my vows to you."

Tears burn in my eyes, hot and relentless, as I respond, "And I love you, endlessly." My voice breaks. "Tomorrow, we start anew. We're not just continuing where we left off, but forging our way forward. We'll do this because we owe it to our families. And we owe it to *us*."

He kisses me again, with a passion so fierce it steals my breath. Each touch reignites the fire within me, a fire only he has the power to kindle.

"Jesus," he mutters, shaking his head when we finally break the kiss. "I will not make love to you the night before our wedding. We have to save ourselves for the big day." His voice becomes a growl. "But you're not making it any easier for me."

I kiss him again, teasingly, this time smiling when he pinches my ass to punish me for being so sassy.

"I suppose I deserved that," he groans, adjusting himself beneath me.

I rest my head on his chest and feel his strong arms around me.

"You pretended to only speak Russian to keep your distance, didn't you?"

"Mmm."

"And that didn't work. So then you pretended to be my bodyguard, but even that wasn't a very good ruse because you did, indeed, function as my bodyguard."

"Yes."

"And *then* you pretended to be my husband. . ."

"Which also didn't work because I could not pretend to be something of such great significance without actually embracing the role."

Of course he couldn't. It would contradict everything in him.

We sit in the quiet for long moments, half shrouded in bushes that flank the walk with vibrant green, the evening sky darkening with every second that passes. Clouds pass by overhead, gray wisps barely visible in the dark blue of an evening sky. The scent of roses in full bloom, late summer's farewell, linger in the air, a gentle breeze stirring the petals around us. Amidst the fading sun and chirping crickets, I grant forgiveness. It seems fitting to be in a garden, a place that promises new life.

"I didn't want you to say that you loved me, even though I already knew I loved you. I feared you'd be hurt even worse than I knew you were going to be. I couldn't bear the thought of anything hurting you anymore."

I nod against his chest. "I know that now. I know. It hurt at first, but we couldn't state our love for one another when we were still so tied to those lies."

"Yes. But I don't ever want you to doubt my love for you."

"If ever I do," I say with a smile. "I'll remember the way you threw your whole body in front of me. Instinctively. As if it were the only option."

He smiles sadly.

"I love roses," I whisper, as our fingers entwine. "They're so classy and sturdy. They have a timeless beauty and are rich in meaning. I love that they're around your family estate."

"Our friends planted them years ago. My mother loved them for similar reasons."

"I love your mother, too," I whisper, earning me a fervent kiss on my forehead.

"She doesn't know you yet, but when she does, she will love you, too."

I look at our hands touching: his, bigger and rougher and etched with ink, and mine paler, smaller, with a few ink stains from a recent run-in with a defiant pen during a lab.

"It's bad luck for us to make love before our wedding night," he repeats seriously. It seems he adheres to Russian traditions more than I do but at the same time, I want to respect that. "You will stay with your mother, as is tradition, and I will stay with my brothers. And tomorrow, my love? Tomorrow, Vera, we wed."

CHAPTER TWENTY-NINE

"ALRIGHT," Polina says. She stands in front of me in a pale pink dress that somehow magnifies the brilliant blue of her eyes. "Let's see how I did."

I turn around to face the mirror and my mother. Mom covers her mouth with her hand and stares.

"Vera," she breathes. "You look like you should've modeled for one of those magazines yourself."

I blush and stare at my reflection. Harper, adjusting the flowers in my hair, smiles brightly. "I definitely understood the assignment," she says cheerfully in a singsong voice. "Didn't I? Thank you, thank you very much. She can do more than shoot a pretty gun, eh?"

Polina grins. "I helped, girlfriend. It wasn't all on you."

Harper rolls her eyes. "I did her hair and makeup! But yes, you got the dress, so we can go halfsies on the credit."

"Absolutely," I say with a playful smile. "You both deserve a medal."

Polina winks. "I'll take a cash bonus instead."

Harper chuckles. "Deal. Just remember that it was me who spent hours perfecting those waves."

I turn to the side as if somehow another angle will make it easier for me to understand that the beautiful woman in front of the mirror. . . is me. Gone is the wild, untamed hair I pin up in a weird bun ninety percent of the time because I can't be bothered. Gone is the pale face that never gets enough sun and the tired eyes from lack of sleep. My hair is sleek and wavy, my face bright and shining. I'm glowing. . . though that isn't all makeup.

"Yeah, girls," I say in a stunned whisper. "You did good. This dress is exactly what I wanted." Simple. Sophisticated. Elegant.

Harper nods with satisfaction. "And I can even walk in these heels," I say, looking down at the pretty satin shoes that peek out from beneath the flowing silky hem of my dress, little kitten heels Harper promised me I'd like.

"Your groom has sent you a bouquet," Aria says from the door. She grins and hands me a large bouquet of red roses.

"Now," Polina says as she hands me the flowers. "Brief refresher on Russian wedding traditions."

My mother giggles, but I groan. "You aren't going to hold him hostage again, are you?"

"No, no, he passed that part. But we do have a few superstitions, and they matter. They matter a *lot*. Okay?"

"Okay," I say with a grin. "Let's hear it."

"When you leave the house for the wedding, which will be held outside, you cannot look back. It's bad luck."

I nod. "Easy enough."

"It's raining!" my mother says excitedly. She even claps her hands.

"Oh no!" I rush to the window, but she shakes her head.

"No, no, Vera, it's good luck, I promise."

I look out the window and see it's overcast and drizzling, so it's not that bad. "During the wedding ceremony, we'll tie a knot in a handkerchief that symbolizes your marriage bond. We also have a few things we do during the reception itself that will bring good luck."

"Like breaking dishes?" I definitely heard about that some-where. I think I saw a video somewhere of a bride gleefully smashing dishes.

"Mm-hmm. Yep. Don't worry, we'll show you," Mom reas-sures me.

"Perfect." I hold my head high as we head outside. When I first got here, the only familiar face was my mother's, but I know the others now, at least a little. Aria's impish grin inspires me. Harper's lovely smile makes me feel welcome. Polina's sturdy, calming presence makes me feel like I'm one of them.

Outside, the late summer afternoon is warm and inviting. My heart beats so quickly that I feel a bit woozy. My nerves are already on edge, so the presence of all of those guards, not even bothering to hide their weapons, makes me uneasy.

My mother stands at the front beside Ekaterina. The matriarchs of our families. They look regal and graceful as always, their presence alone inspiring to me. I swallow hard and stare straight ahead, gripping the bouquet of crimson-red roses in my hands. Tall trees and blooming flowers surround us, creating a romantic and picturesque setting. The imposing home behind us smacks of regal sophistication, which honestly is fitting. Against a backdrop of lush green gardens with a hint of the golden hue of late autumn, our guests wait.

With such short notice my sister couldn't come, so I know hardly anyone. I don't really care who's here. All that I care about is Nikko, who's waiting for me at the altar, dressed in a charcoal gray suit that fits him to perfection. Even from here, I can see the broad span of his shoulders and the hard planes of his muscles, barely contained in civilized clothing. I lick my lips.

I walk to where the ceremony will take place in a designated garden area, where rows and rows of white chairs are adorned with white flowers. The Romanovs have pulled out all the stops for our Russian wedding, even on short notice. The archway that waits for me takes my breath away, overflowing with cascading flowers in shades of ivory and blush. The gentle breeze carries the scent of roses from the garden.

It's a picture-perfect day. A picture-perfect setting. And while a string quartet plays instrumental music in the background, I can't help but notice the palpable tension in the air.

Nikko and I are the lucky ones. We found love in the midst of hatred and truth in the midst of chaos.

I walk toward my future husband, waiting beneath the floral archway and surrounded by his brothers. It's only the first of two weddings between our families, but in many ways, our union forges us together. Forward.

I can't help but wonder what my father would've thought.

My mother stands ahead of me and I am prepared, proud even, to walk down the aisle alone. It feels fitting, really. I am making this choice. I am the one solidifying the link between his family and mine.

Outside, the late afternoon showers have stopped and the warm sun shines down on us. Our guests are standing when I reach Nikko. He reaches for my hands, and I don't know if it's on purpose or instinct, but he moves his body in front of mine to shield me from the crowd. "You look beautiful," he says, bending down to kiss my cheek.

"Thank you," I whisper.

Our vows pass in a blur. I hold his gaze and speak with honesty and conviction. I hear every word he says when he repeats his. The priest officiates, and Nikko's brothers are on constant alert, scanning the crowd for any trouble. As the ceremony proceeds, I notice a few subtle things—whispers among the guests and a few sidelong glances. Hints of tension in the air. Maybe not everyone's pleased with this union, but we've made our decision. I've heard of some commotion at previous ceremonies, but ours goes off without a hitch.

Nikko stands beside Viktor, the intimidating one who bears a few scars and looks as strong as an ox. His best man. Lev and Ollie stand nearby as well—Lev, the youngest, sober and a bit aloof, and Ollie, with his piercing green eyes and enigmatic presence.

I wonder which one of them will marry my sister. I grin when one of his brothers places a gold crown on his head. I take mine as well, and even though we laugh, I feel the weight of that symbolism.

Queen. King. Rulers.

Nikko holds my hand in the air like a prized fighter, and the next thing I know, I'm swept off my feet. "I present to you our newly married couple, Mr. and Mrs. Romanov!" I squeal with laughter, and he practically runs with me to the reception area just as the clouds break open again and our good luck rain pours down in buckets. He's absolutely soaked but manages to shield me from the downpour so I'm still mostly dry as we make it to the main home.

Uniformed staff stand waiting by the bar, and large round tables are filled with coordinating flowers. "So that's it," I say, grinning up at Nikko as he stares down at me. His hair is soaked, and there are large splotches of water all over his dress coat. He shrugs it off and tosses it on a chair. I let my eyes feast on his chiseled body that's been practically poured into a tailored dress shirt.

"Mmm," I say in a low whisper. I fist his tie and yank him over to me. "Tell me we can skip the ceremony, husband?"

It feels natural to call him that after pretending for all this time. It's hard to believe that he is, indeed, my husband now. I'd guess it's going to take me a while to fully embrace that.

We're soon pulled into the festivities and let them do all their traditions. We break our dishes—a strange tradition, but one we follow nonetheless. It isn't until we're picking the pieces up together, also a part of the tradition, that the symbolism of our actions really hits me.

Picking up the broken pieces, we clean up the mess. . . together.

We start again. . . together.

We tie the literal knot in a handkerchief to strengthen the marriage bond, and Mikhail presents us with a loaf of bread and salt, supposedly a symbol of hospitality and prosperity. We take a bite together to signify our willingness to break bread together.

By the time we get to tossing the bouquet and garter to the crowd, one of the only traditions familiar enough to me, I feel like I could fall asleep standing up. Just like in traditional American weddings, whoever catches it is the next to marry. Though the single women nearly push each other out of the way to catch it, the bouquet lands squarely in Viktor's large, rough hands.

He and Nikko share a look. Ekaterina's eyes go wide. Mikhail only nods.

We will see about that, then.

The celebration continues with music, dancing, and a lavish dinner featuring gourmet, traditional Russian dishes, as well as decadent American fare. Even the cake looks like it was taken out of the pages of a glossy catalog—tall, immaculately white, and decorated with shaved chocolate.

We take our first dance in the center of the room under a canopy of twinkling fairy lights. It feels. . . magical.

As the evening transitions into night, the garden is illuminated with soft lighting, creating a warm and inviting atmosphere. Though this is by no means a typical wedding, it feels. . . homey. Familiar. Comfortable. Guests begin to leave, and soon, it's mostly family and close friends who remain.

"It's time," Nikko finally says.

"Time?"

I hear a horn blare outside the large window. I turn and laugh out loud at the sight of the car elaborately decorated with ribbons and flowers, even a little plush teddy tied to the antenna and two large golden rings hanging by ribbons in the back window.

"My brothers really outdid themselves," he says with a groan. "And yes. It's time for us to head to our honeymoon. We need some time to ourselves." He reaches for my hand. "We'll have to come back here again soon, but for now, I want to take you somewhere where just the two of us can finally rest."

I smile at him and whisper in his ear, "You've never said anything sexier."

My mother approaches us. "Come and visit?"

"Of course I will," I tell her. "We'll likely only spend half our time in Russia anyway."

She smiles. "I'll take it!"

"Plus, someone has to help you get ready for Lydia's wedding."

She sighs. "Indeed."

Ekaterina kisses Nikko, then me. "Thank you," she whispers in my ear. "He loves you so."

Polina, Aria, and Harper all give me huge hugs and their cell phone numbers, and Harper hands me a bag she's packed with "all the essentials."

"I want you to tell me all about that research you're doing when you come back," Polina says. "I can't wait to hear it."

"You can count on it."

His brothers aren't quite as warm and fuzzy, but it's probably because of the possessive grip Nikko has on me. He's sort of exuding a "touch her, and I will fucking kill you" vibe to literally everyone, so it makes sense Mikhail and the rest only wave from a distance. Nikko has, after all, fought through hell and back to be where he is now.

Finally, we turn and face the darkness of the night, barely lit by the overhead twinkling of stars and the garden lighting. Hand in hand. . . our journey has only just begun.

EPILOGUE

Vera

A WEEK FLUTTERS by since the wedding—seven days as Nikko's wife, and I can hardly believe where we are, who we are.

Vera Romanov... his wife. Though I'd almost felt like his wife when we pretended, and it often even felt real, nothing could have prepared me for how it really is.

Each morning, I wake up to the soft light filtering through the curtains, casting a warm glow that seems to highlight the new ring on my finger. The simple act of waking next to Nikko, feeling the steady rhythm of his breathing, and seeing the calm on his face as he sleeps is a daily reminder of the profound change in our lives. It's both surreal and deeply comforting.

I like calling him by his real name. It brings a layer of authenticity to everything, a freshness that makes my heart swell. Here, in the rustic charm of The Cove, our days are filled with laughter, shared stories, and the casual comfort of familiarity. I grew up not far from here. This is a side of life Nikko hasn't often experienced, yet he fits in seamlessly, his usual guarded demeanor softened by the easy camaraderie and open hearts of my family.

He takes me to his home. I love it here. It's large and spacious, clean and simple, warm and comforting...like him.

It's the kind of place that honors old memories and hearkens new ones. As we mingle with his family, Nikko's hand finds mine and squeezes.

"I don't know if I ever thought this could be real. I wouldn't let myself believe it."

I lean over and kiss his cheek. "Believe it."

However, despite the joy and celebration, there's an undercurrent of something else—something reflected in the eyes of Viktor, who has taken his duties as best man from the wedding into a kind of solemn guardianship even here. He visits often, and for some reason, keeps asking me about my family, my home, and on his third visit, my sister Lydia. His large, heavy frame leans against the rough wood of the doorway, his eyes occasionally scanning the perimeter before returning to observe the festivities with reserved detachment.

I approach him.

"Viktor, are you all right?" I ask as I reach him, noting the way his posture stiffens slightly, ready to revert to his role if needed.

He gives a slight nod, his gaze flickering to meet mine before looking away. "Fine, yes."

Nikko approaches us, a drink in hand, his presence an immediate comfort. "What's going on?"

"I want to ask you about your sister Lydia. What do you know of her engagement?"

"Lydia? Oh. I don't know much about it except that it was arranged by my father. It's new, and she doesn't know her fiancé that well... when she went to boarding school, we grew apart."

"Are you concerned about the plans Mikhail has?" Nikko asks.

"Yes," Viktor confirms, his jaw tightening. "Her engagement poses issues with our alliance." The men exchange a look I don't quite comprehend.

"We'll have to discuss this," Nikko says his tone firm yet compassionate.

Viktor nods, a brief smile breaking through his usual sternness. "I know, and I'm grateful for that. One wrong move and we could unsettle more than just family dynamics."

The gravity of his words lingers between us.

Later, as the night draws to a close and the last of the guests are leaving, I stand beside Nikko, looking out at the starlit sky. The cool breeze off the ocean is refreshing, yet my thoughts are warm with the love and support of the people around us. Despite the challenges ahead, I feel a profound sense of belonging and purpose, tinged with an air of sadness for what I mourn. Vera Ivanova is no more. Vera Romanova stands in her place.

Who is she?

Hand in hand, we begin to walk along a dimly lit path that circles the perimeter of our house. Nikko squeezes my hand gently, an unspoken affirmation of the connection that pulses between us.

"Do you think it's really possible?" I ask, my voice barely above a whisper, "Everything we talked about—our future, the kids, even the dogs?"

Nikko stops, turning to face me, his eyes reflecting the moonlight. "Children aren't an option. I have to catch up to my brothers."

I laugh out loud. "Catch up? Like it's some sort of contest?"

The look he gives me is half serious, half teasing. "You don't really know my brothers yet. And yes Vera, it's all possible. If there's one thing I've learned, it's that with you, anything is possible." His tone is earnest, filled with that deep, resonant certainty that always seems to steady my more tumultuous thoughts.

I smile, leaning into him. "I want all of it, Nikko. The bustling days filled with purpose, and quiet evenings like this, just us and the world standing still."

He brushes a strand of hair from my face. "And we'll have it all. We'll build it together."

"And the porch?" I tease lightly, caught up in the beauty of our shared dreams.

"The porch will be there, overlooking the best sunsets, with space for two rocking chairs—yours and mine," he promises, a playful glint in his eye. "And a bunch of little ones."

"A *bunch*?"

He shrugs. "Four, right?"

"Sounds right." I grin.

We resume walking, our steps slow and measured. "I want our kids to grow up knowing they can be whoever they want and that we love them uncondtionally."

"And with a mom who reads them more stories than they know what to do with," Nikko adds, chuckling.

"*Every* fairy tale. And maybe I'll teach them to type with more than just their index fingers."

He grins, and my heart turns in my chest.

"What was Viktor talking about with Lydia?"

Nikko sobers. "Your marriage to me poses a problem with her affiliation with the *Ledyanoye Bratstvo*. It may be something we need to dissolve. But that is for another day."

"Ahh."

"I love you, Vera Romanova," Nikko says, his voice low and full of emotion as we make it back to our home.

"And I love you, Nikko Romanov," I reply, my heart swelling with an indescribable joy.

Hand in hand, we stand, eager and ready for whatever happens next, with the certain belief that as long as we are together, we can face anything.

THE END

PROLOGUE
Ten Years Earlier

THEY WOULD PAY and pay dearly. Every last fucking one of them.

The purr of luxury cars and the rhythmic click of heels and polished shoes mingled with the swish of neatly-pressed uniforms while Viktor maintained his distance.

Head down, dressed in nondescript, inexpensive clothing with his hands buried in his pockets, he looked like a nobody. Just like he'd planned. No one at Liberty Ridge Academy would give him a passing glance.

He glanced at his watch. Though he'd come early before his session with his mentor Kolya, time was ticking. Kolya detested tardiness and it mattered to him to show on time.

Where was she?

Sometimes she'd be cloaked in a scarf and a knee-length sweater, concealing her figure as though shielding herself from the relentless, judgmental gaze of her peers. But today, she was conspicuously absent from the usual flurry of student arrivals.

His pace slowed, and he moved away from the throng, even though most students steered clear of him. He was a giant among them, a decade their senior and twice the size of the biggest varsity football player.

Fortunately, the lack of surveillance at the school was laughable. Anyone paying attention would have noticed the imposing young man who was always there. Always watching.

"Here she comes," one of the boys announced in a snide whisper about ten feet ahead of Viktor. "The fat girl with the big tits."

Viktor clenched his fist in a surge of protective fury and made a fact: he'd deal with that fucker first.

He had only been training with Kolya for three months, but he had already begun to develop hard muscle under Kolya's tutelage. It would come in handy when he cornered that asshole in the dark alley between school and home.

Viktor's eyes narrowed as the familiar Lincoln purred to a stop at the curb. He held his breath. She was here, brought by her father. Viktor refocused his attention, his gaze icy and menacing as he contemplated knocking the boy's teeth out. He cracked his knuckles, tension rolling off him in waves.

One of the boys shot him a wary glance before nudging his friend as the car door swung open.

"Sit up straight," her father commanded from the backseat. "You represent the Ivanov family with *dignity*."

Viktor's breathing became labored. Time stood still for a moment when he saw her.

His angel.

Lydia Ivanova. The most beautiful girl he'd ever seen. The girl who lived in his dreams. The object of his utter obsession. He stroked the gold earring in his pocket and pricked his finger with the post to keep him focused.

Each tiny pain was a tether, keeping his thoughts sharp and his desire in check.

Viktor's mind was a constant whirlwind of thoughts about her: her scent, the way her eyes, a striking emerald flecked with hazel, flickered with a mix of defiance and vulnerability. He knew her every expression, every quirk. He had watched her for months, always from the shadows, always unseen.

He knew it was wrong, the way he tracked her movements, the way he collected items she had touched—like this earring, lost one summer night and now a permanent fixture in his pocket.

He was her shadow, her silent sentry, driven by a need he didn't understand, a desire so deep, it bordered on madness.

"Back off, motherfucker," he said softly under his breath when Sterling Eldridge took a step toward her. "Back the fuck *off*."

Lydia was fire, in more ways than one. He'd watched the way her eyes lit up when she set things ablaze, the joy and freedom she found in the flames. It was a part of her he loved, the dark side she showed no one.

His fingers tightened around the earring, the sharp sting grounding him.

She stood facing her classmates, a defiant spark igniting her emerald gaze as she swung one long leg out, then the other, her plaid uniform skirt grazing the top of her knees. Her glasses perched precariously on the edge of her nose. When she tossed her head, thick waves bobbing defiantly in the breeze, her chin lifted in silent challenge.

Fat girl with the big tits.

Viktor's blood boiled at the thought. She was *amazing*.

Despite her father's harsh, dismissive tone—always scolding, always belittling—she stood proud and tall. He fucking loved that about her.

But today from his vantage point under the shelter of a thick maple, he saw the sheen of tears in her eyes. A public scolding only added to the torment inflicted by her cruel classmates.

Fucking losers.

"Awww," one of the said under his breath to the other. "Is she gonna cry?"

Viktor's hand curled into a fist.

He would be victim number two.

He noted the golden Lincoln purring at the curb and narrowed his eyes before he zeroed back in on the boy with the big mouth and imagined what he'd look like missing his two front teeth. Viktor cracked his knuckles and rolled his neck. It would feel so fucking good to when his fist connected with flesh and bone.

As Lydia walked toward the school, one of the books fell from the large pile. She bent to pick it up.

"Lydia," her father muttered. "Don't be so damn clumsy."

Always scolding, always dismissive and harsh. Viktor didn't know how anyone could withstand the constant berating. Did it make her feel small and unworthy? From what he'd seen, her father was relentless.

In his eyes, Lydia was neither overweight nor clumsy — she'd developed earlier than her other classmates, all curves and voluptuous temptation, and she simply hadn't grown into her own body yet.

And who the hell were they, anyway? Who decided what her body should look like and who decided it didn't meet some set of random fucking expectations?

She was *perfect*.

Viktor stood taller and glanced at the time. He had seven and a half more minutes before he'd have to jog to get there on time.

Lydia's father frowned and sat up straighter. "I'll be here to pick you up today. We have something urgent to discuss," her father said, glancing at his watch.

"Yes, Father," she said in a clear, graceful voice. "See you then."

As the car left, she stepped forward and wobbled. A few of the boys made derisive comment. The leader winked at a tall, slender blonde girl exiting a silver Mercedes behind Lydia. They shared a look when the girl pressed her finger on her nose and wrinkled it at the girl, as if mimicking a pig. Snickers erupted all around them.

Fucking spoiled, pretentious brats. Viktor delighted in imagining how he would punish them all.

"Lydia! You okay?" A thin girl a full head shorter than Lydia sidled up beside her. Maybe he'd spare that one.

"I'm good, thanks," she said in that beautiful voice that haunted his dreams.

The first bell rang. It was time to go. If he showed up late, he'd be in deep shit. Kolya didn't warn twice.

The blonde walked in front of the boys, standing tall and flaunting her breasts. She'd left a few of the buttons on her uniform shirt undone, her meager breasts push up to flaunt. Pretending to sneeze, she made a big production of scattering tissues in Lydia's direction. Laughter erupted all round them. Lydia's pretty cheeks pinked.

Viktor's growl rumbled deep in his chest. This particular girl had been hitting at Lydia stuffing her bra for weeks now. Jealousy was an evil little bitch.

"Morning, Lydia," the girl said with fake camaraderie. "Need help?"

"No." Lydia held herself erect, not trusting the girl. She held her head high and turned away. The boys watching on and snickered.

"Fine," the girl said, shaking her head. "Not sure why you have to bring so many home anyway. Show-off," she muttered under her breath. She flicked her hair over her shoulder and turned to walk away as one of the boys, the tallest and obvious leader of the group, discreetly stuck his foot out.

Viktor risked coming out of the shadows. If he could — *fuck.*

Lydia stumbled but quickly righted herself. Her cheeks flushed, she turned on the boy.

"You fucking asshole! You did that on purpose!"

Pride surged in his chest.

Atta girl.

"Lydia!" A sharp voice came from several paces ahead where a tall woman with her hair in a merciless bun at the nape of her neck marched over to them. Snickers erupted all around them as she approached. "Come here at once."

Viktor's gaze hardened. Lydia might have stood up to him today, but it left her more vulnerable than ever to the cruelty of her classmates. His protective instinct, already fiercely attuned to her, flared. He could not stand by while she was mocked and isolated.

Stepping forward, his presence immediately silenced the group. His voice, when he spoke, was low but carried an unmistakable threat. "You find something funny? Maybe you'd like to share the joke with me."

The snickers died in their throats. Lydia, her gaze flicking briefly from the teacher heading her way to Viktor, seemed to straighten even more, her eyes meeting his with a silent thank you that said she knew, at least for today, she wasn't alone against them.

No words passed between them, only a quiet understanding before her teacher reached her.

"This is the last straw, Ms. Ivanov," the woman said severely. "But soon you'll be no bother to me. Perhaps your father will tell you of his recent decision and how it impacts your attendance here."

Lydia stared and paled. "They were—"

"I don't care what they were doing," the teacher dismissed.

Viktor kept careful note of all of them. The tall pompous football player. The stuck-up blonde. The critical teacher.

They would all pay and he would take his sweet time making it hurt.

"What are you talking about?" Lydia marched after the teacher. Her bag was slightly open, and a few papers and a slim, well-worn paperback book fell to the ground. Viktor bent and picked them up, but when he went to give them to her, she was gone.

Her classmates scattered like scared little ants.

He tucked the under his arm and headed to meet Kolya and face the consequences for being late.

He came the next day.

And the next.

And the next.

But she never returned.

CHAPTER ONE
Present Day

Viktor

"Name a price," Mikhail says. "I owe you, Viktor. It's time."

Mikhail looks at me over the fuzzy head of his sleeping son and says, "I indebted to you for everything."

I shake my head slightly, dismissing the weight of his gratitude. "You don't owe me. I did what I had to do. I did what you needed me to do. It was crucial that I take care of what's yours, because we're family, and you know that." I pop the top of a Hennessy and drink half of it in a few gulps.

I look out into the dark blue-black haze of a late September evening, the lights of the city twinkling in the distance from our vantage point in The Cove. We've had a tumultuous few months with a brief pause for our brother Nikko's wedding, but now it's time for us to continue to make our moves. We've made great strides here in The Cove and it's time we kick things up.

Since our father's death, we've been doing everything in our power to strengthen our ties and put down roots as the most powerful family in The Cove, nestled between Coney Island and Manhattan.

Every day that passes counts. Every strategic move a power play.

Mikhail's voice grows softer, more earnest. "You saved my wife's life, Viktor."

I shift in my seat, feeling the unease settle over me. "Family does for family. You'd have done the same for me," I respond, my eyes briefly meeting his before settling on the infant. "Just make sure you keep them safe. That's all I ask."

The room falls silent, the magnitude of my request left lingering. Mikhail nods, his expression solemn. "I will. And anything you need, Viktor, it's yours. You name it."

The other brothers present – Lev, and Aleksandr – listen intently to our conversation. I can sense Lev getting restless beside me, tapping his foot as if he's holding himself back from interrupting.

"You guys don't get it." Lev speaks up from the back of the office, his voice cutting through the previous chatter. Our youngest brother often keeps to himself but misses nothing. We've grown closer the past few months while my brother Nikko was stationed in Moscow.

"Leave it, Lev." I shake my head. *Jesus.*

"What are you talking about?" Aleks asks, his curiosity piqued. Head of cyber security, he prides himself on noting everything but he's been deep in the weeds researching a new development on the West Coast and hasn't looked up from his laptop.

Lev continues, his voice firm and clear. "He doesn't want money. He doesn't want *things*. Viktor doesn't want any of that. He already has his own house, he has everything he needs... well, almost everything that he needs."

The room falls into a brief silence as everyone processes Lev's insight, waiting for him to reveal what it is that I still need. I look away, my jaw tensing. He's read my fucking mind. When Mikhail offered me the proverbial Genie's lamp, I immediately knew what I would wish for when I rubbed the golden sides.

I'd only need one wish.

"Fuck," I mutter under my breath. My brothers hide nothing from each other. I won't hide this.

"Lydia Ivanova," Mikhail says quietly, almost reverently.

Silence reins for long moments before Aleksandr speaks up. "Is she available? Has anything changed?"

Lev shakes his head, "No."

Mikhail growls. "Since when does that fucking matter? You know our mantra."

Aleks's lips twist into a grim smile, his gaze hardening. "No one and nothing stands in our way."

I stand up abruptly, my voice low and resolute, "I don't need anything. I don't need any*one*. It's too risky."

Blowback from the LB, the group to which Lydia's been promised, is more powerful than we are and known for their ruthlessness. The retribution if we intervened would be swift and severe.

But before I can continue, Lev interrupts. He's smaller in

stature than I am but a force to be reckoned with. His eyes gleam with intensity, his arms crossed on his chest.

"Youv've taken your eyes off the prize, brother. You haven't seen what Ollie and Aleks have." He leans forward. "Do you have any idea what Timur Yudin plans on doing with her when they're married? What he plans to do to the Ivanovs?"

I draw in a sharp breath, willing my racing pulse to slow the way my mentor Kolya taught me to do when I was just a boy who didn't know his own strength.

It doesn't help.

"I get it," Lev presses on, his fierce gaze burning into mine. "It would fucking kill you to see a woman like her treated like property. And if you killed Yudin like you want to, the blowback to the rest of us would be brutal."

I dig my fingernails into the palms of my hands. He goes on.

"Yudin plans on sharing her with his men. He's a filthy, sick son of a bitch. He's already filmed her and shared it. He's got on in his crew that jerks off every fucking night to pictures of her on his phone."

"Where?" I growl. "Who?"

"Sit down, Viktor."

I shake my head and Aleks puts his hand on Mikhail's arm. "Let him. He'll turn into the fucking Hulk right here in front of you if you don't."

I pace, trying to let the rage bleed off me.

"He plans on decimating the Ivanovs. He's an insidious fucking snake and already made strategic moves by infiltrating their ranks and spreading misinformation to sow distrust within their leadership. By marrying into the Ivanov family, he gains access to their secrets and vulnerabilities. And unlike us," he says, pausing for emphasis. "He doesn't plan on strengthening by collaboration. He plans on decimating for his personal gain. Over time, he'll destroy them. Sabotage business deals, assassinate the Ivanov power players." He shakes his head and lowers his voice.

"You've watched Mikhail, Aleks, and now Nikko get married. We've grown in strength here in The Cove, and we all know joining forces with the Ivanovs is complicated." He shakes his head and looks to Mikhail. "Lydia Ivanovo's marriage to that self-centered prick would fragment our control as well. She'd be used and discarded" He looks to me next. "We *have* to intervene and fucking end this before their marriage."

Aleks and Mikhail share another look, an unspoken understanding passing between them as they consider Lev's words and the implications they carry.

I don't even want to think of actually...*having her*. If I let myself hope, if it doesn't happen... My mouth goes dry.

I pace in the office and shake my head. "*Fuck.*"

"Her marriage to him will bring severe consequences," Lev counters. "If we secure the hand of both Ivanov women, you know what that means for us."

I do. It means creating a foundation that decades of influence and legacy couldn't rival. It means allowing brutal devstation to our friends and family.

But it's complicated. So fucking complicated.

Mikhail holds my gaze. "Tell me what you know about Yudin."

I look away, my jaw tense. "I've stayed away."

I had to.

Watching her go anywhere near him sends my blood to boiling and my gaze grows hazy. I have to focus on protecting my family and can't risk going nuclear on a man who means nothing to me. I can't expend energy on a situation that's out of my control.

I've watched. I've watched so carefully, but from a distance. "He hasn't hurt her and that's all that matters."

Timur Yudin buys her nice things, makes sure she has a guard on her, albeit it a weaker one that I would have, and has never once raised a hand to her. I would know. If he did, I'd rip his dick off and shove it down his throat so he choked on it while I slit his throat.

"Yet," Aleks says, shaking his head. "Aria's got a file on him. We researched heavily after Nikko's marriage to Vera."

My skin prickles and I swivel my gaze to Aleks.

Aria, Mikhail's wife, is our head of cyber security and excellent at what she does. When our brother Nikko married Lydia's sister Vera Ivanova, it became necessary to zone in on whoever might pose a threat to us.

I look away, not wanting to listen to the details.

What good will it do? I'll only want to fucking torture every cell in his body before I murder him with my own bare hands. I hate him for being near her. I despise him for not being worthy of her. If I find out one goddamn detail about him—

"He's a master at orchestrating these deadly catastrophes," Aleks says, his voice icy. "He makes sure people in his stable have fatal accidents, then he swoops in and collects hidden insurance policies."

I shake my head. Fucking douchebag move, but it's not out of the ordinary to—

Aleks goes on, relentless. "He stages human trafficking. He sells women and children as if they're cattle. He's a top trader in the black market."

I clench my jaw and stare straight ahead. The fucking asshole. I'm no saint, but anyone involved in human trafficking deserves to be dealt with severely. He'll live to regret every vile action he's taken. No one harms the innocent on my watch.

And I want her. I want her so fucking bad it consumes my every thought. If I can't have her... if she ends up with that self-serving, sadistic prick —

Lev speaks up. "There's more. Don't shut this down, Viktor, and fucking listen." My gaze snaps to his. "Three months ago, his lawyer got him acquitted on accusations of ownership of child pornography, but he's guilty as fuck. He's just untouchable. Too much money and too much power."

"*Fuck,*" I growl.

Aleksandr delivers the final blow. "Aria uncovered accusations that were deeply buried. He brutally assaulted his last girlfriend. She faked her death to escape, but he found her.

When he did, he broke her jaw before she threw herself into oncoming traffic."

Bile rises in my throat with the effort of restraining myself.

"It's not a question of *if* he will hurt her, Viktor, but *when*."

"You've been tailing him?" I growl. "Where is he?"

Aleks frowns, making a few clicks on his keyboard. "Two hours north of here. Near the Mid-Hudson Bridge." He reaches for his phone without breaking eye contact with Mikhail, signaling the gravity of the decision. He dials quickly, and the room falls silent, waiting for the call to connect.

"Nikko," Aleksandr begins when the call is picked up, "we need to discuss the Ivanov situation."

Nikko, always quick on the uptake, responds, "I've been waiting for this call. Go."

Mikhail takes over, his voice firm, "It's about Lydia. We need to secure her for Viktor." He fills him in.

Nikko pauses, the gears turning as he considers the implications, especially given his ties with Lydia's sister. "Alright, I see the angle. I'll set things in motion. But remember, this isn't just about owing us; it's about aligning our families for the long term." He needs the Ivaonov's buy-in. After the death of their *Pakhan,* new leadership has taken position, and Nikko is the only one that has a working relationship with them. He'll know how to play this.

They go on to discuss the details and how they'll make it happen while my mind races with possibilities. There's a faint buzzing in the back of my mind, a combination of disbelief in what we're about to do and the need to find Timur Yudin and destroy him.

As the call ends, the atmosphere in the room shifts from tension to a more calculated focus. Mikhail looks around, ensuring everyone is on the same page. "Nikko will handle the arrangements. We need to be strategic and careful. This isn't just about acquiring what Viktor wants but about positioning ourselves favorably within the community and ensuring long-term alliances."

"And dealing with the fucking blowback from Yudin," I mutter.

Aleksandr nods in agreement, his mind already racing through potential scenarios. "We have to consider every move as part of a larger game. Lydia is the key piece. Not only does Viktor get what he desires, but her connection through marriage ties us to a powerful family, strengthening our influence."

Lev, usually the quietest, seems fueled with his need to see this happen, adds, "And we need to keep this clean. No loose ends that can come back to haunt us."

Easier said than done.

I've been silently listening but finally have to speak up, my voice low and contemplative. "Make sure Lydia is treated with respect in this process."

I'll take good care of her. Such good care of her.

My brothers nod, understanding the delicate balance of fear and favor they need to maintain. This isn't just another acquisition; this was personal, and it has to be handled with precision.

Mikhail's expression darkens as he leans forward, the lightness of our earlier considerations gone. "While we aim to manage this smoothly, understand that Lydia will likely not come willingly. We'll need to compel her."

Of course she wouldn't. She might see us, or me in particular, as a threat. She's fiercely independent and resists being controlled or used in any of her family's political moves or machinations. Being forced to marry me after her engagement to Morozov will likely piss her off. Who knows what she thinks about me? Given what I know about her, she doesn't easily trust and almost never lets her guard down.

This won't be easy.

Aleks smiles. "You know... we can align this necessity with an old Russian prophecy known to both our families, which we can use to our advantage."

Aleksandr, intrigued, raises an eyebrow. "A prophecy? Explain."

Mikhail nods, a grim smile touching his lips. "Yes, the prophecy known to families that hail from Moscow speaks of a 'Scourge'—a great turmoil that one family will endure, only to be saved by an alliance through marriage. It's vague enough to instill fear and acceptance. It's believed that rejecting the prophesied union will bring disaster, and embracing it will restore balance and prosperity."

I shake my head. "That's ridiculous. We're all too pragmatic to believe in old prophesies. No. If I'm going to have Lydia —" I pause and get my shit together before I continue. "I want it out in the open. I want to solidify our alliance with the Ivanov family like Nikko did, and for the same reason." I shake my head. "She can't go to that monster."

I'll do way more than fuck him over.

I dislike manipulation and typically prefer brute force. But this situation requires a delicate touch. "I want the Ivanovs to believe that aligning with us is not only inevitable but beneficial."

I shake my head, still disbelieving that this could work, that Lydia... could be mine.

"And if it doesn't work?" I try to keep my tone light, pretending that what hangs in the balance could make or literally fucking break me. I fail. My voice cracks.

"It will work," Mikhail says. "I promise you."

When I finally leave Mikhail's office, I'm weary but energized.

Lydia Ivanova.

I drive to my home, an apartment in a high-rise on the Manhattan border. I walk up the brick steps on autopilot, barely noticing where I'm going or what I'm doing.

Nikita, my large, muscular Tibetan Mastiff, meets me at the door. I scratch her ears. "Give me five," I tell her. I need a minute before we go for a walk. I take the stairs to my bedroom two at a time and walk straight to the closet hidden deep in the back of my bedroom.

I slip the key into the lock. The door creaks open on its hinges. I give myself a moment to lean against the worn wood and take in a deep breath before I let my gaze roam over every damn piece I've collected.

A nearly empty bottle of *Opulence* I lifted from her locker at the gym a year ago. A lipstick-stained napkin I confiscated at a coffee shop where she met her mother a few months ago. A torn page from a notebook she carries with the simplest of shopping lists on it. A disposable, empty coffee cup with her name scribbled on the side in permanent marker. A ticket stub from a concert she snuck into when she was still a teen here in America. Her photograph from her senior year in high school and a more recent one I found online and had made into a print. Her copy of *Wuthering Heights* she left behind all those years ago that I've read so many times the pages are falling apart.

Lydia's shrine.

I lift the bottle. The heady, intense fragrance is her signature scent. I lift it and give myself the luxury of a deep, cleansing breath of it. Just smelling it conjures up the mental image I have of her.

I let myself linger through the shrine. I finger the napkin and press it to my lips. I read her shopping list and recite it from memory.

Chocolate

Coffee

Oranges

Something for dinner

I run my thumb along the edge of the coffee cup, where I imagine her lips graced. I place them all back own with reverence and stare at the picture of her as a teen and compare it with the way she looks now.

She's only grown more beautiful, more exquisite, more sensual with time. Curvy and lush, she's imposing yet graceful. Her long, dark hair cascades over should in waves, her eyes expressive and intense. She favors flowing tops and dresses that accentuate her curves.

Lydia.

With a sigh, I place everything back with precision, shut the door, and lock it behind me. I stifle a yelp when I almost trample Nikita beneath my feet.

"Jesus," I mutter, my heart hammering in my chest. "You should give me some notice you're there. *God.*"

I look at the locked door with a frown. I turn around and face the bedroom. It's hard to even believe, but if this works... if Mikhail actually pulls it off and Lydia becomes mine... I might need a bit of a feminine touch to this room.

And fucking safety meaures put in place.

I snap on Nikita's leash and head out to take her for a walk when my phone rings.

"We spoke with Zofia." Zofia Ivanova, my sister-in-law Vera and Lydia's mother, is the Ivanov family matriarch in the wake of her husband's death. She and my brother Nikko are the ones that make all major decisions.

"And?" My heart smashes against my rib cage, my mouth instantly dry.

My phone rings with a call from my brother Nikko as I get out at the entrance to my home a few miles from the Romanov family headquarters.

"Yeah?"

"Her mother's amenable to the idea but I need more time. I'm working on it. Let's assume this is a go and work accordingly."

I swallow hard.

"Alright. Thanks."

"But you know we need to destroy Yudin, Viktor. You know what he'll do in retaliation. We can't leave a single shred of him behind."

I nod. "Consider it done."

CHAPTER TWO

Lydia

I fiddle with my engagement ring, spinning it around on my finger, and stare. Diamonds inlaid in yellow gold, they sparkle under the overhead lights. I know they must've cost a fortune. Timur Yudin, a man of high tastes and a high-ranking captain of the *Ledyanoye Bratstvo*, doesn't do cheap.

My belly churns with nerves as I wait for him. The guard he's stationed by me stand scrolling through their phones as I sit at a quiet table by myself. Timur said he'd be here any minute, and instructed me to go and wait for him. He seemed a bit guarded but that's not unlike him after a busy day of work.

I pick up my phone and pretend to make a call, then surreptitiously put my phone camera on so I can look myself over to make sure I'm flawless. Timur doesn't like anything less that perfection.

I'm wearing a soft green dress that highlights my curves and emphasizes the green in my eyes. My make-up's flawless, not a hair out of place.

I finish checking myself over, and when satisfied, put my phone back down. When he arrives, he won't like it if I'm on my phone. I'm expected to pay attention to him.

The flicker of the candle on the table gets my attention. I'm drawn to the orange flame behind frosted glass. I reach out and run the tip of my polished fingernail around the base of the candle. I pause and note a drip of wax.

My heart races.

It's not one of those fake electric candles, but real fire. If I took the edge of this tablecloth and touched the flame, I know exactly what would happen. First, it would smoke—

I close my eyes and draw my hand back as if it the glass itself scalded me. I hate that my mind goes there when I'm stressed or under pressure.

No.

I worked too hard and too long to go back there now. I can't.

I won't.

I can still hear my mother's tearful plea while my father slammed my suitcases into the back of the car that took me to boarding school. *"Why, Lydia? Why did you do it?"*

I heard the questions she didn't ask as clearly as I heard the ones she did.

Where did I go wrong?

I take another sip of wine, aware that I've liked only traded one vice for another, but I don't fucking care.

I take a few minutes to look around the upscale restaurant. It's difficult to get into *Le Jardin de Lumière*, but I'm excited because the name reminds me of Beauty and the Beast, my childhood favorite. Who am I kidding? It's my favorite even now in adulthood. They're booking six months out here, but Timur likes expensive, hard-to-get things, so it makes sense he would want to come here. I'd expect no less from him.

Quiet instrumental music plays in the background. The tables are set with fine china and crystal wine glasses, the utter picture of sophistication. The basket of fragrant, warm bread accompanied by slabs of homemade butter topped with crystalized truffle salt. *Delicious.*

My phone buzzes with a text. My heart leaps, thinking it might be Timur, but when I look at the screen, I sigh.

> Vera: Lydia, can you talk now?

Vera gets so caught up in her studies she doesn't talk to me for weeks at a time, and now that she has a break she wants to chat? I shoot her a quick response.

> I can't now, I'm meeting Timur for dinner, but I'll call you when we're done.

I'm still holding my phone when I hear his familiar voice behind me. I quickly tuck it in my purse.

"Lydia. Thank you for waiting so patiently." He stands tall and imposing behind me with an air of unapproachable strength. I turn to face my handsome fiancé, once more appreciating his features are sharp and defined with high cheekbones and a strong, clean-shaven jawline. Dressed impeccably in a tailored suit, he exudes confidence and sophistication, his demeanor composed but with an icy detachment that can be intimidating to those who don't know him. I know him, though. I know him well.

I stand and give him the full effect of my smile.

"Hi. How was your day?"

With a smile, he bends and kisses my cheek. My heart flutters at his nearness. Timur Yudin is all grace and refinement, a gentleman in every sense of the word. His hand rests on the small of my back for a brief second before he takes his seat. He always holds my chair out for me, so I stand a bit awkwardly before I realize he must've forgotten.

I clumsily sit in front of him.

"You're looking quite nice tonight, Mr. Yudin," I say flirtatiously. He smiles coldly when the waiter approaches.

Normally attentive and gentlemanly, his behavior takes me off guard. Timur addresses the waiter. *"Bonjour, je voudrais un verre de vin rouge et une sortie, s'il vous plaît."*

I cringe when the waiter looks confused. Timur just accidentally ordered an exit instead of an appetizer. I don't want to correct him in public, but he's made a mistake.

I quickly amend. *"Je voudrais un verre de vin rouge et une entrée, s'il vous plaît."*

The waiter bows and takes his leave. Timur levels his gaze at me with an air of coldness so sharp, I shiver.

"Do not ever do that again," he snaps.

"Do what?" I look at him in surprise.

"Correct me in public."

I laugh. "Timur, you ordered an exit instead of an appetizer. I was hardly correcting you, just making sure—"

His hand reaches out and snatches my wrist. "Are you talking back to me, too, now?"

I blink in surprise. "No."

Sometimes he reminds me of my father, and I *hate* that. Though Timur is handsome and polished and treats me well, he occasionally has a bit of a cold streak when stressed.

"What is it, Timur? You seem troubled," I say gently. I lay my hand on his. "What's going on?"

He shakes his head. "I'm guessing you haven't spoken with your mother."

I blink. "No. Why?"

He looks away, his jaw taut. "Oh, you'll see. Did you order yet?"

Why does my belly dip to my toes.

"Timur. What is it? What do you need to tell me?"

His gaze hardens. "I asked you if you ordered yet."

I shake my head. "No, I was waiting for you."

He blows out a breath. "Of course you were."

I look at him in surprise. My phone buzzes and buzzes in my purse. When Timur scowls at me, I silence it.

"What is wrong?" I ask, my anger rising. I don't like not knowing what's going on, and it seems like he's lying to me.

He only shakes his head. "It doesn't matter. Order. Something light, Lydia."

My cheeks color and I suddenly lose my appetite. We've only known each other for a few months. Not long before my father's sudden and tragic death, he arranged for our wedding. Timur has been the perfect gentleman, attentive and generous, even if a bit cold sometimes. But he's never been like this before. He's definitely never commented on my food choices.

I look down at my full figure, my bust spilling out of dress I wore to accentuate my curves.

I thought he liked my curves.

"You want me to choose something light?"

He smiles, but his eyes remain cold. "I'm teasing. Choose whatever you want. You know that." He mutters something under his breath.

What the hell?

"Timur," I say in a little voice. Who is this man and what's become of the man I'd actually grown used to and was looking forward to marrying?

The waiter comes back with a wine menu.

"I worry about you, you know," Timur says, as he butters a roll and places half of it on my plate. It's a lot less butter than I would use, and only half the bread, but the gesture seems almost sweet.

"Oh?" I take a bite even as my stomach clenches. The food tastes like ash in my mouth. "Why?"

"We're getting married soon and the weight of responsibility will fall heavily on you to manage our home, our social engagements, and eventually, our children. And the little hobbies you have aren't becoming of the wife I know you could be."

My *little hobbies?*

I drop the bread, my appetite gone. "I don't know what the fuck you're talking about," I snap.

"There you go again," he says, his eyes on me heated. "Losing your temper." He leans in and rests his chin in his hand. "I'm going to be your husband. I'm only expressing concern for you, Lydia. There's no need to lose your temper." He gives a casual shrug but his tone is anything but. "I'd hate to have to lose mine."

Was that a threat?

I stare at him, my jaw slack.

The candle flickers between us. Beckoning.

"Look," I say in a low voice so as not to draw the attention of everyone around us. "I don't know what happened to you to cause you to behave this way, but I've had a few drinks and I need to use the bathroom. I'm going to just take a little break and when I return, let's have a civilized conversation, shall we?"

It's hard to issue an ultimatum to a man that has more power in his left thumb than I do in my entire life, but I'm over this.

I stand but he grabs my wrist again, even harder than before.

"Sit *down*, Lydia." When I don't, he gentles his voice. "I'm sorry. I had a bad day at work. Sit down and tell me about your day."

He almost convinced me. There's something about that suave, persuasive voice of his that almost convinced me it was only a slip-up and my real fiancé is going to come back. But I need a little bit of a breather.

I jerk my wrist away from him, getting the attention of several people nearby.

"I'm just using the restroom," I say. "Please let me go."

He reaches for me but a waiter comes by, so to save face he plasters a smile on his face. For once I'm happy he's always more concerned with appearances than anything else. "Go. Come right back."

A crowd of women passes in front of me. I take the opportunity to step right into the middle of them and head to the bathroom before he can pull me back.

What's happened and why is he behaving this way?

I feel sick to my stomach and wish, not for the first time, I had someone to confide in. I wish my sister and I were still close, like we were when we were children, but now that she's married into the Romanov family, that's impossible. Timur has forbidden it.

I stare at my reflection in the mirror and take a deep breath.

He's obviously in a bad mood, but he's never been like this before.

I dab at my lips with lip gloss, trying to quell my rising nerves.

I reach for my phone, wishing again I could call Vera. I have no friends, and my mother and I were never close.

It doesn't matter. So he was...what, impatient? Crass? A man's entitled to the occasional bad temper, isn't he? I'm certainly not a ball of sunshine every waking hour.

Up until now, he's always treated me well.

Maybe I just have unrealistic expectations. It's a fluke. A bad night.

It will be fine. I'll go back out and my charming fiancé will order dinner for me and we'll forget this ever happened. I'm starving. Maybe I'm exaggerating things in my mind.

I tap the screen and stare at five missed calls and as many missed texts.

What the hell?

My blood runs cold.

> Vera: Lydia, you are in danger. Come home.
> I'm sending a car for you now. You have to
> leave. Please. I'll explain everything

Come home? I'm two hours away from home.

I'm in danger? I look around the spacious, luxury bathroom. It's well-lit with marble flooring that gleams under soft, ambient overhead lighting. The walls are adorned with large, oval-shaped mirrors in gilded frames. The polished countertops boast bouquets of fresh flowers. It seems too elegant, too refined, for me to be here and in... danger.

Still, I walk to the stall and open it, sliding the lock in place behind me. I open my purse and eye the lighter and pepper spray I always carry with me. I have some measure of protection, anyway.

I check the rest of my messages.

> Lydia, please call me. It's urgent

And then another text from a number I don't recognize.

> Lydia, this is Nikko Romanov, your brother-in-law. It is imperative we secure your location and bring you to safety.

What the hell is going on?

I jump when the door to the bathroom opens and I hear the click of heels on the tiled floor. I hold my breath as the footsteps approach. I reach in my bag and take out my pepper spray, my finger trembling on the trigger. But I only hear a door to a stall shut.

I'm losing my mind.

I put the pepper spray back.

I've made this into something much, much bigger than it actually is. I'm at a fancy restaurant. With the man I'm going to marry. Vera's being dramatic, or influenced by her new husband.

With trembling fingers, I text Vera back.

> Okay what is going on?

> It's too much to text and something I don't want to communicate this way. I don't know if your phone is tapped. It's important to come home so we can chat. Are you alright? Are you safe?

I blink. My phone...tapped?

I'm hiding in a bathroom stall. My fiancé is acting strange, and my phone's blowing up with cryptic messages about my safety. No, of course I'm not alright.

> I'm fine, don't worry. I'll call you after dinner, okay?

I slide my phone into my bag and leave the stall. The door opens again, letting in another woman dressed in a silky ivory cocktail dress but I barely notice her. Timur stands outside the door, leaning casually up against the wall, his hands in his pockets.

I go to him.

"I need to call my sister soon. She said she needs to talk with me," I tell him when I exit. The pinched expression on his face has vanished and instead, he looks like the polished, civilized man who proposed to me bathed in sunset hues on a beach in Maui. I breathe out a sigh of relief.

"Oh? Our first dish has arrived. Can it wait? You said you were starving. I'll expedite the delivery of the rest of our food and we'll leave early so you can call her."

He ushers me back to our table, matching my strides as we walk hand in hand. I wonder if I imagined the grumpiness from before. This is the Timur I can't wait to be with.

"Thank you. I could tell she'd rather talk to me in person."

Timur leans in and reaches for my hand. "I'm sorry, Lydia. I shouldn't have been so rude before. I had a day from hell." He smiles at me, his warm brown eyes crinkling around the edges. A little dimple in his cheek flashes at me. I'm not sure why something makes my stomach dip with nerves and a prickle of fear skate across the back of my neck.

This is Timur. My future husband. He's never hurt me. Maybe I had too much to drink.

"Forgive me?"

"Of course."

My phone buzzes again and Timur scowls. He hates cell phones and especially hates being interrupted.

"Sorry. She's really worried."

"About what?" he asks, as he takes a stuffed mushroom and slides one onto my plate. I'd rather eat two, but he's distracted.

"No idea." I reach for another roll to go with the mushroom but he scowls disapprovingly.

"What?"

"The wedding's coming and you said you were watching your carbs," he says with a shrug.

My cheeks flush pink. "Eating low carb made me feel like I had the flu. I hated it."

Why am I explaining this to him? Shouldn't he accept me for who I am?

When my phone buzzes again, Timur looks near apoplectic. His eyes burn into me, his cheeks flushed.

"What the fuck is —"

"It's fine, It's fine," I tell him, shaking my head. "I'll shut it off."

I polish off the wine in my glass to steady my rising nerves. In a normal situation, he's sending me all kinds of red flags, but we're not a regular couple in an ordinary situation and I know that well.

"She's just worried, said something about me not being safe."

He nods but doesn't look too bothered. "You're safe when you're with me. I stationed a guard here for you before I came. She should stop watching the news."

"She doesn't watch the news."

Timur's lips thin. He doesn't like being contradicted.

My food feels too dry in my mouth. I swallow with effort.

A chill shivers down my spine, and I don't understand why. I push my wine away. I don't want anything interfering with my ability to think straight. It's a strange, strange night.

I'm not in danger. I'm with my fiancé and bodyguards. "You'll keep me safe, won't you?"

Timur leans forward and holds my hand. "Of course I will, Lydia. Always."

Pre-Order your copy of 'Scorch: A Dark Bratva Forced Marriage Marriage Romance" by scanning the QR code below (Available July 12, 2024):

Fueled by dark chocolate and even darker coffee, USA Today bestselling author Jane Henry writes what she loves to read – character-driven, unputdownable romance featuring dominant alpha males and the powerful heroines who bring them to their knees. She's believed in the power of love and romance since Belle won over the beast, and finally decided to write love stories of her own.

Scan the QR Code below to receive Jane's Newsletter & be notified of upcoming new releases & special offers!

Be sure to visit me at www.janehenryromance.com, too!

www.ingramcontent.com/pod-product-compliance
Lightning Source LLC
Chambersburg PA
CBHW070409310726

48977CB00003B/614